Praise for
THE WEDDING PHOTOGRAPHER

AN AMAZON INDIA MEMORABLE BOOK OF 2016

'Brings together all the ingredients that make for a
heady, romantic story'
The Hindu

'Keeps the reader enraptured till the end'
HT City, New Delhi

'With a breezy style reminiscent of Anuja Chauhan, the
novel is exactly the kind of humorous read one needs
after a rigorous day at work'
Telegraph

'A pacy work of fiction . . . sure to keep the
reader glued'
Tribune

'Take a long glass of fresh lime soda and put your feet
up, maybe lie down in a hammock and sip this book,
page by page'
Asian Age

'For readers who love a frothy romantic comedy, this is
the perfect book'
Deccan Chronicle

'If you have grown up reading Mills and Boon or Nora Roberts . . . you are surely going to love [this] novel'
HT City, Kolkata

'[A] very good rom-com'
New Indian Express

'This refreshing novel . . . is a treat'
Wedding Vows

'Has all the elements of a breezy rom-com'
Verve

PENGUIN BOOKS
MAN OF HER MATCH

Sakshama Puri Dhariwal is the author of *The Wedding Photographer*. She was born in Delhi and raised in a cricket-crazy family. She has an MBA in marketing and has worked as a brand manager for e-commerce, media and telecom companies. Sakshama currently lives in San Francisco with her husband and daughter. *Man of Her Match* is her second novel.

MAN OF *her* MATCH

SAKSHAMA PURI DHARIWAL

PENGUIN BOOKS

An imprint of Penguin Random House

PENGUIN BOOKS

USA | Canada | UK | Ireland | Australia
New Zealand | India | South Africa | China | Singapore

Penguin Books is part of the Penguin Random House group of companies
whose addresses can be found at global.penguinrandomhouse.com

Published by Penguin Random House India Pvt. Ltd
4th Floor, Capital Tower 1, MG Road,
Gurugram 122 002, Haryana, India

Penguin
Random House
India

First published in Penguin Books by Penguin Random House India 2017

ISBN 9780143426257

Typeset in Sabon by Manipal Digital Systems, Manipal
Printed at Repro India Limited

www.penguin.co.in

This is a legitimate digitally printed version of the book and therefore might not
have certain extra finishing on the cover.

For Arpit,
the man of my match

MAN OF *her* MATCH

May 1996

Eight-year-old Nidhi Marwah rushed to the boundary wall she shared with Mrs Walia next door, and pressed her chin to the top brick, craning her neck for a better view. A Maruti van had just pulled into Mrs Walia's driveway, and Nidhi was bursting with curiosity to know what, or rather whom, *it had brought with it.*

She turned to her trio of trusted comrades and whispered, 'I can't see anything! Tell me what's happening.'

Mahendra Rao, the family's chauffeur of fifteen years, lowered his head to hers, eyes fixated on the scene unfolding in front of him. 'A man has stepped out of the front seat. He looks like the driver. He is unloading suitcases from the dicky.'

'There is a child in the back seat, Nidhi Baby,' narrated Mangal Singh, the pot-bellied cook. 'I think she is a girl your age.'

'Tum andhi ho gayi hai, Mangal,' the family's Nepalese security guard, Bhimsen Thapa, scoffed, mixing up the gender pronouns, as he often did while speaking Hindi. 'She is not a girl, she is a boy!'

'Maybe she is a girl with short hair, Nepali,' Mangal Singh countered. 'Like Nidhi Baby.'

A shiver of excitement caused Nidhi to drop the cricket bat she was holding. 'I'm finally going to have a friend!'

Rao gave her a hurt look, twirling his handlebar moustache in affront. 'We are your friends.'

'Ummm, I meant a friend my age,' Nidhi clarified.

'Odie is your age,' Bhimsen reminded her.

'Odie is a dog,' Nidhi said, rolling her eyes.

As fond as Nidhi was of the Trio, they could be a real pain sometimes. Last week, Nidhi had dragged Mangal Singh out of the kitchen to play basketball at the newly installed hoop in the driveway, but Mangal just could not wrap his head around the rules. He ran without dribbling the ball and kept hurling it at the hoop like in a shot-put contest. Then, three days ago, Nidhi had gathered the Trio to play football with her, but they kept kicking the ball outside the house and then fighting over who would go and retrieve it.

So, naturally, Nidhi's excitement was justified.

'Maybe she will go to the same school as me!' Nidhi burst out, her face flushed with exhilaration.

The Trio exchanged a look of deep concern for their de facto ward, the only child of workaholic lawyer Balraj Marwah. Balraj seldom saw Nidhi awake, and when he did, it was mostly to admonish her about her latest mischief, or to issue more edicts in her already over-disciplined life. And even though Nidhi was friendly and extroverted, her tomboyish personality made her an outsider for both genders—the girls thought she was too much like a boy and the boys thought she wasn't boy enough. Hence Nidhi's tendency to pin her hopes on every new arrival in her school, or her neighbourhood. She stalked and poked and pestered and pleaded with every new kid, till they either caved in or asked to be left alone—more often than not, unfortunately, the latter.

Nidhi glanced at the worry-stricken faces of the Trio in confusion. 'What?'

'Uh, maybe she is just here for the summer holidays, Nidhi Baby,' Mangal said, in a belated attempt to manage her expectations.

'Tell me about her! What does she look like?' Nidhi asked, her green eyes alight with interest.

'She is stepping out of the car,' Rao whispered, then narrowed his eyes in confusion. 'But she is not a she.' He turned to Mangal in disgust, confirming his suspicions about Mangal's deteriorating vision. 'She is a he.'

'Ha! Boli thi na.' Bhimsen smirked, thrilled about this minor victory over his Indian counterparts.

Nidhi jumped up and down in her spot in an attempt to catch a glimpse of her new neighbour.

The young boy was as tall as Nidhi, with a longish mop of untidy brown hair very similar to hers. Dressed in jeans and a plaid shirt, he walked towards the main door of Mrs Walia's house, shoulders drooped and eyes focused on the ground.

Nidhi panicked. What if he disappeared into the house before she had a chance to introduce herself?

'Hi!' she shouted. 'I'm Nidhi.'

The boy turned for a fleeting second before resuming his dispassionate walk into the house.

Nidhi shot Bhimsen a forlorn look and the guard gave her a reassuring smile. 'Maruti ki driver Nepali hai, Nidhi Baby. I will get all information from him!'

Nidhi watched a variety of emotions—surprise, sorrow and sympathy—flicker over Bhimsen's *wrinkled face as he exchanged a few quick words with the Nepalese driver. When he returned, she jabbed her elbow into Bhimsen's ribs and looked at him expectantly. 'What did he say?'*

'The boy's name is Vikram, and Mrs Walia is his grandmother. He used to live in Mumbai with his parents, but they died in a car accident a few days ago. Driver ko itna hi pata hai.'

Nidhi's face fell. 'That's really sad.' Then she thought of something. 'But if he's Walia Aunty's grandson, why hasn't he ever visited before?'

'Pata nahi,' Bhimsen replied. 'The driver didn't say.'

'It's because . . .' Rao's voice trailed off.

'Because?' Nidhi prodded.

Because Vikram's father, a Punjabi, had married a Rajput woman without Mrs Walia's consent, resulting in a decade-long feud between mother and son.

'Because Mrs Walia had a falling-out with her son before Vikram was born,' Rao explained.

'How do you know?' Mangal asked pointedly.

The same way he got most of his information—by eavesdropping on his employer's conversations in the car.

'I heard it somewhere,' Rao evaded.

'It doesn't matter, because Vikram and I are going to be best friends!' Nidhi said confidently. 'I just know it, Rao Uncle.'

Rao gave her an affectionate smile. 'And how do you know that, Nidhi Baby?'

'Because among all his other luggage, I'm pretty sure I saw a cricket kitbag!'

March 2014

Vikram Walia grabbed his kitbag from the conveyor belt at Terminal 3 of the New Delhi airport and slung it over his shoulder, before following his manager towards the exit. He had a mild headache from the sugar-coated rebuke he had received during the two-hour flight from Mumbai to Delhi, and he was in no mood for a prolonged lecture.

'I have pulled major strings-vings to take Aamir Khan off this campaign,' his manager-cum-agent, Monty Bhalla, had told him repeatedly. 'This is best opportunity to repair damage you have . . . ummm, damage that *has been done* to your image.'

'The reason Aamir Khan *refused* to do the campaign,' Vikram corrected Monty, 'is because he wants to focus on the next season of *Satyamev Jayate*. One of the advantages of being kicked off the team is that I have plenty of time to read newspapers.'

Monty had grinned sheepishly before rattling off the details of the corporate social responsibility campaign he was gunning for Vikram to endorse. Vikram mentally switched off, nodding along absently, as he often did when his flamboyant manager inundated him with superfluous details of potential brand endorsements. Between the jingling of Monty's gold bracelet as he gesticulated madly

5

and the gleaming of his varicoloured rings, Vikram had caught the following gist: if he agreed to sign with the brand in question, he would end up spending a couple of weeks on a campaign without receiving a single penny. It seemed like a big waste of time to Vikram, but given his 'conduct' over the last few weeks, he had no leverage to negotiate, not even with his own manager.

As they neared the airport exit, Vikram automatically slipped on a cap and sunglasses, preparing himself for the inevitable onslaught of the paparazzi.

'Vikram, how are you coping with the five-match ban?'

'Are you dating Natasha Sahay?'

'Is Shaan Kapoor pressing charges?'

'Is umpire Mark McCoy pressing charges?'

'How long are you in Delhi?'

'Do you think the number thirteen is unlucky for you?'

'Will the ban be extended?'

'Will you be allowed to play the South Africa series?'

Monty stepped in front of Vikram with practised ease and held up his pudgy, metal-adorned hands to block the non-stop camera flashes and fiery questions. 'No *cum-ment*, no *cum-ment*.' He winked at a couple of journalists who were friends and mouthed, 'I'll call you later,' before ushering Vikram into the back seat of a black Mercedes Benz.

As soon as the car started moving, Vikram held up a hand, pre-emptively cutting off whatever his manager was about to say. 'Not now, Monty.'

Monty nodded agreeably, realizing that he had pushed his client far enough for one day. He took out a small bottle of medication from his pocket and swallowed a couple of pills, silently dwelling on the events of the past seven days. At the beginning of the week, as a show of indignation over an LBW decision in a match against Sri Lanka, Vikram had roughly shouldered past an umpire on his way back to the pavilion. As per the International Cricket Council's code of conduct for players, technically, this would have constituted a level 2 offence—'showing serious dissent at an umpire's decision'—and resulted in Vikram having to forgo his match fee. However, due to a series of prior incidents, and Vikram's general disregard for rules, the ICC categorized the misdemeanour as a level 3 offence—'intimidation of an umpire'—resulting in the much harsher five-match ban, effectively causing Vikram to sit out the rest of the series.

And if that wasn't bad enough, three days ago, Vikram had engaged in an unprovoked brawl with Bollywood actor Shaan Kapoor, punching him square on the jaw at a crowded nightclub in Mumbai. A fan-posted video of the incident had gone viral, causing the Board of Control for Cricket in India to set up a disciplinary hearing at the end of the month. If the hearing didn't go in his favour, Vikram's ban could be extended further for 'conduct unbecoming of an Indian cricketer'.

So whether Vikram agreed to it or not, Aamir Khan pulling out of *News Today*'s EducateIndia programme was a blessing for Monty's belligerent client. While the deal wouldn't pay Vikram anything in cash, it was a masterstroke as far as mending his tarnished image was concerned. The programme would help position Vikram as a proponent of education for underprivileged children and, since it was an internal brand campaign, the newspaper would ensure large-format ads on a daily basis—each carrying Vikram's smiling face. Recently, Vikram's bad-boy image had slumped to such depths that a news article had called him 'a bad influence on Virat Kohli'. So this campaign was the perfect opportunity to present Vikram in a positive light. All he needed to do was charm *News Today*'s marketing team into believing he was the right man for the job.

'Absolutely not!' Nidhi said in disbelief.

'Why not?' Dibakar Roy, her boss and marketing head of *News Today*, asked, furrowing his brows in surprise.

'Dibakar, we'd be better off having *no* brand ambassador than *this* brand ambassador,' she said, genuinely horrified.

Dibakar looked unperturbed and she mentally mouthed his next words: 'Your idealism is your most endearing quality, Nidhi.'

'Thanks, Dibakar,' she said, trying not to let the sarcasm in her head seep into her voice. 'But I'm just being realistic.' She walked around his desk and handed him that day's *Delhi Today*, the entertainment and lifestyle supplement of *News Today*. 'Have you seen this?'

Without looking at the newspaper, Dibakar nodded. 'Of course. So what?'

'*So what*? Allow me to read out some of the tweets from the trending hashtag "Walia Ki Gaaliyan".'

Famous for his unflappable patience, Dibakar listened to Nidhi read out excerpts from the article he had already skimmed through that morning.

'"The only thing more colourful than #WaliaKiGaaliyan is a rainbow. On Govinda's shirt. In a David Dhawan film."'

When Dibakar gave no reaction, Nidhi continued, '"Why will Vikram Walia never be invited to Arnab Goswami's show? Because he's the only person who can outshout Arnab. #WaliaKiGaaliyan".'

She glanced up at Dibakar, but he was watching her with a patronizing smile, like a parent waiting for a child to deliver the punchline of their joke.

'Oh, this one's my favourite. "What was Vikram Walia's first word? The F-word. #WaliaKiGaaliyan".'

Dibakar cracked a smile at that but said nothing.

'*This* is the guy you think should be the face of EducateIn? A guy who barely cleared his board exams?'

'Because he was too occupied winning the Under-19 World Cup,' Dibakar pointed out calmly, smoothing his French beard with his index finger and thumb.

'He's a loose cannon!' Nidhi argued ardently, gesturing to the newspaper. 'How can you possibly expect *him* to represent such a serious cause? We need someone who can be a good role model for the kids. We're trying to steer them to a life of education and learning, not abusive language and violence!'

Dibakar nodded patiently and reached for the newspaper, pretending to read the article headlined 'Walia Packs a Punch'. The front page of *Delhi Today* carried an elaborate photo essay of Walia's many altercations—with opposing players, umpires, the crowd, even journalists. And then there was a screen grab of the famous YouTube video of Walia punching an A-grade movie star.

In theory, Dibakar agreed with Nidhi. Walia *was* a loose cannon and couldn't be relied upon for championing such an important cause. But practically speaking, Aamir Khan's last-minute exit from the project had wreaked havoc on the campaign's timeline. Not only would they have to defer the launch by two weeks, they would even have to risk rolling out a series of ads pushing a cause that was highly pertinent yet too common to garner the interest it deserved without celebrity backing.

'As usual, you have a valid point,' Dibakar began, and Nidhi instinctively knew his polite compliment was intended to soften the blow of his oncoming refusal. 'But since we have so much riding on this campaign from a brand image perspective, I think going with one of the most popular cricketers in the country might be the best recourse. Sure, it is a risk, but . . .'

'Larger the risk, greater the reward,' Nidhi finished in a glib tone.

'Exactly!' Dibakar beamed approvingly.

Nidhi was undeterred. 'Vikram Walia is an obnoxious, self-centred, spoiled Casanova. Do you remember the incident with the Brazilian models?' she charged on, making air quotes around the word 'models'.

'Who knows how much truth there was in that?' Dibakar shrugged.

She threw him an exasperated look. 'How can you say that? There were eighty dozen photos!'

'Photos of women stepping out of his apartment. Walia wasn't *in* any of those photos. Maybe he wasn't even at home,' Dibakar reasoned.

'Do you think I'm naive enough to believe that those Brazilian escorts were actually *cleaning ladies*?' Nidhi sputtered.

Dibakar suppressed a smile.

'Come on, Dibakar!'

'I doubt that the man dating Natasha Sahay is wasting his time with escorts—Brazilian, or any other nationality,' Dibakar smiled.

'It doesn't matter who he's dating,' Nidhi said, ignoring his attempt at humour. 'He's known for his sexual exploits, offensive language, and foul temper on *and* off the field. I don't think he's the right fit for our brand,' she finished a little desperately.

'He thinks he is.'

Nidhi blinked. 'He does?'

'His manager does, anyway.'

'Then maybe his *manager* should endorse EducateIn. He would be an infinitely better choice than the biggest celebrity brat in the country!'

Dibakar sighed. 'Are you done?'

Not even close. But she could see from Dibakar's flustered expression that he'd had enough.

'Yes,' Nidhi relented with visible reluctance. 'But if our brand scores plummet because of him, I'm not responsible!'

'Nidhi, he is the biggest cricket star in the country. And we are getting him for *free*.'

'Because he wants to remedy his tainted public image, not because he cares about educating India.'

'He does a lot of charity work, you know?'

Nidhi frowned. 'I've never heard anything like that.'

'Because he does it quietly, away from the public eye. He doesn't do it for the PR,' Dibakar said with a smug smile.

'Is that the reason he wants to endorse EducateIn? Because it's "away from the public eye"?' Nidhi countered dryly.

'His motivations are irrelevant. Having him as the face of our brand is going to get us more eyeballs than we can ever amass on our own.'

'And what about the eyeballs *he* will get? We're planning three full-page ads a week—it's a win-win for *him*!'

Dibakar narrowed his eyes, watching her carefully. 'What is your problem with Vikram Walia?'

'Nothing,' Nidhi grumbled.

'Good, because he'll be here at 3 p.m. tomorrow. Now run-run and get your notebook so we can discuss the arrangements for tomorrow's meeting.'

Nidhi intentionally walked out of Dibakar's cabin at an unnaturally slow pace. He was always asking her to 'run-run and do this' or 'run-run and do that', and it annoyed her no end. Especially on a day when a project so close to her heart had basically fallen apart.

Damn you, Aamir Khan, for ruining my life.

Vikram lounged on his grandmother's bedraggled beige sofa, propping his legs up on the old glass coffee table.

Even though Dadi had passed away three years ago, he could almost hear her bearing down on him, her voice a high-pitched shriek, *'Feet off the table!'*

Instinctively, Vikram lowered his feet.

'How long are we going to stay here?' Monty asked, looking around at the dingy, old living room with obvious distaste.

'As long as we're in Delhi, we'll stay here,' Vikram said.

'Don't joke!' Monty gasped, taking out his handkerchief to wipe the beads of sweat from his brow. It was fifteen degrees outside.

'I'm serious. The DDCA is only ten kilometres from here and I'll be training there with Coach.'

'We will be in Dilli for *kam-se-kam* two weeks. Don't you think it is better if we stay in a *hotul*?' Monty suggested.

'Staying at home is the only way I can stomach living in this city,' Vikram said with disgust.

Monty raised an eyebrow. 'Didn't you grow up in Dilli?'

'Unfortunately.' Vikram nodded, absently placing his feet on the table.

'Are you deaf?' Dadi's voice rang in his ears. *'Take your feet off the table this instant! This is not your house—at least not until I am dead!'*

Vikram's exact response to that during his last visit had been, *'And when do you think that blessed event will take place?'*

His grandmother had burst out laughing at his insolence.

Vikram smiled at the memory and took his feet off the table.

'Why don't you just sell this house?' Monty asked.

'Because . . .' Vikram's voice trailed off.

Come to think of it, why hadn't he sold the house? Located by the Ring Road in Lajpat Nagar, the house was around 1000 square yards, and even though it had been constructed in the late fifties, it had two floors, a large garden flanked by shisham trees and a driveway on the side long enough to park four cars. Sure, the bushes and trees in the garden required pruning, the large cracks in the driveway needed to be filled, and the interior of the house could use a complete overhaul, but Vikram was certain the house would fetch a few crores, at least.

'The going rate for main road *kothi* in Lajpat Nagar is eighty crores,' Monty said, reaching for his pills.

Vikram looked up in surprise. '*Sach mein?*' He glanced around at the cracks in the walls, the paint hanging off the wooden doors, the innumerable dents and scratches in the marble below his feet and back at Monty. 'This house will fetch eighty crores?'

'This house will not even fetch eighty *rupees*.' Monty grimaced, popping an anti-anxiety pill. 'The land is worth eighty crores. And if a builder constructs sexy apartments here, he could sell it for much more.'

'Wow.'

'How can you be so clueless about your own finances?' Monty asked, looking appalled.

'That's what I have you for.' Vikram grinned.

After leading the Under-19 team to a World Cup win, Vikram's life had changed. Not only because he was recruited for the national team, but also because he was inundated with endorsement offers. Overwhelmed by the sudden and unprecedented attention from sponsors, Vikram had turned for guidance to his coach, who referred him to his second cousin from Kapurthala. And that is how Monty Bhalla became Vikram's first, and only, manager.

Unlike many of his teammates who, upon gaining fame and success, had moved on to professional sports management companies, Vikram had retained Monty. The guy was sharp, well connected and incredibly enterprising, which is why it didn't irk Vikram in the least that his commission was 5 per cent higher than the industry norm. But what made the extra fee absolutely worth it was the one trait Vikram attributed utmost importance to, the one trait that money couldn't buy—loyalty.

Monty's sole interest in life was Vikram's well-being, which included improving his game, increasing his wealth and enhancing his public image—the latter being the only department Monty sometimes struggled with. Not that Vikram could blame him.

While most of his teammates' managers were thirty-year-olds in crisp business suits who spoke impeccable English, Vikram had Monty Bhalla.

At forty-one, divorced and without kids, Monty was always seen in bright Hawaiian shirts—the first four buttons of which, irrespective of the weather, were always open—and more jewellery than most women. Monty's accent could only be understood by a trained Punjabi ear, but luckily for Vikram, his grandmother had spoken English almost exactly as Monty did, without any attention to grammar.

'If you are sure you will never move back to Dilli, I can put out offer in market?'

'I'm absolutely certain. I'm not a Delhi person,' Vikram said.

'Okay. Let me make some inquiries,' Monty said, whipping out his phone.

'Before that, could you please find me a gym nearby?'

'Gold's Gym at Defence Colony. I already spoke to their security team.'

'Thanks. Could you also leave a message with Singhal's secretary? I've been trying his cell phone for the past two days,' Vikram said, referring to his best friend.

'Already done. He is in Japan for one week, he will be back next Monday,' Monty said.

'What's that son of a bitch doing in Japan?' Vikram wondered out loud.

Monty chuckled. 'Rohan Singhal is no longer small fish. He is rubbing shoulders with big-time global investors. Market *mein* rumour *hai ki* Shopcart.com is going to raise one billion dollar.'

'Wow. No wonder the asshole has been avoiding my calls,' Vikram joked.

'I have *ultimate* idea!' Monty exclaimed and Vikram smiled at the way his manager's face lit up. 'Ultimate' was Monty's go-to adjective to describe anything he deemed even remotely cool. 'Why don't you become brand ambassador of Shopcart?' Monty suggested, already working out the mechanics of the deal in his head.

'I think Singhal can do much better than an out-of-work cricketer like me,' Vikram said dryly.

'But you are second-highest-paid sportsman in India. And if Rohan has one billion dollar, he can pukka afford you!' Monty explained, visibly excited.

'If Singhal ever stooped to the likes of me, I would do it for free!' Vikram chuckled, knowing the proposition would drive Monty crazy.

'Again joke!' Monty complained, looking genuinely worried. 'That's five crores right there.'

'So sell the house for five crores extra.' Vikram shrugged.

Monty went almost purple with anxiety. '*Lekin* Vikram—'

'I'm going upstairs to take a nap.'

'But can we talk about—'

Vikram shook his head firmly, signalling the end of the conversation. 'You can take the master bedroom downstairs.'

'Wah. Thanks,' Monty said ungratefully.

Vikram grinned at him and strode up the stairs to his childhood bedroom. He looked at the mantel, still filled with his trophies and medals. Framed certificates and newspaper clippings of his achievements decorated the walls, and his old bat rested artlessly in a corner. He walked over and lifted the bat, a little surprised by how light it felt in his hands. Running his hands over the Kashmir willow and the discoloured SG sticker, he smiled to himself.

He took a step towards the window and found it jammed. He struggled with it for a few minutes, pushing hard at the pane, until the stubborn thing finally creaked open. He closed his eyes against the waft of the cool March breeze that sneaked in. But his tranquil smile transformed into a bitter scowl as soon as he opened his eyes. His window, located on the side of the house, right above his driveway, directly faced that of his next-door neighbour and arch enemy Nidhi Marwah. True, it had been twelve years since he had last seen her, so maybe 'arch enemy' was a tad extreme. But frankly, if he never saw her again, it would be too soon.

Pushing away thoughts of her from his mind, Vikram flopped down on his bed and instantly fell into a deep slumber.

'Bhimsen,' Nidhi whispered to the snoring guard. 'Open the gate!'

The snoring only got louder.

Typical, Nidhi thought with a sigh. If a burglar walked into the house right now, Bhimsen would sleep through the entire robbery, then wake up the next morning and argue that he had *not* been snoring in his sleep.

'Bhimsen!' Nidhi hissed, louder this time, hoping to be heard over the late-night nineties' music blaring through the guard's radio. But the man didn't so much as flinch. Instead, he continued to breathe in tandem with *'Haye Hukku Haye Hukku Haye Haye.'*

It was nearly 11 p.m. and, in a few minutes, Nidhi's father would be getting ready for bed. On most nights, he didn't really bother to check in on her, but if this was one of those rare occasions when he knocked on her door to wish her goodnight, she was in big trouble.

Nidhi wasn't allowed to stay out of the house after 10 p.m. without prior permission, and she absolutely did not want her father to find out that she had spent the last couple of hours drinking with her friends Risha and Tanvi. So the present situation did not bode well for Nidhi.

'Time for plan B,' she muttered to herself, dialling the cook's cell phone number. 'Mangal Singh?' she whispered into the phone.

'Yes, Nidhi Baby?' he whispered back.

'Why are you whispering?' she asked.

'Because you are whispering,' he answered.

Nidhi bit back a laugh. 'Is Papa asleep?'

'No, Nidhi Baby. But he is getting ready for bed.'

'I'm outside the main gate and, as usual, Bhimsen is fast asleep. I'm going to climb over the gate and walk down the driveway. Can you let me in through the side entrance?' Nidhi asked.

'Okay,' he said.

'Okay,' Nidhi responded.

'Okay,' he repeated.

'Why aren't you hanging up?' she demanded.

'Because you are not hanging up,' he said.

'Phone *rakho* and come to the door!' she said in a loud whisper.

'Okay.'

Nidhi slung her backpack over both shoulders, starting her climb over the wrought-iron gate with seeming confidence. Unfortunately, as she was crossing over, one of her belt loops got caught on a spike. She gave a small yelp as she hung, half suspended in the air.

Oblivious to the pair of scrutinizing eyes at the window of the Walias' house, Nidhi tried to untangle herself. 'Dammit!' she hissed, then clamped a hand over her mouth.

With an amused smile, Vikram watched a girl climb over the Marwahs' gate, get stuck in one of its spikes, finally undo herself and scamper stealthily to the side entrance. It was dark, so he couldn't really make out her features, but her silhouette was definitely sexy. Before Vikram had the opportunity to apprise the rest of her lithe figure, someone opened the door and let her in. It looked like the Marwahs had a hot houseguest. Or maybe a new tenant.

Because the girl Vikram had just seen looked nothing like the tomboyish daughter of Balraj Marwah.

June 1996

Nidhi dragged her feet through the Walias' garden, promising herself that this was the last time.

For an entire month, Nidhi had knocked on Vikram's door every day, asking him to come out and play. During the first week, he had slammed the door in her face without a response. Over the following week, he had at least said, 'No, thanks,' before closing the door. The third week, he had left the door ajar, listening to her rather convincing sales pitch.

'I taught Odie how to fetch. Do you want to come play with him?' or 'Do you want to check out our new basketball hoop?' or 'Bhimsen has a black eye because the football hit him in the face yesterday! Do you want to see it?'

When Nidhi knocked this time, Vikram opened the door with a sigh. 'What is it now?'

She gave him a bright smile. 'Do you want to play doubles badminton?' He opened his mouth to answer, but Nidhi pre-empted his refusal and charged ahead, 'We have only three racquets, so the last time, Mangal Singh had to use the mosquito swatter. It was really annoying because after a while he lost interest in the shuttlecock and started whacking mosquitoes. Bhimsen was worried that Mangal would collect all the dead mosquitoes and use them in pulao instead of jeera.'

A smile tugged at Vikram's lips.

'So what do you say?' Nidhi asked hopefully.

'You can borrow my racquet,' Vikram said, deliberately misunderstanding her question.

If this were any other day, Nidhi would have jumped at the chance. After all, a borrowed racquet guaranteed another audience with him when she returned it.

But Nidhi's little heart had taken all the rejection it could handle, so she shook her head. 'No, thanks. I'll manage with what I have.'

When she entered her own garden, the Trio saw her crestfallen face, and their expectant smiles turned reassuring.

'It's okay, Nidhi Baby. The four of us will play!' Mangal Singh said.

'No, it's fine. You all can go back to work,' Nidhi said, slumping down on the grass, with her elbows on her knees and her face between her palms, a portrait of dejection.

'Come on, Nidhi Baby,' Rao chimed in. 'It will be fun.'

'I don't think so,' Nidhi whispered.

'You can be on my team and we will beat these Indians very-very badly!' Bhimsen said, trying to goad her into admitting that she too was Indian and thus could never play against India.

Nidhi plucked out a fistful of grass and shook her head. 'I'm not in the mood.'

'That's too bad,' spoke a voice from behind her. 'I was hoping to beat you.'

Nidhi jerked her head around. Standing at the gate with a badminton racquet in his hand—and a friendly grin on his face—was Vikram.

March 2014

News Today Office Messenger Chat
Participants: Nidhi13, Risha_K

Nidhi13: You're the worst friend in the world.

Risha_K: Hey, don't blame me! The first rhyme my dad ever taught me was 'Whisky before beer, have no fear; beer before whisky, very risky'. But did you listen to me? Of course not!

Nidhi13: I want to sleep for the next three weeks. Or at least until the throbbing in my head subsides.

Risha_K: I'm only working half-day today, so I'm going home to sleep as soon as this conversation is over. PS: Please make it quick.

Nidhi13: You journalists and your flexi timings. Some people have all the luck.

Risha_K: We also get paid about half of what you marketing folks get paid, so suck it up.

Nidhi13: How's Shorty doing?

Risha_K: I'm sure her liver of steel is unscathed. She's probably pacing up and down the length of the 17th floor shouting threats into her Bluetooth.

Nidhi13: I'll bet. This is the worst day for a hangover. I would've never drunk so much if Aamir Khan hadn't betrayed my trust.

Risha_K: Vikram Walia is a great alternative.

Nidhi13: For the nine-millionth time, no, he's not. He's an ass.

Risha_K: Haven't seen his ass, but I'm sure it's as glorious as his six-foot frame. He's super hot.

Nidhi13: And that should be the criteria for selecting a brand ambassador?

Risha_K: So you agree he's hot?

Nidhi13: Absolutely not.

Risha_K: And you don't find his crooked smile sexy?

Nidhi13: What is the media's obsession with his 'crooked smile'? How can a crooked smile be sexy? It doesn't even make sense!

Risha_K: And you don't think his abs are downright perfect?

Nidhi13: He's a stupid, shallow playboy.

Risha_K: Wow. What's your problem with him?

Nidhi13: Nothing. Dibakar is on his way to my workstation, so I gotta 'run-run'.

Nidhi minimized the chat window and turned to Dibakar.

'Hello, Nidhi!'

'Hi, Dibakar.'

'Can we go over the list?'

'Again?' she asked.

'I just want to make sure we haven't missed anything.'

How could they have missed something in the last half hour since they had gone over the list? Ignoring the pounding in her head, Nidhi reached for her notebook and read out the items: 'Shammi kebabs and mushroom patties from Wenger's, grilled shrimp from Dhaba by Claridges—although, again, I *really* don't think we need the shrimp—chocolate pecan brownies from the Taj Mansingh coffee shop, banoffee pie from Big Chill, and four types of coffee from Starbucks.'

'What about tea?'

'The pantry is stocked with a variety of teas.'

'And cookies too?'

Nidhi nodded.

'Have we forgotten anything?'

'Yes.'

'What?' Dibakar asked, looking mildly panicked.

'A waitress uniform for me,' Nidhi said sweetly.

'Not the time for jokes, young lady!' he said with a feeble smile. 'Wait, we forgot one thing.'

'What?'

'Mineral water.'

Nidhi shook her head. 'No, I already had the conference room lined up with bottles of Bisleri.'

'*Bisleri*?' Dibakar blanched. 'No, Nidhi, we need Evian!'

Nidhi's eyes widened. 'Are you serious? The campaign is meant to raise funds for the education of underprivileged kids. Should we be wasting money on *imported water*?'

'We need Evian,' he repeated firmly. 'Or Himalayan, at the very least.'

'But, Dibakar,' she argued, 'cricketers have great immunity; they drink tap water all the time and never fall sick.'

Nidhi didn't know that for a fact, but it sounded plausible.

'You don't understand,' Dibakar said, and Nidhi thought that was the only sentence they had agreed upon all day. 'We are about to give him a taste of experiential marketing,' Dibakar continued gleefully.

'Really?' Nidhi asked, and instantly regretted her rhetorical question.

'It's like the sizzle of a sizzler,' he began, and Nidhi silently mouthed along the latter half of the sentence she had heard a million times, 'you can't taste it, but it adds to the experience.'

'In that case, I better go organize the water,' she said with sham gravity, not because she actually intended to, but because she needed a break from his incessant micro-management.

Dibakar nodded approvingly, scampering off to his large cabin with mincing steps, greeting everyone along the way with a beatific smile.

Nidhi walked in the direction of the sports editorial department, and spotted the associate sports editor Sameer Singh. She rested her chin on the wall of his cubicle. 'Hey, Sam.'

Sam stood up and gave her a dazzling smile. 'To what do I owe this pleasure, hot stuff?'

Most of Sam's conversations began with 'You're so hot' and ended with 'Why don't you just date me already?' Nidhi humoured him because he was harmless, but also because he was one of the few in editorial who didn't acknowledge the Chinese wall between marketing and editorial.

Over the years, Sam had become a good friend, and Nidhi shared a healthy professional equation with him. He was approachable and reasonable, and didn't throw his weight around just because he could. Unlike his boss, sports editor Sukhdeep Pal Singh Baweja, who was a cantankerous asshole in a permanent bad mood, known for coming to work either drunk or stoned, or both. Nidhi hated interacting with Sukhi because, aside from the aforementioned traits, he was just plain difficult to work with. He was always ready with a snide remark or an insulting comment, and his tone was forever dripping with boredom or distaste.

And even though he was only in his late thirties, his prematurely grey ponytail, unkempt beard and perpetual scowl made him appear closer to sixty. In her three years at *News Today*, Nidhi hadn't seen him smile even once.

But despite his obnoxious personality, Sukhi was the apple of Editor-in-chief Jay Soman's eye. Primarily because Jay shared Sukhi's no-nonsense attitude, but also because Sukhi's contacts with various sports bodies, particularly the BCCI, made him indispensable to the sports ed team.

'Vijay texted saying they are twenty minutes away,' Nidhi said, referring to the cricket correspondent. 'Will Sukhi make it in time for the Vikram Walia meeting?' she asked.

'Only Sukhi knows the answer to that,' Sam said dryly. 'Yesterday he showed up for a meeting fifty minutes late. And guess who the meeting was with?'

Nidhi arched an eyebrow. 'Don't tell me it was with Jay?'

'Yup. And you know the reason Sukhi gave for his tardiness?'

'Flat tyre?' Nidhi hazarded.

'He said he got into an argument with his weed guy.'

Nidhi's eyes widened. 'No way! How did Jay react?'

'He lit a cigarette, took a drag and passed it on to Sukhi, as though the excuse was perfectly legit,' Sam said with disgust.

'Wow. If he's late for Walia's meeting, he better come up with something more creative,' Nidhi said.

Sam shook his head. 'Walia is an important guy, so Sukhi will probably show up before time.'

'He can be such a pain,' Nidhi muttered. 'At least make sure *you* come early.'

'Coming early isn't something I'm usually known for,' Sam said, wiggling his eyebrows.

Nidhi rolled her eyes. 'Real grown-up, Sam. Be there or I'm going to unleash Dibakar on you.'

Sam feigned a shudder. 'I can't handle his chummy smiles and sugary friendliness. They grate on my nerves.'

'You can't handle Sukhi's grouchiness and you can't handle Dibakar's niceness. What *can* you handle?'

'Your spiciness,' he said without missing a beat.

Nidhi laughed. The man was incorrigible. 'Stop it!'

'Never,' he said dramatically.

Nidhi threw him a helpless smile. 'Marketing conference room in twenty minutes.'

'By the way,' Sam called out, and Nidhi turned around expectantly. 'Nice skirt.'

'Twenty minutes, Sam,' she reminded him firmly before walking away.

Inside the conference room, Nidhi arranged the EducateIndia literature and double-checked the projector. She gasped when she caught sight of her desktop wallpaper—a shirtless image of Vikram Walia.

'Oh ha ha, very funny,' she yelled to her colleagues seated behind the wall of the conference room. The faint laughter that followed confirmed their attempt to prank her. Shaking her head, she changed the wallpaper back to the sensible (even if less aesthetically appealing) Windows default—rolling green hill beneath a blue sky.

That morning, Nidhi had asked Dibakar to give Anusha, the summer intern, a chance to present the EducateIndia proposal to Vikram, but Dibakar had refused point-blank. Apparently, Anusha was not 'ready'.

'But it will be a great learning opportunity for her,' Nidhi had argued.

Dibakar shook his head firmly. 'You know I'm a reasonable person, Nidhi. This is not negotiable. You will present to Vikram.'

Dibakar was always pretending to be flexible and democratic, but he ran the marketing department on his own whims and fancies. Realizing it was a lost cause, Nidhi had just shrugged.

In the long run, Nidhi's goal was to move away from news media marketing to social marketing, and EducateIndia was a step in the right direction. So there was no way she was going to let a spoilt celebrity like Vikram Walia damage her campaign. He might be a rich cricketer with a hot Bollywood girlfriend, but as far as Nidhi was concerned, he was a lemon.

Life had handed her a lemon in the form of Walia, and Nidhi intended to make the best goddamn lemonade anyone had ever tasted. No one would stand in her way, not even Walia.

Over the years, Nidhi's animosity towards Vikram had faded into indifference. His face was plastered on every newspaper, magazine and billboard in the country, and he was often seen on TV brushing his pearly white teeth or shampooing his perfect hair. Nidhi was so used to seeing Vikram all around her that their forthcoming confrontation didn't faze her in the least. He had broken her heart and walked out of her life, but she had been a fourteen-year-old girl when that had happened. She was now a twenty-six-year-old woman, and a thorough professional at that.

So, superstar or not, Vikram Walia stood no chance in the face of Nidhi's steely resolve. And given that it had been over a decade since they had last seen each other, Nidhi had even entertained the possibility that Vikram might not recognize her.

A few minutes later, the marketing and sports editorial teams—including Sukhi, thankfully—stood in a neat row in the conference room to greet Vikram Walia and his manager, Monty Bhalla. Since she would be making the presentation, Nidhi was standing farthest from the door, next to the projection screen.

Nidhi had spent the last two days preparing for the meeting. She had conditioned herself to treat Vikram like any other client and keep their interaction purely impersonal. In addition to that, she had gone over the presentation half a dozen times, memorizing every bullet point on each slide and every number on each spreadsheet. She was confident that she would breeze through the meeting and Vikram would be out of here in less than an hour—signed, sealed, delivered.

Unfortunately, while Nidhi was quite over-prepared to do her job, she turned out to be grossly underprepared for her reaction to seeing Vikram in person. The moment Vikram sauntered into the conference room, Nidhi stopped breathing. Even though he was clad in khaki pants and a casual white t-shirt, unwittingly, Nidhi's gaze clung to him. Her heart hammered relentlessly in her chest, her head started spinning and her knees threatened to buckle under her. She struggled to compose herself as memories flashed before her like a rapid, disordered slideshow.

Sitting on the charpoy in Dadi's garden, eating mangoes directly from the bucket. Buying Pan Pasand from Lalaji ki dukaan. Sharing a plate of chhole bhature at Nagpal Corner. Devouring a dozen golgappe at Central Market.

And just as Nidhi was wondering why all her memories were food-related, snatches of past conversations pushed forth in staccato.

'You can borrow my racquet.'

'I like you the way you are.'

'Don't worry, Nidhi. I'll fix it.'

'I never want to see you again!'

'I hate you!'

Nidhi took a deep breath and placed her palms on the table, steadying herself as Vikram bestowed the lazy glamour of his lopsided smile on each member of the *News Today* team, warmly shaking their hands, and politely taking the visiting cards they were handing him.

'Sukhi Paaji, good to see you again,' he said with a friendly smile at Sukhi.

'Pleasure to meet you, Dibakar,' he said formally, glancing down at Dibakar's card, seemingly to get the name right.

'Nice to meet you, Sameer,' he said with a quick peek at Sam's card.

As soon as Vikram's gaze locked on Nidhi, his entire frame went rigid. A cold sneer replaced his amiable smile, and his eyes filled with cynical distaste as they raked over her.

So much for not recognizing her.

Vikram took the visiting card she was holding out, but without bothering to glance at it, he said, 'Nidhi, a pleasure.'

Sans pleasure.

Nidhi clasped his hand and a spark shot through her entire body. Knowing that every eye in the room was on her—and that Vikram's eyes in particular seemed to hold some sort of a challenge—she resisted the urge to jerk her hand away immediately.

Oh, boy. This was going to be a long meeting.

Vikram struggled to keep his anger under control. He fought the overwhelming urge to storm out of the conference room—only because he was unwilling to give Nidhi Marwah the satisfaction of thinking that she had the slightest impact on him.

From the corner of his eye, Vikram conducted a thorough perusal of her physical appearance—albeit a detached, clinical assessment. A grey pencil skirt had replaced the baggy shorts she had always worn as a kid, a pair of gleaming black stilettos had substituted her worn-out sneakers, and her trademark messy bob had grown into chestnut-brown waves that bounced around her shoulders as she turned to share something on the projection screen.

Over the past few minutes, Nidhi had stood at the helm of the conference room, taking them through the marketing plan. A plan that, incidentally, Vikram had not heard a single word of. Not because he wasn't interested in educating underprivileged children, but because he couldn't take his eyes off her damned legs.

Clinical, my ass.

Vikram almost hadn't recognized her. But while the rest of her appearance had transformed drastically, there was one thing about her that was unchanged.

Her eyes.

Her deep, dark, piercing green eyes. Eyes that, he had once thought, could peer into his very soul.

Vikram clenched his fists, furious with himself. Twelve years ago, this girl had ruthlessly crushed his heart, and yet here he was today, a besotted fool, waxing poetic about her eyes.

Vikram suddenly realized that there was complete silence in the room and five pairs of eyes were watching him curiously. He cleared his throat. 'Sorry, what was the question?'

The bald Bengali man gave Vikram a genial smile. 'Would you like some snacks?'

Absently glancing at the elaborate spread of food in front of him, Vikram shook his head. 'I'm good, thanks.'

The Bengali looked disappointed. 'How about some tea or coffee?'

Vikram shot a quick look at the visiting cards he had arranged to correspond with the *News Today* team's seating arrangement. 'Thanks, Dibakar, but I don't drink tea or coffee.'

Nidhi snorted. Or coughed. Vikram couldn't be certain which, but there was no way to confirm without looking directly at her. And that he would not do.

Dibakar seemed positively crushed. 'Have *something*, Vikram.'

Vikram studied the lavish assortment of snacks on the table with an inward groan. His late lunch was still sitting in his stomach and he didn't really feel like eating, so only out of politeness, he reached for the food item he found most appetizing. Dibakar cringed at his choice, but Vikram ignored him and twisted open the Bourbon biscuit, licking the chocolate clean before popping it into his mouth.

Nidhi inhaled sharply as a strong vision flashed before her.

It was the summer they had turned eleven. Nidhi had just been proclaimed captain of the girls' cricket team and she sprinted home from the bus stop, bursting with excitement to give her father the good news. Vikram waited outside her father's study, with his ear pressed against the door, eavesdropping shamelessly. Inside the study, Nidhi handed the letter of appointment to her father and he read through the 'good news' before looking up to speak one cold, callous syllable. 'No.'

'But why?' she cried in disbelief.

'Because you waste enough time playing sports with the Walia boy as it is.'

Nidhi tried to reason with him, but in return she received a harshly worded lecture. She was losing focus on her studies by concentrating on fruitless endeavours. And then her father commanded her to walk over to the paper shredder and destroy the letter. Nidhi's eyes welled up at the cruelty of his suggestion. 'I won't accept the position, but at least let me save the letter!' she begged.

'Memorabilia is for sentimental fools,' her father said.

'Is that the reason we don't have a picture of my mother?' Nidhi challenged, even as her chin quivered with suppressed anguish.

A shadow of pain flashed over her father's face, but it was gone before Nidhi could be sure. With a blank expression, he crossed his arms over his chest, patiently waiting for his order to be obeyed. In a deliberate act of defiance, Nidhi threw the letter on the floor and ran out of the study, shoving past a stunned Vikram.

Nidhi locked herself in her room and cried her eyes out even as Vikram sat outside her bedroom door for hours, whispering soft, comforting words to her, his voice laced with worry. When that didn't work, he tried to tease her and make her laugh. When Nidhi didn't respond to his jokes, he finally used the ace up his sleeve.

'I have a really cool surprise, but you have to come out to get it. If you don't want it, I'll just give it to someone else,' he said.

It was curiosity that finally drew Nidhi out of her room.

'What is it?' she asked, her green eyes brightening with interest. Vikram brought his hands forward and showed her the big surprise—two packets of Bourbon biscuits.

Nidhi gasped with excitement at the sight of the 'special guest' biscuits they weren't allowed to touch. 'How did you get these?'

Vikram chuckled at her expression. 'Dadi forgot the steel ka dabba on the kitchen counter, so I swiped them!'

'But won't you get into trouble?'

Vikram shrugged. 'It's worth it.'

Forgotten was her shattered dream of being cricket captain as she lay in the garden with Odie on one side and Vikram on the other. They stared at the colourful evening sky, licking the chocolate off each Bourbon biscuit, chomping happily till not a crumb was left in either packet.

'Nidhi?'

Nidhi shook away the reverie and turned to Dibakar. 'Yes?'

'My apologies for the interruption,' Dibakar said, hinting for her to proceed.

She nodded and returned her attention to the projection screen. Over the next few minutes, she blitzed through the remainder of her slides with effortless aplomb. At the end of the presentation, Monty bombarded them with rapid-fire questions about Vikram's visibility through media and editorial coverage, which Nidhi and Sam took turns responding to.

'So Vikram will need to make himself available on three days this month, Nidhiji?' Monty confirmed, glancing down at his notes.

'Four is ideal,' Nidhi said, 'but if he's busy, we can work with three.'

Noticing the subtle emphasis she had laid on the word 'busy', Vikram raised an arrogant eyebrow.

'Do you have a question?' Nidhi asked formally.

It was the first time she had addressed him directly and Vikram's jaw clenched in response. 'Yes,' he said shortly.

She nodded. 'Go ahead.'

He made unwavering eye contact with her. 'Why do I get the feeling that you're not keen on me?'

Sukhi sniggered.

Nidhi's mouth hung open. '*Excuse me?*'

Vikram gave her a bored look. 'Is it correct that Aamir Khan walked out of this campaign at the last minute?'

'Yes,' she said tentatively.

'Do you believe he was a better fit?' Vikram challenged.

'Of course, not!' Dibakar chimed in. 'We think—'

'Just a second. I want Nidhi to answer the question. Do you *personally* feel that Aamir Khan was a better fit for this campaign?'

Nidhi turned to Dibakar helplessly. He mouthed 'no'.

'It's a yes or no question,' Vikram drawled.

Nidhi raised her chin a notch. 'Yes.'

Anger flashed in Vikram's eyes along with something else Nidhi couldn't identify, before he turned to the other occupants of the room. 'Maybe I should ask Aamir to reconsider.'

Laughter rang through the room, defusing the tension.

'Can you?' Nidhi asked hopefully.

'She's joking,' Dibakar said with a nervous laugh, watching Vikram's narrowed eyes.

'Yes,' Nidhi lied. 'Joking.'

Vikram stood up and they all rose to their feet expectantly. There was a deafening silence in the room as everyone waited for him to speak.

'I need a single point of contact. Who will it be?' he asked, looking Nidhi square in the eye.

She didn't flinch. 'Me.'

'Wonderful,' he said dryly. 'I can't wait.'

March 1998

Diary of Nidhi Marwah
Age 10

I got into a big fight today.

Actually, I got into two big fights today. The first one was with the worst human being in the world: Raghav Reddy. That idiot bowled a yorker and made me lose my wicket, but that's not what the fight was about. When I was walking off the pitch, he said to me, 'Maybe you should start playing with me instead of Walia. That stupid orphan is ruining your game.'

So I punched Reddy. I hit him so hard that he went flying into the wickets. Then I tackled him to the ground and continued to pound him till my knuckles were bloody and swollen. Vikram came running from the non-striker's end and grabbed me by the waist, but I kept kicking and screaming as he dragged me away.

To be honest, I actually wanted to hit Reddy with my bat, but Coach would've killed me for disrespecting the equipment. After that, both Reddy and I got sent to the principal's office and now I have to write a 300-word essay on 'The Effects of Violence in the Community', and an apology letter to Reddy. Yeah, right, like I would ever apologize to that stupid jerk!

Then on the walk back home, Vikram got mad at me because I wouldn't tell him why I punched Reddy. Maybe I should've told him and made him write the stupid essay instead.

And then—okay, so I just realized I got into three fights today—I had an argument with Papa because he said I'm wasting time on sports instead of concentrating on my studies. He was furious about the gash I got on my cheek during my scuffle with Reddy. And when I told Papa the reason I had punched Reddy, he was even more angry. 'This is all because of that Walia boy—his bad temper is rubbing off on you! Look at the way you dress, look at the way you walk. Constantly wearing dirt-stained clothes and playing basketball with that ill-mannered ruffian. You never got into fights before he moved in next door. And now practically every week I receive a letter from your school about some skirmish or misdemeanour. I'm going to have a talk with his grandmother!'

I thought that was a bit excessive, but I know Papa sometimes takes out his work stress on me. So instead of arguing with him, I apologized for getting into a fight—which, I kind of did feel bad about—and went up to my room to do my homework.

After some time, Vikram started throwing pebbles at my window, so I opened it and asked him what his problem was.

'Wanna shoot hoops?' he hollered, dribbling a basketball in the driveway. He gave me a goofy smile, like we hadn't just fought a few hours before.

'Sure!' I called out from the window.

We never stay mad at each other for long. That's why we're best friends.

March 2014

10 a.m.

From: Nidhi Marwah <nidhi.marwah@newstoday.in>
To: Monty Bhalla <montybhalla73@gmail.com>
Subject: News Today EducateIn Marketing Plan

Dear Monty,

Please find attached:
1. Marketing plan (as discussed during the meeting)
2. Minutes of the meeting
Vikram is required to be physically present on the following dates:
(a) Stock photo shoot: March 3, i.e. tomorrow (confirmed as per our conversation on Saturday morning—the studio has been booked accordingly)
(b) Rural school visit: March 8
(c) CEO meet-and-greet: March 11
Please let me know if these dates work. Please also share the address where I can send the promotional material for Vikram's approval.

Warm regards,
Nidhi Marwah
Sr Brand Manager, *News Today*

4.45 p.m.

From: Nidhi Marwah <nidhi.marwah@newstoday.in>
To: Monty Bhalla <montybhalla73@gmail.com>
Subject: Re: News Today EducateIn Marketing Plan

Dear Monty,

I haven't heard from you all day and you're not answering your phone either!
Please confirm that Vikram will be present at the shoot tomorrow morning at 11. I've texted the address to your phone.

Regards,
Nidhi

8.30 p.m.

From: Nidhi Marwah <nidhi.marwah@newstoday.in>
To: Monty Bhalla <montybhalla73@gmail.com>
Subject: Re: News Today EducateIn Marketing Plan

Dear Monty,

Please confirm about tomorrow asap! I've already paid the advance for the studio. We'll lose a lot of money if the shoot doesn't happen tomorrow!!!

Nidhi

8.32 p.m.

From: Nidhi Marwah <nidhi.marwah@newstoday.in>
To: Risha Kohli <risha.kohli@newstoday.in>; Tanvi Bedi <tempid321_tanvi@newstoday.in>

Subject: Meet me downstairs in five . . .

. . . I need a drink.

'This is exactly why I hate working with celebrities. They are inconsiderate, egotistical and completely unprofessional!' Nidhi said emphatically.

Risha nodded in agreement. 'Thanks to my Page 3 beat, I constantly have to deal with self-proclaimed celebrities who have a tiny brain and a huge sense of self-importance.'

Tanvi, Nidhi's college friend and temporary colleague, grunted in agreement before gulping down her beer, signalling their waiter to bring another round by moving her index finger in a rapid circular motion.

'What's with you, Shorty?' Risha asked Tanvi.

'"A tiny brain and a huge sense of self-importance" sounds like someone else we know,' Tanvi grumbled, pushing back a curly black strand of hair into the clip that held together her mane of unruly locks.

'What did Lady K do now?' Nidhi asked, referring to the owner and chairperson of the *News Today* group, and Tanvi's current client, Kamini Singhvi, nicknamed 'Lady K' by the *NT* employees.

In the early nineties, Lady K had inherited the media group from her father, newspaper mogul, Bhanu Bhandari. While old BB had been an equanimous sort of man, his only child, Kamini, was hot-tempered, impatient and extremely demanding. And even though

Lady K only visited the office for three hours every weekday (11.25 a.m. to 2.25 p.m., including a twenty-minute lunch break), anyone on the seventeenth floor could tell you that it was the most stressful three hours of their day—especially the current secretary, because Lady K went through secretaries faster than most women went through nail polish. Past examples included:

Ratna Dinkar, aged thirty-five, fired for forgetting to remind Lady K to initial the annexure pages of an acquisition contract.

Shivshankar Laxmipathy, aged fifty-seven, retired early. But in truth, fired for having a weak bladder.

Kiran Sandhu, aged twenty-six, fired for giggling when she handed Shah Rukh Khan his misplaced cigarette lighter during a meeting with Lady K and he thanked her with, 'Tu hai meri Kiran!'

And then there was poor Peter D'souza, aged forty-nine, who had stood up abruptly during the board meeting, turned to his employer and said, 'God is watching you,' before collapsing to the floor.

Allegedly, Lady K had calmly asked the CEO to have Peter's unconscious body removed from the boardroom before proceeding with business as usual.

Her current secretary was fifty-one-year-old Bushra Syed, who had, by some miracle, managed to hold her position for the last six years.

And fortunately for Tanvi, she got along with Bushra just fine. As the wedding planner of Lady K's son, Tanvi was temporarily stationed at the News Today office, and permanently at Lady K's beck and call.

At 5'2", the only thing small about Tanvi was her frame. Which is why Riya Sridharan, Tanvi's boss and owner of the prestigious Iris Wedding Planners, had nominated Tanvi to 'handle' Kamini Singhvi. Tanvi had a big personality that intimidated most people; she was blunt, outspoken and, her famous Punjabi temper notwithstanding, an absolute professional.

Her professionalism, incidentally, was pretty much the only thing Tanvi had in common with Nidhi's other best friend, Risha.

Risha, at 5'8", was naturally responsible for coining Tanvi's moniker, 'Shorty'. Risha's wavy, glossy brown hair fell all the way to her waist, while Tanvi spent most days struggling to tame her shoulder-length raven curls. Risha's big, expressive hazel eyes against smooth olive skin were in stark contrast with Tanvi's elf-like features—almond-shaped brown eyes and a dainty nose on a beautiful, dusky complexion.

And as far as dissimilarities went, the girls' physical appearance was just the tip of the iceberg.

Risha had an open personality and was quick to make friends, whereas Tanvi's attitude was sceptical at best, mistrusting at worst. While Risha was gentle and tactful in her dealings with people, Tanvi spoke without a filter and her vocabulary was punctuated by several four-letter words. And though Risha always chose to look at the bright side of life, Tanvi preferred to call herself a 'realist'.

But Nidhi loved both girls equally, and was grateful for the balance they brought in her life.

'What did Lady K do now?' Nidhi repeated.

'She threw the latest invite in my face,' Tanvi answered.

Nidhi and Risha laughed.

'No, seriously,' Tanvi continued, her tone resigned, 'she crumpled it into a ball and threw it in my fucking face. It narrowly missed my eye.'

'*Kameeni* Singhvi,' Risha muttered, angry on her friend's behalf.

'By the way,' Nidhi remembered suddenly, 'rumour has it that the budget for the wedding flowers is thirty lakhs?'

'That rumour is inaccurate.' Tanvi snorted.

'Of course, it is. No one can spend thirty lakhs on flowers!' Risha said, rolling her eyes.

'Yes, because some people can spend *ninety* lakhs on flowers,' Tanvi deadpanned.

Nidhi choked on her beer. 'No way! What kind of flowers cost that much? A zillion orchids?'

'"Orchids are so middle class,"' Tanvi said disdainfully, in a perfect imitation of Lady K. '"We'll import flame lilies from Madagascar."'

Risha's mouth hung open. 'What the hell is a flame lily?'

'Some bullshit overpriced flower.' Tanvi shrugged.

Nidhi, having googled the flower in question, turned her phone to show Tanvi. 'Wikipedia says it's available in Tamil Nadu! Why import it from Madagascar?'

'Because it's on the verge of extinction in India, and if anyone finds out they tried to procure a protected species, it won't reflect well on the Singhvis.'

'What a waste of money. Why don't they just get standard *genda phool*? They're so pretty!' Risha contended.

'Because it's beneath Kameeni to use *normal* flowers like genda phool,' Tanvi explained. 'Which is why she also made me order three thousand super-rare Dutch tulips that only bloom in March and have a two-week life span. So we're gonna store them in a specially built air-conditioned greenhouse until the goddamn wedding.'

'It says here,' Nidhi said, reading off her phone, 'that the flame lily is fatal if ingested and has been used to commit murder!'

'Thanks for the idea, but I've already considered and rejected it. Unfortunately, Lady K only takes food and drinks directly from Bushra's hands,' Tanvi said dryly.

Risha gave her a sympathetic look. 'I'm sorry, Shorty. Want a bite of my chocolate mousse?' she asked, eating a spoonful and washing it down with beer.

Tanvi cringed. 'How can you have dessert with beer?'

Risha shrugged, tossing back her French braid. 'I can have dessert with anything.'

So true.

'I wish I'd saved yesterday's leftover banoffee pie for you,' Nidhi said. 'You should've seen Dibakar, he practically doubled over with gratitude when Vikram signed the deal. The only person unperturbed was Sukhi. For some reason, Vikram was treating him with utmost respect. For a man known for abusing journalists, he was being way too deferential to Sukhi.'

Risha laughed. 'That's not because Sukhi is a journalist, silly! It's because he's an ex-cricketer. He played a few international matches before his shoulder injury rendered him useless. Cricketers have this weird bro code.'

'That explains it. Vikram kept calling Sukhi "Paaji" and nodding along reverentially to everything he said.

While leaving the conference room, Vikram asked Sukhi if they could catch up, and Sukhi swept Vikram away to his cabin where, according to Sam, they sat for thirty minutes. Sam thinks they went out for drinks after that.'

'You and Sam sure talk a lot,' Risha said pointedly.

Nidhi shrugged. 'Mostly just water-cooler conversations. He's fun to hang out with.'

'You should totally date him,' Risha suggested.

'He's not my type,' Nidhi said.

'Who the hell *is* your type?' Tanvi asked.

Involuntarily, Vikram's face appeared in front of Nidhi. She took a long sip of her drink, processing the day's events.

Her intense reaction to seeing him earlier that day had caught her off guard. On television, his intentionally groomed stubble and perfectly styled hair had always seemed too metrosexual for Nidhi's taste. But in real life, it made him appear elegantly masculine and devastatingly handsome. And then there was that incredible, chiselled physique. Even in his simple white t-shirt, Nidhi had been able to trace the hard contours of his body with her eyes. No wonder fashion brands were throwing money at him to pose on their billboards. Come to think of it, he would be perfect for a sexy underwear ad—muscular biceps, well-defined pecs, rock-hard abs . . .

'What are you thinking about?' Tanvi asked suspiciously.

'Nothing,' Nidhi said guiltily.

Risha narrowed her eyes.

'I have to tell you guys something,' Nidhi said, taking a deep breath and wondering where she should begin.

Maybe at age eight, when the boys in school had refused to let Nidhi play with them and Vikram had said, 'If she doesn't play, I don't play.' That, in the boys' eyes, was the worse of the two evils because Vikram was the best player on the team. So they had reluctantly conceded to let Nidhi and Vikram open the batting together.

Or age ten, when Nidhi had nicknamed him 'Viks ki Goli' and driven him crazy by singing the ad jingle every day for a month. '*Viks ki goli lo, khich-khich door karo . . .!*'

Or age twelve, when the girls in school had started badgering Nidhi for information about Vikram.

Or age thirteen, when Vikram had used shoe polish to cover an obscene mural of Nidhi in the boys' toilet.

Or age fourteen, when he had kissed her for the first time. When he had held her in his arms after burying Odie. When she had cried herself to sleep every night for several months after he had callously demolished her young heart and disappeared from her life.

Maybe it was the alcohol. Maybe it was all the memories that suddenly swam up from the recesses of her heart, even as she fought to suppress them. Maybe it was the overwhelming amount of history they had shared in the six years that they had been best friends.

Or maybe it was the fact that Nidhi had locked away the chapter of Vikram Walia so deep inside her that talking about it would entail completely baring her soul.

So Nidhi chickened out.

She went instead with another update she had been intending to share with her friends. 'Papa wants me to meet a boy.'

'Oh,' Risha said, sitting up with interest. 'Who?'

'A lawyer at Papa's firm.'

'And?' Tanvi prodded.

'I don't know much about him, but Papa thinks he's pretty great. His exact words were "focussed, diligent and enterprising".'

'Basically, a dead bore,' Tanvi said with her characteristic candour.

Risha, the eternal optimist, turned to Nidhi with an excited smile. 'Did you see a photo?'

'Yup. He's tall and beefy. Too beefy, in fact. Looks a bit like a gym instructor, actually,' Nidhi said.

Risha watched her friend carefully. 'So, simple. Don't meet him.'

Nidhi shrugged. 'Trust me, I'm not exactly dying to, but—'

'But you can't say "no" to your dad,' Risha finished automatically.

Nidhi stared into her beer mug and nodded softly.

Tanvi exchanged a look with Risha before speaking bluntly. 'You need to stop being so scared of him.'

'I'm not scared of him. I just . . . don't want to disappoint him.'

'Why are you so worried about disappointing him?' Risha asked gently.

Because my mother leaving us was the biggest disappointment of his life. And he is always comparing me to her, waiting for me to slip up and do something he won't approve of. But all that is nothing compared to the throat-constricting fear I live with on a daily basis—the fear of losing him.

'I don't want to hurt him,' Nidhi said, trying to sound casual.

'He's lucky to have you, Nidhi,' Tanvi said brusquely. 'You're practically perfect.'

Nidhi gave her a sheepish grin. 'Not *that* perfect. I had to climb over the gate again the other night!'

Risha laughed. 'I'm glad my adventurous side is rubbing off on you.'

'Speaking of which, when is your next photography excursion?' Nidhi asked.

'Actually, I have some great news,' Risha smiled. 'You know Anuj from the online editorial team?'

'What about him?'

'His brother is getting married next month and he wants me to shoot the wedding!'

Nidhi's face lit up with excitement. 'Are you serious? That's so great!'

'Well done, Rish,' Tanvi said, flashing a rare smile. 'You're finally a wedding photographer.'

Risha nodded happily. 'Thanks. I'm super excited!'

'This calls for celebratory shots,' Tanvi announced, waving their waiter over.

Risha groaned. 'Not again.'

'Hey, if I can jump over the gate once, I can do it again!' Nidhi assured her.

From his bedroom window, Vikram watched with a strange combination of amusement and curiosity as Nidhi climbed over the gate of her house.

In a skirt.

What possessed a twenty-six-year-old woman to sneak into her own home at 11 p.m.? Vikram wondered, as Nidhi bent down to take off her heels and tip-toed through the driveway, waiting for her trusted compadre to come to her rescue.

Surely Nidhi wasn't still bound by a silly curfew Vikram frowned.

The door opened and a familiar face looked around surreptitiously before letting Nidhi in.

Mangal Singh.

Warmth and fondness swept over Vikram at the sight of the old cook.

With Nidhi's father working long hours and travelling for days at a time, the Trio had practically raised Nidhi. Come to think of it, they had sort of raised Vikram too.

When Vikram had moved to Delhi after his parents' death—broken, bitter and alone—Nidhi and the Trio had welcomed him into their home with open arms. Rao Uncle drove Nidhi wherever she wanted to go, but also sneaked the car out for 'servicing' if Vikram needed a ride back from one of his inter-school matches. Mangal Singh's culinary endeavours accounted for Nidhi's preferences, but also included Vikram's favourites. And good old Bhimsen had always kept an eye on the adults' whereabouts, giving Nidhi and Vikram a timely heads-up to ditch whatever mischief they were up to and run back to their books.

With the earthy Trio as her friends and playmates, it was no surprise that Nidhi had been a tomboy at that age. While other girls played with dolls, Nidhi played with cricket bats and hockey sticks. While other girls applied make-up to their faces, Nidhi wiped sweat from hers. While other girls flirted with boys in the corridor, Nidhi shoved them fiercely on the basketball court.

So Vikram could only wonder what had inspired the change in her. How had a feisty tomboy suddenly transformed into such a knockout?

The transformation was hardly 'sudden', Vikram thought objectively. It had been twelve years since he had last seen her. Even though it felt like just yesterday.

An admiring smile tugged at his lips as he recalled the traces of defiance in Nidhi's stormy green eyes when she had haughtily admitted, in a room full of people, that Vikram wasn't the best choice for the campaign. That he wasn't *her* choice for the campaign. She had seemed so confident and composed that Vikram couldn't resist goading her by asking why she wasn't 'keen' on him. And the resultant crack in her composure, though brief, had been immensely gratifying.

She was passionate about her job, that much had been evident in the meeting. But other than that, he didn't know anything about her. Except that she seemed to prefer climbing *over* gates, instead of walking in through them like regular girls.

Inadvertently, Vikram smiled. Nidhi Marwah had never been a 'regular' girl.

'What are you doing?' Monty's query made Vikram whirl around.

'Nothing.'

'Are you spying on neighbours?'

'What do you want?' Vikram snapped.

'Why you told me not to reply-sheply to *News Today* girl's email?'

'Nidhi.'

Monty shot him a surprised look. 'You remember her name? You never remember names.'

Vikram ignored that. 'Let her know I'll be there tomorrow, but don't give her an address for correspondence yet.'

'Why?'

Because that would take the fun away from spying on her.

'Because I haven't decided whether or not I want to move to a hotel,' Vikram lied.

Monty's face brightened. 'Let's move, please! I can't sleep in this house. Whole night strange noises keep coming. *Aisa lagta hai* whole house will fall on my head and I will die in my sleep.'

'You won't,' Vikram said confidently.

Monty hobbled out of the room, muttering something about *'assi crore ka bhooth bangla'*.

Vikram returned his attention to the window and observed the Marwahs' sprawling mansion. The red-brick facade seemed spanking new—the ledges of its front windows painted a pristine white. The lush green garden was fenced by perfectly clipped hedges, the flower beds were sprinkled with petunias of different colours, and the pavers in the driveway appeared to be freshly installed. The only thing that stuck out like a sore thumb in the charming scene was the rusty old basketball hoop hanging at the end of the long driveway.

Suddenly, the lights in Nidhi's room came on. Her window was open and though the lavender curtains were drawn, they fluttered gently in the breeze, offering Vikram sporadic peeks into her world.

She took off her long earrings and placed them on the dresser. She plugged her phone into the charger. She pulled her hair back into a ponytail. She untucked her blouse from her skirt and glanced at her open window.

Vikram ducked beneath the window sill, swearing under his breath when his head hit the ledge. He heard the faint sound of her window closing and the bolt sliding into place with a sharp crack.

He slid to the floor, trying to rationalize the sudden thaw in his feelings towards Nidhi. Maybe the events that had transpired twelve years ago had impacted Vikram so profoundly because of his young age. But he was no longer an idealistic teenager, wearing his heart on his sleeve.

Even though the stories of Vikram's sexual conquests had been vastly exaggerated by the media, by the age of twenty-six, he had been with quite a few women. Mostly practical, experienced women who knew not to expect anything from him other than dinner and good sex. Sometimes just the latter. Vikram didn't do relationships and he made that abundantly clear from the beginning. His profession gave him access to numerous beautiful women and Vikram had, admittedly, been spoiled by their attention and ministrations.

So maybe this thaw wasn't a thaw at all, but a natural physical reaction to a beautiful woman. An *incredibly* beautiful woman who, incidentally, didn't seem affected by him in the least.

Vikram glanced at her window. Though her lights were still on, he couldn't see beyond the curtained window pane.

He thought of the last time he had been inside her room. God, had it really been *twelve years*? His hands tightened on the ledge as memories of that terrible night washed over him.

Is it true, Nidhi? he had asked, shaking her roughly by the shoulders.

Guilt had filled her green eyes. *Yes.*

Vikram's jaw hardened as he recalled the event, vivid in his mind as the day it had occurred. That one crystal-clear memory was enough to wipe away the fleeting warmth Vikram had felt towards Nidhi.

He reached out and closed the window, and, with it, once again shut her out of his heart.

February 2000

Nidhi was very nervous.

This was the first slumber party she had been invited to, and she was desperate to make a good impression. It was twice as important because, by some miracle, her father had given her permission for a sleepover—something she'd assumed he would be dead against. But Palak's father worked at Balraj's law firm, perhaps that was why he had agreed.

Nidhi had spent the afternoon with Vikram, 'rehearsing' for the sleepover. She made a list of conversation topics, ranging from Sweet Valley books to lip balm versus lip gloss, to the latest Bollywood sensation—some actor called Ritwik Roshan. Basically everything Nidhi assumed twelve-year-old girls were interested in.

Vikram had told her not to bother. 'Just be yourself.'

Nidhi snorted at that. 'Thanks for the lame advice, Viks. No one has ever liked me for "being myself", not even Papa.'

An inscrutable look crossed Vikram's face before he shrugged. 'I like you the way you are.'

But Viks didn't count because he was her best friend. He had no choice but to like her the way she was. Unless he wanted his butt kicked.

At Palak's house, Nidhi was greeted by four girls, all of whom seemed uncharacteristically excited to see her. Even though the school year was about to end, they hadn't shown the slightest inclination in talking to Nidhi before then. It didn't take long before she realized that the reason for inviting her over wasn't because this group of popular girls was interested in getting to know Nidhi. It was because they were interested in getting to know Vikram.

'Where did he go to school before this?' one of the girls asked.

'Mumbai,' Nidhi responded, fishing in the nearly empty packet of Uncle Chipps for crumbs.

'How did he get that scar?' Palak wanted to know.

'He was in a car accident a few years ago,' Nidhi said, licking the residual masala off her fingers.

'Is it true that he's an orphan?' whispered another girl.

'No, it's not!' Nidhi snapped. 'He has a family that loves him.'

It was the truth, because Vikram had Dadi. And he had Nidhi.

'Does he have a girlfriend?' The fourth girl giggled.

'No,' Nidhi said.

'Why not?'

Because girls are lame, Nidhi thought, looking at the concrete evidence right in front of her. 'Because he's busy with sports and stuff.' She shrugged.

'Does he like girls who play sports?' Palak asked.

'Ummm,' Nidhi stalled, thinking about that. 'I guess so.'

The girls giggled among themselves and Nidhi resisted the temptation to roll her eyes. Why were they so interested in Vikram, anyway? He was always covered in dirt and grass stains, and he perpetually smelt like a cricket field.

He was also really competitive, sometimes unpleasantly so. Over the years, Nidhi had learned that it was better to play on Vikram's team than against him, because it sucked to be at the receiving end of his aggression and temper. Plus, since he mostly ended up winning, it was in Nidhi's interest be his teammate.

But what these girls saw in that messy, smelly fighter-cock was beyond Nidhi.

'He's so *cute!*' they squealed, poring over his yearbook photos.

Nidhi peered at the picture of him holding up the 'Cricketer of the Year' trophy and wrinkled her nose. 'He's alright.' When the girls stared at her like she was demented, Nidhi hastily adopted a dreamy expression. 'I mean, yes. So *cute!*'

They giggled, returning their attention to the yearbook.

Maybe he's a little cute, Nidhi thought, remembering the day they had given Odie a bath together. Odie kept licking Vikram's face and Vikram had fallen to the floor, laughing in resignation as the mongrel drenched him in saliva. Nidhi thought of the day her father had made her reject the captaincy of the girls' cricket team. Vikram had slid little notes under her door to get her attention and, at one point, even a Vicks ki goli as he sang, 'Viks ki goli lo, khich-khich door karo . . .'

Nidhi felt a strange flutter in her stomach. Assuming it was a hunger pang, she reached for another packet of chips.

March 2014

Vikram answered the phone in his sleep. 'Huh-lo.'

'Good morning, sleepyhead!' said a cheerful voice on the other end.

'Nuts!' he croaked, sitting up in bed. 'How's it going?'

'We just finished the first schedule. I'm at the Jodhpur airport, heading back to Mumbai,' Natasha Sahay responded.

'Great. No trouble with Kapoor, I hope?'

'Nope. We only had one scene together, so it was fine.'

'Let me know if you need me to come, okay? As you're aware, I have all the time in the world,' Vikram said drolly.

Natasha laughed. 'Awww, sweetie, hang in there. You'll be back on your feet in no time!'

'So you haven't heard?'

'Heard what?'

'BCCI is conducting a disciplinary hearing because of the Kapoor incident.'

'Oh God! I am *so* sorry, Vikram. I feel terrible about it! I wish I hadn't—'

'It's not your fault, Nuts,' Vikram interrupted.

'It *is* my fault!' she said, sounding distraught. 'I never should've—'

'Natasha, stop it,' he said firmly. 'You're one of my closest friends. And Kapoor is an asshole who deserved what he got. In fact, I feel bad that I only got in one punch!'

She chuckled at that. 'The make-up guys have been complaining about his black eye.'

'Too bad it's just his eye and not his front teeth,' he gritted. 'I'll aim better next time.'

'Don't you dare!' she warned with a laugh. 'By the way, he asked me about us.'

'What about us?'

'Same old. "What's going on between the two of you?"'

'Tell him to mind his own fucking business,' Vikram said blandly.

'I did. But what's the source of these rumours? I have a strong feeling our managers are behind them,' Natasha whispered.

'I'm sure they are. Monty has told me a thousand times that being romantically linked to you will improve my image. Although I can't, for the life of me, see how it will benefit you.'

'Well, I suppose anyone would be a step up from Shaan Kapoor,' she teased.

'Can't argue with that.' He smiled, and then added playfully, 'Plus I've been told I'm easy on the eyes.'

'Can't argue with *that*,' she rejoindered with a gentle laugh. 'By the way, how are you liking your favourite city in the world?'

'Oh, you mean the city where "rickshaw" means "cycle rickshaw"?'

'So what do they call a regular rick?'

'"Auto." But it doesn't matter, because you don't see any of those after sunset.'

'That's absurd.'

'I can't get out of here soon enough,' Vikram groaned. 'People are supremely lazy, everything closes at midnight, there's no vada pao, and most importantly, there's no ocean. I can't wait to go back home.'

'When are you back?'

'In about ten days, to see Donna.'

'Okay, let me time my appointment with yours.'

'I'll ask Monty to do it.'

'Thanks, sweetie. We're boarding now, call you later, okay?'

'Okay, Nuts. Take care of yourself,' he said fondly, hanging up the phone.

Vikram slipped out of bed and walked downstairs to find Monty sitting at the dining table, chewing on a piece of French toast. He shot Vikram a murderous look. 'This tastes like *gatta*.'

Vikram swallowed a laugh. 'How do you know what cardboard tastes like?'

Monty's glare intensified.

'Don't be so spoilt, Monty.' Vikram chuckled. 'Remember when we had no money and French toast was a delicacy?'

Monty gave him a dirty look. 'Why aren't you ready? I'm going to drop you off at shoot and go run some errands.'

'What errands?'

'Meeting journalists to do damage control. For Shaan Kapoor wala episode.'

Vikram shrugged. 'He had it coming.'

'You know that and I know that. But how will public find out? Unless Natashaji—'

'Leave her out of it, Monty,' Vikram said.

'Lekin Vikram, if we present her version to media, I can *grentee* it will alter public opinion. More important, your disciplinary hearing will be—'

'I said, leave Natasha out of it!' Vikram bit out.

Monty sighed and reached for his bottle of pills, swallowing two with his coffee.

'Easy on the medication, tiger,' Vikram warned, heading upstairs to shower.

Nidhi paced up and down the length of the studio furiously. It was 1 p.m. and there was no sign of Vikram Walia or his Bappi Lahiri clone. She had called Monty half a dozen times, but his phone had gone unanswered.

She flopped into the chair and shot the photographer an apologetic look. 'I'm so sorry, Anoop.'

Anoop shrugged. 'Don't apologize to me, babe. You're the one paying for my time.'

Nidhi gave a resigned sigh. 'How I wish we were working with Aamir Khan. Apparently, he's the most professional celebrity in the entire industry. Unlike this Vikram Walia—arrogant, self-entitled, first-rate jerk.'

'Sorry, I'm late,' a deep voice spoke from behind her.

Nidhi's eyes widened and she froze in her seat, praying to God that Vikram hadn't heard her comment.

'Hi, Vikram,' Anoop said, struggling to keep a straight face, as he walked up to shake Vikram's hand. 'I'm Anoop.'

Nidhi stood up and turned slowly. 'Uh, hi.'

'Hello,' Vikram said formally.

Phew. He hadn't heard her.

'I'll show you to the green room,' Nidhi said.

Vikram shrugged indifferently and followed her.

'Were you stuck in traffic?' she asked, attempting polite conversation.

'No.'

Great. He didn't even offer an excuse for being late.

'Will Monty be joining us?'

'No.'

Oh-kay! So he clearly wasn't one for small talk.

A few minutes later, when Vikram made his way to the set dressed in jeans, a white button-down and a navy blue blazer jacket, Nidhi tried not to stare. Even in his casual attire, she thought he could easily be on the cover of *Vogue*.

Oh wait, he already was last month.

Nidhi was utterly surprised by his attitude during the shoot. Say what you would about his hot-headedness on the cricket field and his improper outbursts off it, in the studio, Vikram Walia was a complete professional. Aside from being extremely camera-friendly, he was responsive to the crew and, unlikely most celebrities, didn't disrupt the shoot by constantly texting on his phone. Nidhi felt a reluctant stab of respect for his work ethic.

At the end of the shoot, they all gathered around Anoop's monitor to go over his work.

'The pictures look great, Anoop,' Vikram said with genuine admiration.

'Thanks, man,' Anoop replied modestly.

The *News Today* creative director, Khalid, pointed to something on the screen. 'How would you feel about airbrushing that?'

'What are you referring to?' Vikram asked, peering at the screen.

'The scar on your eyebrow,' Khalid clarified.

'No!' Nidhi burst out, before she could stop herself.

All three men turned to her in unison, surprised by the intensity of her protest.

'Ummm,' she mumbled, 'I mean, I don't think we should.'

Khalid shook his head. 'We need a soft, happy feel to the campaign, and the scar makes him appear harsh. We should get rid of it unless, of course, Vikram has an objection.'

Vikram shrugged. 'I don't care, man. It's your call.'

'No,' Nidhi said firmly. 'We need the scar.'

'Why?' Khalid asked.

Because it's a symbol of his strength. A talisman that represents everything he went through before he got where he is today.

Unaware of Vikram's inquisitive gaze, Nidhi said, 'Because it makes him seem more human. People like weaknesses and imperfections in celebrities because it takes them off their pedestal and makes them more relatable.'

'Hmmm.' Khalid nodded. 'Fair enough. What do you think, Vikram?'

Nidhi thought she saw Vikram's features soften briefly before his face became impassive and he said, 'I think I need a drink.'

The men laughed and nodded in agreement.

'You coming along, Nidhi?' Anoop asked.

Protocol suggested that, as brand manager, Nidhi be present while—and pay for—entertaining the celebrity. But she didn't want to spend any more time in Vikram's presence than absolutely necessary, so she said, 'Uh, I have stuff to do.'

'What stuff?' Anoop asked.

'Office stuff,' Nidhi evaded.

'Sounds important,' Vikram said dryly, before turning around and walking towards the green room.

'What's wrong with you?' Khalid hissed in Nidhi's ear. 'He's our brand ambassador. Stop being so rude!'

'Fine,' Nidhi muttered. 'One drink.'

At the private room of a bar in Hauz Khas Village, seated across the table from Nidhi, Vikram watched her slender fingers wrap themselves around a lager glass. He had always seen her hands calloused from a match or swollen from a fight. He had never seen them like this—smooth, feminine, gentle. He wondered if they felt as soft as they looked.

With every subsequent minute he spent in her company, Vikram became more curious about the reason for Nidhi's metamorphosis. Who was this prim, proper, graceful woman in front of him? And what happened to the combative little spitfire he had played sports with as a kid?

Anoop and Khalid were in an animated debate about the Indian cricket team's performance on foreign soil, and they were occasionally drawing Vikram into the discussion. Nidhi, on the other hand, was staring into her beer. Vikram had tried to initiate conversation with her several times, but to no avail. She wasn't being rude—no, far from it. On the contrary, she was nodding interestedly at whatever he was saying, and responding to his questions with unmitigated politeness. And her reserved cordialness was starting to annoy the hell out of Vikram.

'I'm guessing it's frustrating to sit around when the rest of your team is out there playing,' Anoop said empathetically, when the inevitable subject of Vikram's suspension came up.

'Yes, it's quite frustrating. But then that's what I get for being an *arrogant, self-entitled, first-rate jerk*,' Vikram said, deadpan.

Nidhi choked on her beer. Anoop and Khalid burst out laughing. And Vikram broke into a lazy smile, enjoying the flush that crept up Nidhi's cheeks. She looked up at him, the guilt evident in her jade eyes. And the expression instantly took him back to that night twelve years ago.

Is it true, Nidhi? he had asked.

And the same guilty expression had snuck into her eyes. *Yes.*

Vikram's jaw hardened and he turned away from her.

'I'm sorry,' she said with genuine remorse.

'Sorry that you said it or sorry that I heard it?' he challenged.

'Both,' she admitted.

'It's okay,' he responded brusquely.

An instinct told Nidhi that something other than her rude comment was bothering Vikram. 'What's wrong?' she asked.

'I have a dinner appointment and I'm running late,' he lied, irritated that she could still read him so well.

'Does that mean Natasha Sahay is in town?' Anoop grinned.

'Why would . . .' Vikram's voice trailed off.

Right. He was supposedly dating Natasha.

'Come on, Vikram. You can tell us—off the record,' Khalid chuckled.

Vikram feigned a mysterious smile. 'With you press folks, nothing is ever off the record.'

Nidhi stared into her glass, running her thumb over its rim.

Vikram stood up and reached for his wallet, but Nidhi shook her head. 'I've got this.'

'It was my idea, I'll get it,' Vikram said.

'Absolutely not! You're the brand ambassador, we can't let you pay,' Nidhi argued.

Vikram tossed two thousand rupees on the table. 'Don't worry about it,' he said, his tone clipped.

Wary of the sudden chill in his attitude, Nidhi acquiesced. 'Okay, I appreciate it. Thank you.'

As soon as Vikram disappeared through the back exit, Khalid turned to Nidhi. 'What the hell is your problem with him?'

'You are very *chup-chaap* today,' Monty said between mouthfuls of butter chicken and garlic naan. Vikram had taken pity on the cook, and on poor Monty, and ordered dinner from Moti Mahal.

'Not quiet. Just tired from the shoot,' Vikram lied.

The truth was that his thoughts were occupied by a pair of radiant green eyes. And beautiful, slender fingers. And stunning long legs.

Did the woman have anything in her wardrobe other than short skirts? Vikram wondered irritably. Then he remembered the first night she had climbed over her gate in jeans, and a reluctant smile formed on his lips.

He looked up and found Monty watching him closely. 'What are you thinking?'

'How was your appointment with the journalist?' Vikram asked.

'I met two of them actually—one from *Hindustan Times* and one from *Times of India*. They both think you and Natashaji look *ultimate* together,' Monty said, dipping a piece of naan in his bowl of dal makhani before popping it in his mouth.

'Yeah, maybe cool it with the Natasha stories for a bit,' Vikram said absent-mindedly.

'Lekin why? She is Bollywood's *switty* pie and being seen with her will portray you in positive light.'

'I thought that's what the *News Today* campaign was for,' Vikram pointed out.

'Haan, haan. Just let me get one solid photo of you both in newspaper. *Uske baad, bas*!' Monty promised, biting into a succulent kebab.

'Which reminds me, can you call Donna and make an appointment for Nuts on the same day?'

'Already done.' Monty winked.

'Thanks.'

Monty crunched a pickled onion. 'By the way, I got a call from Mukka Supari. They want to sign you for TV campaign.'

'No,' Vikram said succinctly.

'Lekin listen at least, free *ka ek crore hai*! They don't even want to do shoot or anything. Just slow-motion scene of you punching Shaan Kapoor along with tagline: "Mukka Supari. Shaan Se Khao."'

Vikram gave him a dirty look. 'Wouldn't that tagline work better if Kapoor had punched me?'

'Chalo, at least your sense of humour is intact.' Monty chuckled. '*Vaise*, Vikram, you should seriously consider changing your jersey number. This thirteen number is very bad luck!' he said with an exaggerated shudder.

Vikram rolled his eyes. 'You and your superstitions, Monty. It doesn't matter if thirteen is unlucky for the whole world, it's lucky for *me*.'

Monty kissed the large garnet ring on his middle finger. '*Bhagwan bachaye*.'

'When's the next *News Today* appearance?' Vikram asked casually.

'On Saturday at rural school, seventy kilometres from here,' Monty said.

Four days before I see Nidhi again.

Annoyed that *that* was the first thought to cross his mind, Vikram dragged himself up to his room and lay down on the bed, trying to rationalize his thoughts. Why did he suddenly give a damn about Nidhi?

So what if she had pounced on Khalid for suggesting they Photoshop Vikram's scar? And so what if it had brought back a potent memory that Vikram couldn't get out of his head?

They were fourteen years old, sitting on his grandmother's porch after an emotionally turbulent day. Rao Uncle had driven them to a dog cemetery where they had buried Odie. Nidhi had been crying for hours and Vikram had been trying to repress his own tears. He stroked her back and whispered soothing words to her as she buried her face in his neck and wept. When the harsh sobs subsided to feeble whimpers, he turned her chin up to face him. 'Don't cry, Nidhi. When you cry, your eyes look like algae floating in dirty water,' he teased, and his heart filled with pride when she gave a small, brave smile at his attempt at levity.

'Odie was the only one who loved me unconditionally, Viks,' she whispered. 'He never tried to change me.'

'That's not true, Nidhi,' Vikram said, his voice clogged with emotion. 'I also . . . I don't want you to change.'

In a gesture of gratitude, Nidhi reached up and touched his face, running her fingertips over his jaw, gently rubbing her thumb over his scar.

That's when Vikram leaned in and kissed her. It was a soft, fleeting kiss, with their lips barely touching. It was her first kiss, and his too.

When they parted, Nidhi looked down at her hands shyly, waiting for him to speak.

Vikram remained silent, trying to process the flood of emotions that was suddenly raging through him. In one week, Vikram had to decide whether or not to accept the scholarship to the Mumbai Cricket Academy. So far, it had been a no-brainer—of course, he would move to Mumbai and fulfil his dream of playing professional cricket.

But that kiss had changed everything. That kiss had proved that they were more than just friends. That Nidhi too felt something for him far deeper than just friendship. Vikram couldn't desert her now, when she clearly needed him. But the strangest thing was that even at that young age, Vikram knew that he needed Nidhi more.

'*I'm leaving for Dehradun tomorrow,*' he said, *struggling to remain calm under the storm of feelings that seemed to be engulfing him.*

Nidhi nodded. 'For the cricket camp.'

'*I'll be back in five days,*' he said gruffly. '*Can we talk then?*'

'*Okay, Viks,*' she said softly. '*Thanks for coming with me today.*'

'*Odie was as much mine as he was yours,*' he reminded her with a smile.

Vikram's chest tightened at the memory. For years, the crux of his relationship with Nidhi had been defined by what had happened on the dreadful night that had followed five days later. On the rare occasion that he did allow himself to think about her, that night was all he chose to remember. And invariably, it always drudged up the virulent hatred that he had convinced himself was the only emotion he was capable of feeling for Nidhi.

But thinking about their first kiss had reminded Vikram of all the other things he had forced himself to forget—her earnestness, her tenacity and her loyalty. It had reminded him of all the reasons they had been best friends.

Maybe, Vikram thought rationally, it was time to let go of all the negativity. Perhaps Nidhi hadn't really meant what she had said about him back then. After all, she had been a mere teenager herself.

Whatever the case may be, Vikram realized he couldn't keep pretending that they were strangers. It was time to put the past behind them and move on.

'Hi, Papa,' Nidhi said, striding into her father's study. 'You wanted to see me?'

Balraj Marwah nodded, gesturing for her to take a seat. He spent the next few minutes finishing the email he had been typing, before turning his attention to his daughter. 'You have a lunch appointment with Kuku this Saturday.'

'*Who?*' Nidhi asked, stifling the sudden urge to laugh at the name.

'Kamal Kukreja, junior partner at Marwah & Mehta. I informed you about him last week.'

'He goes by *Kuku?*' Nidhi asked, bewildered.

'He shares his first name with one of the senior partners, so we call him Kuku to avoid confusion.'

'Oh,' Nidhi said, biting back a smile. 'Unfortunately, I have a work commitment on Saturday during the day, but I can do dinner instead.'

'Why are you working on a Saturday?' her father asked, raising a suspicious eyebrow.

'Because we're visiting a rural school for a social-marketing campaign, and Saturday works best.' No point telling her father about Vikram; Balraj had never liked him much.

'Where is this place?' her father demanded, standing up to his full height of six feet.

Nidhi immediately recognized the intimidation tactic, and since she didn't want to be forbidden from going, she shook her head reassuringly. 'It's not very far. I'll be back before dinner.'

'Okay, but take Rao with you,' Balraj said in a tone that invited no argument. 'I'll be operating from the Mumbai office for the next two weeks and you can make use of Rao's services while I'm away.'

'Will you be back in time for your check-up with Dr Krishnan?' she asked, referring to his cardiologist.

Balraj nodded distractedly.

'Great.' Nidhi smiled approvingly. 'Is there anything else?'

He shook his head. 'I'll ask Kuku to touch base with you. You can mutually decide the mechanics of your meeting.'

How romantic, Nidhi thought, slipping out of her father's study.

In her room, she kicked off her heels and dialled Risha's number.

Risha answered on the first ring. 'How was the shoot with Wicked Walia?'

'It wasn't bad, actually. He was quite well behaved,' Nidhi said, walking towards her window.

'That's a surprise,' Risha replied.

Speaking of surprises, the next-door neighbours' lights suddenly came on. The window was shut so Nidhi couldn't see who was inside. Had someone moved into the Walias' house? Had Vikram sold the house? Nidhi made a mental note to ask the Trio about it.

'I'm thinking of throwing a party at home,' Nidhi whispered into the phone. 'Wanna help me plan it?'

'No, thanks,' Risha said dryly. 'Talking to your dad is like taking the witness stand in court.'

Nidhi chuckled at the rather accurate description of her father's conversation skills—a strange combination of perfunctory and peremptory. 'Papa is going to Mumbai for two weeks, so I have the house all to myself.'

'Oooh, sounds like fun! We can invite a bunch of *NT* folks and Shorty and the rest of your DU friends.'

'Exactly. I was thinking we could do a barbecue in the garden. Do you think it's chilly enough for a bonfire?'

'It's more *angeethi* weather than full-fledged bonfire weather.'

'Okay, how about Friday night?'

'Works for me!'

'By the way, the guy my dad is setting me up with—guess his name.'

'Ranbir?'

'I wish.'

'Hrithik?'

'Guess again.'

'Akshay?'

'Kuku.'

Risha burst out laughing. 'As in "*Choli Ke Peeche Kya Hai*"?'

'What?'

'Don't you remember the prelude to the song? It went "Ku-ku-ku-ku-ku-ku-ku-ku"!'

'Oh, God! Thanks, Rish. Now every time I say his name, I'll hear the song in my head!'

August 2001

Diary of Nidhi Marwah
Age 13

Vikram is such a child sometimes.

The fact that Dadi calls me 'Billi' is something I have to live with. But now Vikram has started calling me that too! And the worst part is, the two of them keep giggling about it, like there's some big inside joke. I asked them why they call me that, even though they know I hate cats; they said it's a secret.

Anyway, that's not the only reason he's a child.

Yesterday, I gave Gaurav Sinha a photograph of me. Gaurav said he wanted to make a portrait of me because I'm pretty (which, by the way, is the first time a boy has EVER used that word to describe me), but since Papa won't let me invite him over, I gave Gaurav my photograph instead. What I didn't get was why it made Vikram so upset.

'You don't know what boys are like,' he said, running a hand through his hair. 'You should ask me before you do stupid things like this.'

I told him that I do know what boys are like, since I spend all my time with one. He said that's not the same thing.

Such a child.

March 2014

'What do you mean you can't share it right now?' Nidhi demanded, clutching the receiver of her office landline tighter.

'*Thoda* patience, Nidhiji,' Monty said calmly.

'Monty, the ad has to go to press in two hours. I need Vikram's approval *now*!'

'Lekin he needs to see the ad,' Monty replied.

'I emailed it to you ages ago,' Nidhi reminded him impatiently.

'He needs to see a physical proof. He is very particular about looking good.'

'In that case, maybe he should consider altering his *behaviour* instead of his appearance,' she muttered. 'Look, I've been asking you to share the address since this morning. By now a peon could have gone and come back with Vikram's approval!'

'No pyoon-shoon, Nidhiji. You are talking about best batsman in world cricket,' Monty said in a grave tone.

This from the man who had pitched Vikram as a 'humble, down-to-earth boy from the neighbourhood' during their first meeting.

'Okay, Montyji,' Nidhi gushed in a sing-song voice. 'I will *personally* take the proofs to him, ji. Can you please text me the address, ji?'

'It is very nearby to your house. You live in Lajpat Nagar only, no? Why don't you leave for home and I will SMS you address *immijately*?' Monty suggested.

'Fine,' Nidhi grumbled, reaching for her purse.

Thirty minutes later, as Rao Uncle pulled into the driveway of her house, Nidhi was on the brink of losing her temper. She had been calling Monty non-stop ever since she left work, but the calls had gone unanswered. The next time she saw him, she would wring his fat neck.

She sat on the sofa in the lobby of her home and shoved her face in her hands, acknowledging the harsh reality of her professional life.

The EducateIndia campaign was doomed to fail.

Nidhi's dismal thoughts were interrupted by the faint sound of Mangal Singh and Bhimsen guffawing behind her. 'What are you two giggling about?' she asked.

'*Kuch nahi*, Nidhi Baby,' Mangal said, unable to hide his smile.

Nidhi sighed. 'What's for dinner?'

'Biryani.'

'*Biryani*? You know I don't eat rice at night,' Nidhi said, puzzled.

'It's not for you, Nidhi Baby.' Bhimsen sniggered.

'Papa is in Mumbai. So who is it for?' Nidhi asked curiously.

'Vikram Baba,' he responded.

'*Who?*' Nidhi gasped.

'Vikram Baba is in town,' Mangal Singh said, his chubby face beaming with pride.

'I know,' Nidhi groaned. 'But how do *you* . . .' Her phone beeped and she picked it up, finding the answer to her unfinished question on its screen, in a pithy message from Monty.

68 Lajpat Nagar.

For a moment, Nidhi thought her eyes had deceived her and she was looking at her *own* address, 66 Lajpat Nagar. But as soon as she realized what the difference in that one digit meant, she grabbed the printouts and stormed out of the house, her entire body shaking with restrained anger.

When she barged into the Walias' living room, she found Monty sitting on the sofa. 'Where the hell is he?'

Monty grinned, not seeming the least bit surprised by her appearance or her tone. 'Upstairs in his room.'

Nidhi threw back her shoulders, raised her chin and stomped up the old wooden staircase, not bothering to knock before entering Vikram's room. 'Is this your idea of a joke?' she snapped.

'Hello, Nidhi. Lovely to see you too,' Vikram said, an amused smile playing on his lips.

His long legs were stretched out on the twin-size bed in a lazy posture that was the very embodiment of indolence and relaxation.

Nidhi's temper rose a notch. 'You're staying *here*?'

'Where else would I be staying?'

'Monty said you were staying at home.'

'This *is* my home.'

'Yes, but I didn't realize home meant *here*. I assumed a home more conducive to your . . .'

'To my what?' he challenged.

Your wealth. Your ego. Your sheer arrogance.

'Your taste.'

'Right,' he said dryly.

Nidhi remembered why she was there in the first place. 'I've been chasing you since morning.'

Vikram locked his hands behind his head, looking more carefree than ever. 'Congratulations. The chase is over.'

Nidhi took a deep breath. 'Vikram, this may be just another campaign for you, but it's very important to *News Today*, and very important to me. I've worked on it for the last six months and now when it's finally about to become a reality, I won't let someone like you put it at risk.'

'What does "someone like me" mean, exactly?' Vikram asked casually.

'Look, you might be a big celebrity who is used to getting his way all the time—'

'You think I'm a spoilt brat,' he stated in a flat tone.

She resisted the urge to nod. 'I just think that a certain level of commitment and seriousness is required to—'

'Nidhi,' he said, swinging his legs off the bed and standing up. 'Last week, did you or did you not tell me that you would be my single point of contact?'

A look of confusion crossed her face. 'Of course, I did. And I've been following up with Monty since—'

'You were supposed to be *my* point of contact, not Monty's.'

She gave him an incredulous look. 'But this is standard protocol. We never approach the talent directly, we always go through their manager.'

'That wasn't our deal. I can call your boss and have him jog your memory,' Vikram said, reaching for his cell phone.

'That won't be necessary,' Nidhi said icily.

'Didn't think so,' he said, taking a step closer to her.

Even in heels, Nidhi was several inches shorter than Vikram. He smelt fresh and misty, like a cool ocean breeze, and his broad shoulders seemed to fill the entire room.

'So you, ummm, you . . .' she stuttered, racking her brain for what she had been about to say.

'I, ummm, I?' he prompted with a grin.

'You want me to call you for every little thing? I mean, won't that be really annoying?' she asked.

His eyes locked with hers and he spoke in a quiet voice. 'When has that ever stopped you, Nidhi?'

A shiver ran down her spine.

Was he making a reference to their childhood? Was he actually acknowledging knowing her before their meeting at *News Today*?

'That's true,' she said, graciously accepting his silently offered truce.

'I know this campaign is important to you, and believe me, it's important to me too. I promise not to screw it up,' he said sincerely.

She nodded. 'Thank you.'

'And while we're working together, it would be nice to get along, wouldn't it?' he ventured casually.

'It *really* would,' Nidhi said with such feeling that Vikram chuckled. He took the proofs from her hand and studied them for a couple of minutes before nodding. 'They look great. Go for it.'

'That's it?' she asked, surprised.

'Yup.'

'That was much easier than I thought,' she said bluntly.

A smile spread across his features. '*I'm* much easier than you think.'

And that was the moment when Nidhi *finally* understood what the fuss was all about.

One side of Vikram's mouth curved up in a crooked half-smile so sexy that it sent a jolt of electricity through Nidhi's nervous system. A flush spread over her neck, and her cheeks flared up under his heated gaze.

She turned around abruptly, walking towards the door in her dazed state.

'Nidhi?' he called after her.

She looked at him expectantly, resisting the urge to fan her face.

'Would you like to have dinner on Friday?'

'I can't.'

His smile faded. 'Oh.'

'I mean, I'm throwing a party at my house on Friday. Do you . . . do you wanna come?' she asked tentatively.

'Do you *want* me to come?' he asked, confused by the hesitation in her voice.

'Yes, sure. But it's just going to be a bunch of . . . regular people. Will you be okay with that?'

Vikram's lips twitched. 'I'm a regular person too.'

'I just meant—'

'I know what you meant. I'd love to come.'

'Okay.'

'And Nidhi?'

'What?'

'Text me the address.'

She burst out laughing.

Nidhi watched from across the garden as Vikram humoured Risha's request for a selfie. They were standing by the angeethi, and Risha was laughing at something Vikram had said. Come to think of it, they'd been talking for almost an hour, and Risha had been laughing a lot. Tanvi, on the other hand, was watching Vikram with crossed arms and narrowed eyes filled with suspicion.

Nidhi started walking in their direction, but halfway through the garden, she ran into Sam.

'You are the prettiest girl in the whole world,' he said, bending down to kiss her cheek.

'You come up with the shittiest lines in the whole world,' she replied, imitating his tone.

'That's because I believe in less talk, more *action*.' He smirked.

Nidhi laughed. 'Glad you could make it, Sam.'

'Of course. And I'm glad to see you've got our celebrity wrapped around your little finger. Just like me,' he said with mock solemnity.

Her head jerked up. 'What are you talking about?'

'He can't take his eyes off you. Not that I blame him,' Sam said, raking a slow, appreciative glance over her.

Nidhi flushed. 'Don't be ridiculous! I'm a professional.'

Sam sighed dramatically. 'I'm aware of that. I've been at the receiving end of your *professionalism* for the last two years.'

'I loved the campaign coverage today, by the way,' Nidhi said, trying to change the subject.

'Thanks, but if I wanted to talk shop, I would've gone to Sukhi's house,' Sam said dryly.

'Sure, if you want to hang out at a dingy flat in Paharganj,' Nidhi retorted. 'Which is probably where he lives for easy access to booze, sex and drugs.'

'Actually, he lives in a fancy apartment in Gurgaon. By the way, did I tell you about Chirag?'

'The sports intern?'

'As of yesterday, no longer an intern, but a junior copy editor.'

Nidhi's eyebrows shot up. 'Doesn't that make him the first intern Sukhi has hired in a million years?'

'Yes. That too after assuring Chirag on day one that he had no future at *News Today*.'

'Wow. So then how did he land the job?'

'Sukhi told all the interns that one offer was available for the person who could change certain autocorrect settings on Kabir's laptop,' Sam said, referring to Kabir Bose, editor of *News Today*'s entertainment and lifestyle supplement, *Delhi Today*, and Sukhi's long-term nemesis. Despite having started their careers together as friends, the two men had turned into bitter rivals after spending over a decade at *News Today*.

'What autocorrect settings?' Nidhi wondered.

'Change "what" to "what the fuck".' Sam grinned.

Nidhi's eyes widened. 'No way!'

'Yup. And Chirag succeeded! Apparently Kabir sent an email to Jay asking him "what the fuck time" he was free to meet.' Sam chuckled.

'Sukhi is such an asshole,' Nidhi laughed.

'Sure is. But for reasons unknown, your Mr Walia is a big fan of his,' Sam reminded her.

'A big fan of whom?' an amused voice asked from behind them.

Nidhi spun around and came face-to-face with Vikram. 'Sukhi,' she responded casually, trying not to notice the way his steel-grey V-neck sweater clung to his muscular chest.

'He's a nice guy.' Vikram shrugged.

Nidhi and Sam broke into uncontrollable laughter.

Vikram looked at them in confusion. 'What's so funny?'

'You're the only person in the world who thinks Sukhi is "nice",' Nidhi said, still laughing.

'Nice as a rabid dog,' Sam whispered in her ear.

Vikram crossed his arms over his chest, watching how close Sameer was standing to Nidhi. His arm was slung casually around her shoulder as she giggled at his comment.

Vikram suddenly realized that he had no idea if Nidhi had a boyfriend. Maybe she was dating *this* guy. He was a good-looking fellow, if you were into the hippie types. Kurta and Nehru jacket with distressed jeans. Longish, messy hair. Probably a wine drinker. Definitely an asshole.

'I was just telling Nidhi how pretty she's looking tonight,' Sameer said, watching Vikram intently.

'Yes, she is,' Vikram said, his tone and expression completely blank.

'Talk about a genuine compliment,' Nidhi teased.

Vikram stared moodily into his glass.

'All set for tomorrow?' Sameer asked, referring to the rural-school visit.

Vikram nodded. 'Are you coming too?'

'Unfortunately not. I'll try to bear the separation as best as I can,' Sameer said, cocking his head towards Nidhi.

'Sam!' Nidhi warned.

For some reason, Nidhi's use of the nickname made Vikram want to drive his fist into Sameer's face.

A few hours later, when the party drew to a close and people started heading home, Risha slipped her arm through Nidhi's. 'I love him!'

'Who?' Nidhi asked.

Tanvi rolled her eyes. 'Walia, who else?'

Nidhi felt her stomach clench.

'He's such a great guy!' Risha gushed.

'I'm not impressed,' Tanvi said blandly.

Risha ignored her and went on. 'The music was blaring when I introduced myself and he misheard my name as "Riksha". So the entire night he's been calling me "Auto Rickshaw".' She laughed.

They have their own little nicknames now?

'He's *nothing* like the media describes him. On the contrary, he's really chilled out and fun. The only thing they got right is his movie-star good looks,' Risha said, wiggling her eyebrows.

Nidhi turned to Tanvi expectantly.

'Frankly,' Tanvi admitted with some reluctance, 'I was quite disappointed not to hear a single *gaali* come out of his mouth the entire night.'

'You know how exaggerated newspaper articles can be,' Risha said, resting her elbow on Tanvi's head, emphasizing the six-inch height difference between them.

'A little more loyalty to your profession and a little less to the man-whore, please,' Tanvi said dryly.

'He is *not* a man-whore, he's a complete gentleman,' Risha said defensively.

'Don't listen to her,' Tanvi said to Nidhi. 'She's clearly smitten.'

Nidhi frowned at Risha. 'You do know he has a girlfriend, right?'

'Who cares? You're way cooler than Natasha Sahay!'

'No, I'm . . . wait, what? *I'm* cooler than her?'

'Duh. Of course you are.'

'What are you saying?' Nidhi asked, confused.

'I'm saying that Vikram has been staring at you the entire night and you've been ignoring him.'

Nidhi gave Risha a blank expression.

'So he's a gawking lech. Big surprise,' Tanvi said in a flat tone.

Risha shot her a dirty look before turning to Nidhi. 'We're getting a ride home with Khalid. And *you* should go be a good host now.' She grinned, darting a quick, pointed glance at Vikram.

Nidhi followed Risha's gaze and realized that Vikram was leaning against a tree, sipping a beer and watching her. She felt her cheeks heat up and she hugged Risha goodbye, mostly to hide her face.

'Come on, Shorty.' Risha grinned, dragging a surly Tanvi behind her.

She walked towards Vikram, her legs watery and unstable. 'Hey.'

'Hi.'

'Did you have fun?'

He nodded. 'Your friends are cool. Risha is a particularly nice girl. Super funny too.'

She smiled in agreement. 'She's hilarious.'

'Tanvi, on the other hand, doesn't give a damn that she's a foot shorter than me—and seems ready to set me on fire,' he said dryly.

Nidhi laughed. 'That's her standard first impression, but she grows on you.'

'I noticed you didn't hug her goodbye,' Vikram said.

'She doesn't like hugs. It's a weird personality thing,' Nidhi explained. Then feeling the need to defend her friend, added, 'But she's always got my back.'

'Your boyfriend is nice too,' Vikram said casually.

Nidhi's eyes widened. '*Who*?'

'Sameer.'

She snorted. 'He's not my boyfriend. He's just a habitual flirt.'

Suddenly, Vikram's entire body seemed to relax and he grinned at her. 'Good, because I was just being polite. I don't *really* think he's nice.'

She laughed. 'You haven't changed at all.'

'I haven't?'

'To be fair, I've only known you for a week.'

'A week *and* six years,' he reminded her.

Nidhi stared at the ground, unsure of what to say. She was spared the awkwardness of a response when Bhimsen suddenly appeared in front of them. 'Vikram Baba,' he began, his eyes aglow with excitement. 'Cricket *khelegi*?'

'*Abhi?*' Nidhi asked. 'It's late, Bhimsen. The neighbours will complain.'

Bhimsen looked at her, then at Vikram, then back at her.

Right. Vikram *was* 'the neighbours'.

Nidhi tried a different tack. 'Vikram and I have to wake up very early for work.'

Bhimsen's face fell and Nidhi tried to salvage his mood. 'But we can play some other—'

'She's just scared she'll lose, Bhimsen,' Vikram interjected, a smug smile on his face. 'I'm ready to play.'

'You're joking!' Nidhi groaned.

'I never joke about cricket.' He shrugged.

Mangal Singh came running from inside the house, balancing two bats and a ball in his giant hands. *'Khelein?'*

'Do you want to change?' Vikram asked Nidhi, conducting a deliberate perusal of her appearance, from her blow-dried hair to her short black dress and her knee-high boots.

'Worried you'll be distracted?' she challenged.

'You wish.' Vikram smirked.

They followed the standard rules of gully cricket: one-tip-one-hand, outside out, etc., and it didn't take Vikram long to realize that even though he had joked about it, playing against Nidhi in her current outfit wasn't the wisest of decisions.

He couldn't concentrate on batting because he couldn't take his eyes off her gorgeous legs.

He couldn't concentrate on bowling because her batting stance accentuated every one of her perfect curves.

And he clearly couldn't concentrate on fielding, he realized when he dropped an easy catch, because he was enthralled simply by watching her run barefoot in the driveway.

Vikram and Bhimsen lost the match by twenty-five runs—probably, Vikram thought with disgust, the largest margin by which a professional cricketer had ever lost a five-over gully cricket match.

Nidhi gave Mangal Singh a celebratory high five, then ran up to Vikram and elbowed him in the ribs. 'Try not to cry yourself to sleep, loser!'

Vikram put her in a chokehold and rubbed his knuckles on her hair. 'Don't get too cocky, Billi.'

Nidhi gasped and he let her go immediately.

'What did you just call me?' she asked, her mouth agape.

'Nothing,' he said firmly. 'I'm going home. Will you wake me up in the morning?'

'Absolutely not. Wake up yourself,' she scoffed.

'Okay, but don't blame me if we're late.' He shrugged.

'Use an alarm!' she snapped.

Years of waking up early for net practice had helped Vikram develop such a strong internal body clock that he almost never used an alarm. But Nidhi didn't know that, so he fibbed, 'I always sleep through it.'

'Fine,' Nidhi grumbled. 'I'll wake you up.'

She stormed into the house, muttering to herself. And even though Vikram only caught snatches of her rant— 'supremely annoying' and 'spoilt child'—inexplicably, they made him smile.

August 2001

Diary of Nidhi Marwah
Age 13

Today was the worst day of my life!!!

That jerk Gaurav Sinha painted a dirty cartoon of me in the boys' toilet and all the boys made fun of me all day long! Vikram whacked me on the head with his science book (it's the thickest one) and yelled at me for not listening to him. When he realized I was trying not to cry, he apologized for shouting. I asked him what the painting looked like but he told me not to bother about it. 'Don't worry, Nidhi. I'll fix it.'

Then he took three bottles of black shoe polish and painted over the cartoon. By the time he came out of the boys' toilet, his hands were completely black and there were traces of shoe polish all over his face and his clothes. After that, he got sent to the principal's office for damaging school property and now he needs to write a 300-word essay on 'The Effects of Vandalism in the Community'.

March 2014

The next day, Nidhi knocked on Vikram's door promptly at 6 a.m.

'Come in.'

She was expecting to find him in the same position as last time—sprawled lazily on a bed two inches too short for him. Which is why her eyes popped wide open at the sight that greeted her.

Vikram was standing in front of his closet, hair slightly damp from a shower, wearing jeans.

Just jeans.

He glanced at her. 'Good morning.'

Nidhi gaped at his bare chest.

One corner of Vikram's mouth tilted up and he said, louder this time, 'Good morning.'

'Uh, hey. Good morning,' Nidhi said, turning away from him and walking towards the window to collect herself.

'Wanna help me pick a shirt?' he asked, his voice dripping with amusement.

'No, thanks,' she said, pretending to stare outside the window. 'In fact,' she said, turning around, 'I'm going to wait downstairs.'

Halfway to the door, Vikram caught her wrist and spun her around.

Nidhi's breath froze as she crashed into his hard chest, her face disturbingly close to his. It took every ounce of restraint in her body not to glance down at the abs that *Cosmopolitan India* had described as 'sinfully delicious'.

'Come on, Nidhi. I want to make a good impression on the kids.'

She yanked her wrist free and walked to his closet, then grabbed the first shirt she saw and handed it to him.

'If only you had put half the thought in choosing that shirt as you did in choosing your dress,' Vikram said, giving her formal navy blue dress a thorough once-over.

'How do you . . .' Nidhi's voice trailed off and her expression became accusing. She walked to his window and saw that he had a clear view of her room. She tried to recall if she had left her window open while getting dressed that morning, but Vikram's wolfish smile made it clear that she had.

'You are such a perv!' she snapped, giving him a mutinous glare before making a haughty exit from his room.

A few minutes later, they sped down Delhi's roads with Rao Uncle in the driver's seat, Monty in the passenger seat and Nidhi and Vikram in the back. And even though Vikram didn't think much of Delhi, he couldn't help but be charmed by the sights that ran past his window. Buildings alternating between Victorian and Mughal architecture, wide roads fringed by lush green trees and the elevated metro winding through the city. And, of course, there was one other thing Delhi had to offer that Mumbai didn't: the woman seated next to him.

He watched from the corner of his eye as Nidhi rapidly made and answered calls. She was like a whirlwind. The event-management agency was already at the venue and they kept calling her every few minutes with problems and queries, but nothing seemed to faze her.

'Anoop will get there soon,' she told the event guys calmly when they complained about the photographer's delayed arrival. 'He rides a motorcycle and doesn't take calls while he's on the road.'

'How do you know for sure?' Vikram asked her when she hung up.

'Because I spoke to him before he left. And even if I hadn't, I know he'll be there. He's a thorough professional,' she said.

'As opposed to?' Vikram asked, raising an eyebrow.

She gave him an angelic smile. 'Why do you ask me questions you won't like the answers to?'

He laughed at her impertinent response. 'It seems like you really love your job.'

'I want to do social marketing in the long run, and EducateIn is a good way to start,' she said.

'Yes,' Monty muttered sleepily from his seat. 'Facebook is the future.'

Nidhi chuckled. 'Not social *media* marketing, just social marketing.'

'Hain?' Monty grunted. 'What is *diffrunce*?'

'The focus of social marketing is non-commercial.'

'NGO type?' Monty asked.

'Kind of. To put it very simply, marketing for causes that benefit society and help people,' Nidhi explained.

'It suits you,' Vikram said.

'What makes you say that?' she asked with a surprised smile.

'Even as a kid, you were always trying to help people, whether or not they wanted your help,' he said wryly.

Nidhi gave him a sheepish smile. 'I wasn't that bad.'

Vikram gazed into her eyes. 'You took in a stray and changed his life.'

'On the contrary,' she said, her expression softening, 'Odie changed my life.'

I wasn't talking about Odie.

'Your hand has healed,' Nidhi said randomly, glancing at his right hand.

The first day she'd seen him, his knuckles had been raw and swollen, probably from the shiner he had given Shaan Kapoor.

Vikram flexed his hand unconsciously and gave her a lopsided smile. 'It's odd that while we were growing up, *you* were always the one getting into fights.'

'Only because of the rowdy company I kept.' She grinned, tipping her head in his direction. 'By the way, I've always wondered why Gaurav Sinha didn't show up at school for the rest of week after the lewd cartoon episode.'

He gave a casual shrug. 'Maybe he got conjunctivitis.'

'From the black eye you gave him?' she guessed.

'Probably.' He grinned.

She shot him an accusatory look. 'I knew it!'

'By the way, *I've* always wondered, why did you punch Raghav Reddy in the fifth standard?'

'It doesn't matter,' she said, avoiding his eyes.

'So tell me,' he said evenly.

A shadow crossed her face and she hesitated.

'Come on, Nidhi. Spill.'

'He called you a "stupid orphan".'

Vikram blinked.

'And let me make it very clear that "stupid" is not the word I had an issue with,' she teased.

Vikram opened his mouth to speak, but no words came out. He was astonished by her confession. Not because he thought she was lying, but because if she was speaking the truth, something was terribly amiss.

His thoughts instantly went back to that fateful night and to the moments that had led to their big confrontation.

Nidhi is only friends with you because she feels sorry for you, Balraj Marwah had said.

Why would she feel sorry for me? Vikram had asked defiantly.

The pity on Balraj's face had been unmistakable when he answered Vikram's question. *Because you're an orphan.*

A strange uneasiness settled inside Vikram and every instinct in his body told him something did not add up.

The car jerked to a stop in the parking lot of the NGO-run primary school that was their destination. Vikram turned towards Nidhi but she was already stepping out of the car.

Nidhi watched with a twinge of pride as Vikram interacted with the students.

'Who is the president of the country?' their teacher asked.

'Pranab Mukherjee!' the students sing-songed.

'Wow, even *I* didn't know that!' Vikram joked.

The kids giggled, suspecting that he was being facetious, but not completely certain. He spent a few minutes talking to them about the importance of education and sports. When the time came for Q&A, there was a nervous silence in the room. His audience was evidently worried about asking a question that wasn't 'smart' enough.

'Don't ask me anything too difficult,' Vikram teased, raising both palms in a defensive gesture.

A few kids giggled nervously.

'Does anyone have a question about cricket?' he hinted.

A dozen hands shot up and he laughed, taking their questions one by one. They started with 'Which international cricketer do you admire the most?' and 'How much does your bat weigh?' and gradually progressed to 'Who is your favourite Bollywood actress?'

And Vikram humoured each query with a patient, friendly smile.

Anoop nudged Nidhi's shoulder. 'Someone has a crush on Walia.'

Nidhi gave him a sharp look. 'I do *not*!'

'Really? Then how about picking your jaw up off the floor?' Anoop suggested dryly.

Nidhi blushed.

Okay, so Vikram was kind of adorable with the kids. And kind of adorable in general. But that didn't mean he wasn't a spoilt, self-important brat. Nor did it change the fact that he was dating the most glamorous woman in the country. And, of course, there was the tiny little issue of him trampling over Nidhi's heart when she was fourteen.

An hour later, Vikram finished umpiring a friendly match between the students and then proceeded to show some of the eager ones a few batting techniques.

As they finally walked out of the school gate, Nidhi was mentally congratulating herself on the smooth completion of the event, but the kudos were premature. Because as soon as she stepped out of the premises, Nidhi was engulfed by a large mob of excited villagers gathered at the entrance of the school. Someone pushed her and she felt herself being swallowed up by the restless swarm of eager fans.

'Vikram sir, Vikram sir!' someone shouted.

'Please sir, just one photo, sir!' screamed another fan.

'I love you, Vikram!' pleaded a shrill female voice.

Nidhi shot a worried look at Vikram but he was shielded by three beefy bouncers as they manoeuvred their way through the crowd, towards the car. A sharp elbow jabbed into her ribs, nearly knocking the wind out of her. Attempting to regain her balance, Nidhi tried to see past the scores of screaming devotees as they chanted Vikram's name, imploring him with their words and their eyes for one photograph, one autograph, one look. Nidhi's lungs felt constricted as she found herself being swept by the sea of faceless faces, frantic cries of the fans ringing in her ears—loud, desperate, incessant. Bile rose up in her throat as a hand reached out and clasped her wrist. A moment later, she felt herself being pulled firmly against Vikram, protected by the hard wall of his chest.

Nidhi looked at him blankly, but she saw neither her protector nor her saviour. She saw instead the handsome, glamorous celebrity that inspired obsessive devotion among millions. She saw a complete stranger.

Interlocking his fingers tightly with hers, Vikram said, 'I've got you. Hold on.'

Nidhi managed a catatonic nod.

A few minutes later, the bouncers deposited her and Vikram into the car, and Rao Uncle immediately locked both doors to ward off the frenzied mob. In her hypnotized state, Nidhi stared at Vikram and then at the throng of crazed fans outside. Dozens of them had piled around the car, banging on his window, thumping on her window, begging for just one precious glimpse of their hero.

'Drive!' Vikram snapped at Rao. 'Monty will come in another car.'

As they made their way through the narrow streets outside the school, Vikram watched Nidhi. For the first time in all the years he had known her, her body language lacked the confidence that was core to her personality. And even though at their first meeting in the conference room he had longed to shake her composure, this wasn't what he'd hoped to achieve. At the moment, she looked utterly confused . . . and lost.

Something tugged at Vikram and he instinctively reached for her hand.

Nidhi gasped and recoiled from his touch, pressing back in her seat. She looked at him like she was seeing him for the first time. Like he was a complete stranger.

Vikram cursed under his breath. Over the years, he had gotten used to fans overstepping their boundaries, but this was probably the first time Nidhi had witnessed such madness in person.

Vikram tried to find the words to make it better, but all he could come up with was, 'It's just me, Nidhi.'

She nodded softly, but didn't speak for the rest of the car ride.

WhatsApp Chat

Nidhi Marwah: This is the worst date ever.

Risha Kohli: Ku-ku-ku-ku . . .

Tanvi Bedi: Shit, I can't get that song out of my head.

Nidhi Marwah: Stop that, Rish! I actually tried calling him Kamal but he said he prefers Kuku.

Risha Kohli: What's he like? Send a picture.

Nidhi Marwah: Isn't the fact that I'm texting under the table bad enough? It will look super weird if I suddenly start taking pictures of him.

Tanvi Bedi: Please don't.

Risha Kohli: So describe him then.

Nidhi Marwah: He's really tall and brawny.

Risha Kohli: What's he wearing?

Nidhi Marwah: A charcoal suit.

Risha Kohli: And what's the problem?

Nidhi Marwah: His personality.

Tanvi Bedi: What did you expect from a guy who goes by a shitty name like 'Kuku'?

Nidhi Marwah: He's been talking non-stop for the last fifteen minutes—hasn't even taken a break to eat. I can actually see the congealed layer on top of his soup.

Tanvi Bedi: What the fuck is he rambling about?

Nidhi Marwah: He asked me what I do at *NT* but before I could answer, started talking about how the newspaper industry is on a decline and why I should get out while I can.

Risha Kohli: Rocket scientist.

Nidhi Marwah: And then he asked me how my day was, but before I could respond . . .

Tanvi Bedi: He started talking about how spectacular *his* day was, filled with great achievements such as eradicating poverty and curing cancer?

Nidhi Marwah: Exactly. Or the lawyer equivalent of those achievements, anyway.

Risha Kohli: Such a charmer.

Tanvi Bedi: Sounds like a first-rate asshole.

Nidhi Marwah: And he hasn't exactly been subtle about staring at my chest. His gaze keeps drifting to my cleavage.

Risha Kohli: Well, you do have rather nice boobs.

Nidhi Marwah: Thanks. But it's no longer flattering when his definition of eye contact is eye-to-bust, instead of eye-to-eye.

Tanvi Bedi: Dump the soup on his crotch and get the hell out of there.

Nidhi Marwah: And he has this fake American accent. He keeps calling me 'Niddy'.

Risha Kohli: That's 'shiddy'.

Nidhi Marwah: And he said he doesn't like girls who
                 drink.
Risha Kohli: Are you telling me you've been surviving
                 this dinner without alcohol?
Nidhi Marwah: Obviously.
Tanvi Bedi: Are you fucking crazy??? Order a shot
                RIGHT NOW!
Risha Kohli: Or pay the waiter 100 bucks to spike
                 your mocktail.
Nidhi Marwah: Oh. My. God.
Risha Kohli: Yeah, it's probably not the right thing
                 to do.
Nidhi Marwah: No, not that.
Risha Kohli: Then?
Nidhi Marwah: I can't tell you what he just said.
Tanvi Bedi: What?
Nidhi Marwah: No, I seriously can't tell you.
Risha Kohli: What???
Nidhi Marwah: Lol.
Tanvi Bedi: What's so funny?
Nidhi Marwah: No, as in he literally just *said* the
                 word 'lol'.
Risha Kohli: Okay, I think this qualifies as an SOS. I'm
                 calling you.

Nidhi glanced at her ringing phone and composed her
features in the perfect imitation of partly embarrassed
and partly apologetic. 'Sorry, I need to get this.'

'Sure, sure, no problem,' Kuku said, finally picking
up his soup spoon.

'Hello?' Nidhi said into the phone.

On the other side, Risha sang, 'Ku-ku-ku-ku . . .'

'No, I'm not at home,' Nidhi ad-libbed, biting back a laugh.

Kuku frowned at his soup.

'Choli ke peeche kya hai . . .' Risha crooned.

'Oh, God! Is everything okay?' Nidhi gasped into the phone.

Kuku gave a disgusted shake of his head and gestured to the waiter. 'No! They served me cold soup.'

Suppressing the urge to roll her eyes, Nidhi mouthed, 'I'm on the phone.'

'Oh,' Kuku said, before turning to the waiter and snapping, 'This kind of service is unacceptable! How dare you charge eight hundred rupees for soup and then serve it cold?'

'He sounds like such a nice guy,' Risha said sarcastically. 'You need to leave *right* now.'

'Right now?' Nidhi asked, raising her voice a notch.

Kuku was now berating the waiter and Nidhi was concerned that her ruse was getting upstaged by all his yelling.

'Try standing up and looking around frantically,' Risha suggested.

Nidhi stood up and looked around frantically. 'That's terrible, Risha!' she exclaimed into the phone.

'Is something wrong, Niddy?' Kuku asked. *Finally.*

'Yes, really wrong,' Nidhi said, feigning a worried look.

'About time he caught on,' Risha said dryly.

'What happened?' Kuku asked, placing his hand on hers.

'My friend is feeling unwell, so I have to go see her,' Nidhi explained.

'Oh, that's horrible,' he said, pronouncing 'horrible' as 'hah-rible'. 'I'll come with you.'

'No!' she exclaimed.

'Why not?' he asked, sliding a finger up Nidhi's arm in a gesture that made her inexplicably uncomfortable.

'Ummm, she lives in a women's hostel,' Nidhi improvised hastily, withdrawing her hand. 'And guys are not allowed inside.'

'Nice!' Risha chuckled on the other side of the phone. Since the fierce security guard at Risha's building seldom allowed guys up to her apartment, Nidhi's fib was quite close to the truth.

Kuku frowned before glancing at her chest. 'Can I give you a ride?'

'No, Rao Uncle . . . I mean, the driver is waiting outside. He'll take me,' Nidhi assured him, then spoke urgently into the phone. 'Hang in there, Risha. I'll be there as soon as possible!'

The moment Nidhi reached Risha's house, the girls collapsed into giggles. Nidhi filled Risha in on the details of her disastrous date, and after a few minutes, the conversation invariably shifted to Vikram.

'Honestly, I don't think he's the villain the media makes him out to be,' Risha said.

Nidhi raised an eyebrow. 'You *have* seen the video of him punching Shaan Kapoor, right?'

'Maybe he had a valid reason. Shaan Kapoor does seem like a bit of a sleazeball,' Risha pointed out.

'Clearly you haven't seen the eighty zillion pictures of Vikram's innumerable . . . *groupies*!' Nidhi spat out.

Risha gave her a surprised look. 'What's that got to do with anything? He's a young, good-looking guy—of course, he has female fans.'

For a moment, Nidhi considered telling Risha everything. That Vikram was her first friend, her first kiss, her first love. But the truth was that the morning's events had changed everything.

After witnessing first-hand the adulation and hysteria that surrounded Vikram, Nidhi finally saw him for the celebrity he was. The guy sitting next to her in the car the previous day had been the superstar from the cola commercials and 'man of the match' speeches, not the boy she had grown up with. And Nidhi was even more convinced that Vikram's interest in her, if at all he *was* interested in her, would only last till the time she reciprocated it. Once the chase was over, he would drop her and move on to the next girl. Leaving Nidhi to nurse her broken heart—again. This time, perhaps, irreparably.

So instead of confessing her innermost thoughts about Vikram, Nidhi said, 'I'm just saying, don't fall for his "nice guy" image. These celebrities are total pros at dealing with the media. He knew that a lot of the people at my party were journalists, so, of course, he was nice and charming!'

Risha watched her friend carefully. 'Since when are you such a cynic, Nidhi?'

Since Vikram Walia broke my heart twelve years ago.

But Nidhi wasn't ready to go down that path yet, so she went for a joke instead. 'Hey! It's "Niddy".'

February 2002

Nidhi bit her nails nervously as she waited for her father to finish his telephone conversation.

He had summoned her into his study after dinner, and Nidhi had the uneasy premonition that she was in trouble.

Two days ago, her father had seen her kissing Vikram on the Walias' porch and now Nidhi was tormenting herself over how her father's fury would manifest itself. He had never raised a hand to her but, at the very least, Nidhi was expecting verbal abuse for what she had done.

What had she done? She had just kissed a boy. Girls her age were doing a lot more than just kissing, Nidhi thought, trying to calm herself down.

Her father hung up the phone and the knot in Nidhi's stomach tightened. She jerked erect in her chair.

'How was your day?' Balraj asked her in a pleasant tone.

'It was . . . f-fine,' she stuttered.

'Relax, Nidhi. I haven't called you here to scold you,' he said calmly.

'You haven't?' she asked, surprised.

'I just want to discuss something with you.'

Nidhi gulped.

'What's going on between you and Vikram?'

Her face went bright red with embarrassment.

'It's okay. You can tell me, I'm your father,' he said with a smile so friendly that Nidhi was taken aback. 'We can be friends, can't we?' he asked, watching her shocked expression.

She gave a shy smile and nodded.

'So, tell me. How do you feel about Vikram?'

'I . . . I like him.'

Her father gave her another unusually gentle smile. 'You can be completely honest with me, Nidhi.'

'I love him, Papa,' Nidhi said, her eyes ablaze with feeling. 'He's my best friend. My only friend, really. But I also love him. I've loved him since he moved in next door, and I think I'll always love him.'

She looked down at her hands, feeling a little silly at her sentimental proclamation.

'I see,' Balraj said quietly.

'I'm sorry. I know you don't like him,' Nidhi said awkwardly.

Balraj gave a small smile. 'I don't dislike him, Nidhi. I just don't like his temper.'

'But he doesn't lose his temper as much any more,' Nidhi said, half truthfully.

'Perhaps because you are a good influence on him,' Balraj offered, sounding unconvinced.

Nidhi nodded eagerly. 'Yes, he hasn't gotten into many fights recently.'

'And is he proceeding with his decision to move to Mumbai?'

'I don't know. I mean, he should. He's got a full scholarship to the best cricket academy in the country.

He's really talented and I think he can play for India someday,' she said, chewing on her lip.

Balraj nodded. 'You're a smart girl, Nidhi—mature for your age. I agree that moving to Mumbai is best for him. I must congratulate him on his achievement when he's back from Dehradun. When does he return?'

'On Friday,' Nidhi said, suddenly feeling demure and liberated all at once.

'Great. Now run along, I have to see an important project to completion,' her father said.

Nidhi left his study, impatiently counting the minutes till Vikram's return.

March 2014

Vikram's patience was wearing thin.

He hadn't seen or heard from Nidhi since the previous evening. Her atypical silence had unnerved him, and he wanted to explain the events that had occurred outside the school. He wanted to help her understand that fame wasn't a thing to be taken seriously. On the contrary, it was a side effect, an occupational hazard that didn't change who he was on the inside. Just why he had this urgent need to make explanations to Nidhi is not something Vikram stopped to analyse.

He had tried peeking through her window, but it was closed. When the clock finally struck eleven, he had stood at his window and waited for her to climb over the gate, but she had never appeared.

He had texted her that morning, but she hadn't responded. He had tried calling her, but her phone had been switched off. For a moment, he considered calling her boss to complain about her inaccessibility, but not only did that seem desperate, it was also bound to piss her off.

Which, he thought with a smile, might make it worth it. Colour would rise up her smooth cheeks and her beautiful green eyes would flash like a forest fire as she issued him a stern reprimand.

Vikram returned from his training session with his coach and after a light lunch, went to the gym to work out. When he got back home, he turned on the cricket match between India and Sri Lanka—one that Vikram would've been playing if he hadn't been suspended. To avoid smashing his fist into the screen, he switched off the television and went to the gym. Again.

Around six in the evening, when he finally returned, he walked straight into the Marwahs' house.

Bhimsen leapt from his stool and greeted him excitedly. 'Vikram Baba!'

'*Kya haal hai*, Bhimsen?'

'Match *dekhi*?'

'Haan,' Vikram lied.

'What a victory!'

Vikram's phone was flooded with congratulatory messages from sponsors and media persons about India annihilating Sri Lanka. And while he was thrilled for his teammates, he was too bummed about not playing to respond to any of the texts.

'Where's Nidhi?' Vikram asked Bhimsen, just as Mangal Singh came scurrying out of the house.

'I thought I heard your voice, Vikram Baba. Match *dekha*?' Mangal asked, his face red with elation.

'Yes, yes. Such a great match. What a fantastic win. Best match I've ever seen!' Vikram said with faux enthusiasm. 'Where's Nidhi?'

'She is staying at a friend's house since yesterday,' Mangal said.

Alarm swept over Vikram and he snapped in agitation, 'Which friend?'

'Risha Didi,' Mangal responded, his pudgy face losing some of its colour.

Relief flooded through Vikram, and he smiled at his old friends, trying to make up for his caustic tone a few moments ago. 'Oh. When will she be back?'

'Tomorrow evening,' Mangal said stiffly.

Anxious to compensate for his earlier abruptness, and also because he wanted to catch up on the years of Nidhi he had missed out on, Vikram turned to two-thirds of the Trio and made them an offer they couldn't refuse. 'Would you like to have a drink with me?'

Both men's chests puffed up with pride, and they nodded eagerly.

A few hours later, the three men lay sprawled in Vikram's unkempt garden in different physical positions and levels of inebriation. They discussed Bhimsen's perilous journey crossing the Nepal–India border on foot ('Very-very danger!')—a story Vikram had heard several times before. They spoke about the birth of Mangal Singh's fifth child, born ten months after his most recent visit to his missus ('Late *paida hua*!')—a story Vikram had never heard before. They exchanged views on the upcoming general election, food inflation, item songs and, of course, cricket. The only topic they had *not* touched upon was the one Vikram had orchestrated the entire drinking session for.

Nidhi.

'What were things like after I left Delhi?' Vikram asked, watching the stars in the night sky swim before his eyes.

'Very-very boring,' Bhimsen said. 'Nidhi Baby stopped playing all games with us. Even basketball.'

'Yes,' Mangal Singh slurred. 'That is why the hoop is rusted and broken.'

'And what else?' Vikram probed.

'And the boundary wall became bigger,' Bhimsen said, gesturing to the eight-foot-high wall that separated the Walias' driveway from the Marwahs'. Back then, the wall was half its current height, and Vikram remembered jumping over it all the time as a teenager.

'And Rao got his appendix removed,' Mangal added.

'And you got your cataract removed,' Bhimsen reminded him.

'And also my wisdom teeths,' Mangal said, opening his mouth wide to show the craters that had replaced his wisdom teeth.

Great. Nearly two bottles of Black Label and they were discussing Mangal's dental history.

'What else?' Vikram prodded.

'Balraj Saab's health seriously deteriorated. He underwent two major—'

Vikram cut him off with a more straightforward question. 'What was Nidhi like after I left?'

'Sad,' Bhimsen said. 'Very-very sad. She did not smile for months.'

Mangal Singh nodded. 'She cried in her room every night. She closed the door, but we could hear the sobs. Every morning when the *bai* did *jhaadu-pocha*, the dustbin was full of used tissue papers.'

Vikram felt his heart wrench at the visual. And strangely, the strongest emotion he felt at that moment was guilt. He tried to remind himself that *he* was the wronged party, that Nidhi had stomped on *his* heart.

But all Vikram could see was a fourteen-year-old Nidhi crying herself to sleep every night after he had left.

He tried to clear the whisky-induced haze and settle the events of *that* night once and for all.

Vikram came home from Dehradun on a Friday. He was exhausted, from five days of non-stop cricket, but also from the seven-hour-long bus journey. And yet he dumped his kitbag and luggage in the garden and ran straight to Nidhi's house.

For five days, he hadn't stopped thinking about her: her tear-stricken face, her trusting eyes, her soft fingers against his face. And, of course, that kiss. Vikram hadn't been able to get that kiss out of his head.

Five days apart from Nidhi had convinced Vikram that he was making the right decision. He would stay in Delhi and join a local cricket academy. He would stay back so he could be with Nidhi.

As soon as he entered her house, Bhimsen informed him that Nidhi's father wanted to see Vikram in his study. Surprised by the unprecedented invitation, Vikram haphazardly straightened his clothes and wiped his face with his jersey before knocking on the door to Balraj's study.

'Good evening, Uncle,' Vikram said, when Balraj asked him to enter.

'Hello, Vikram. Good to see you!' Balraj said, a wide smile on his face.

Vikram tried to hide his shock. At best, Balraj had been curt with Vikram, but if he was finally initiating friendship, Vikram wasn't a fool to turn it down.

'How was your trip?' Balraj asked, gesturing for him to take a seat.

Vikram sat down and responded politely, 'It was very good, Uncle. I learnt a lot.'

'When are you going to Mumbai?'

'I . . . I'm not sure if I'm going. I'm thinking of staying here.'

Balraj gave him a tight smile. 'I see.'

The silence lingered in the room and Vikram shook his leg fervently, unable to contain his impatience to see Nidhi. He started to stand but Balraj's voice cracked through the silence like a whip. 'Sit.'

Vikram sat back down and looked at him expectantly.

'I want to speak to you about something.'

'About what?' Vikram ventured.

'I don't want you to be upset with Nidhi. You know girls Nidhi's age often say things they don't mean,' Balraj said.

'What are you talking about?' Vikram asked, feeling anxious.

'You know, the thing Nidhi said about you—she probably didn't mean it,' Balraj said casually.

'What did she say?' Vikram pressed, trying to ignore the strange sensation in the pit of his stomach.

'That she hates you,' Balraj said with quiet conviction.

Rebellion flashed in Vikram's eyes. 'I don't believe you. Nidhi would never say that.'

Balraj shrugged. 'Not to your face.'

'Not even behind my back,' Vikram said fiercely. 'She's my best friend.'

'Nidhi is only friends with you,' Balraj persevered patiently, 'because she feels sorry for you.'

'That's not true!'

'She means well. But she also believes that you've been a very disruptive presence in her life. And if she *didn't pity you so much, she would have told you bluntly how she really feels.'*

'That's not true,' Vikram said, standing up and walking backwards to the door.

Balraj looked him square in the eye. 'It is. You need to know this. It would be wrong of me not to tell you. In fact, she told me that the only reason she kissed you was because she felt sorry for you.'

Vikram broke out in a cold sweat. 'Why would she feel sorry for me?'

Pity filled Balraj's eyes. 'Because you're an orphan.'

'I don't believe you,' Vikram said defiantly, clenching his fists. 'I'm going to ask her right now!'

'Go ahead,' Balraj suggested, and even before he finished the sentence, Vikram was running out the door, taking the stairs up to Nidhi's room, two at a time.

He burst in through her door, anger emanating from his body.

Nidhi leapt up from the bed at the sight of him, and a happy look crossed over her face.

'Is it true, Nidhi?' he said, shaking her roughly by the shoulders. 'Your father told me what you said . . . Is it true?! Is that really how you feel about me?'

Guilt flickered in her treacherous green eyes and she whispered, 'Yes.'

Vikram let go of her abruptly, as though touching her had scalded him. His eyes filled with hatred. 'I never want to see you again.'

Nidhi's eyes widened in shock. 'Why are you saying that, Viks? Is it because of the . . . what happened between us?'

'That stupid kiss? Please. It meant nothing to me!' Vikram spat out.

She looked stung, but Vikram wanted to hurt her as much as she had hurt him, so he added untruthfully, 'I've kissed dozens of girls and they're all better kissers than you!'

Tears welled up in Nidhi's eyes and she reached for him, but Vikram took a firm step back, speaking in a scathing tone, 'You're nothing but a stupid tomboy and I hate you!'

Even as tears streamed down her cheeks, Nidhi raised her chin and replied in a ragged but calm voice, 'Okay.'

Vikram stormed out of her room, slamming the door so hard that it shook on its hinges.

Now, lying in his grandmother's garden twelve years later, even as alcohol streamed through his blood and potentially clouded his judgment, Vikram knew that Nidhi had not wronged him. And the conviction in that unfounded instinct shook him to his very core.

Nidhi was the same girl who had knocked on his door relentlessly for one month, forcing him to come out of his house, and his shell. She was the same girl whose loyalty had compelled her to publically beat up a boy for calling Vikram an 'orphan'. And she was the same girl who, even as Vikram spewed his venom on her and told her that he hated her, stubbornly refused to reciprocate the sentiment.

Vikram had known it twelve years ago when he stood in her father's study, defending her. And he knew it now.

Nidhi was incapable of hatred.

For some reason, Vikram found pride and comfort in that. Because it gave him hope that all was not lost between them.

Nidhi pressed her fingertips to her temples in a futile attempt to postpone the inevitable headache. Dibakar was making her go over the itinerary and menu for the next day's event. For the fourth time.

Admittedly, the event was a big deal. Twenty of the city's biggest CEOs had been invited for a formal meet-and-greet with Vikram. The idea was to encourage corporates to donate to EducateIndia by generating interest in the cause. Vikram had promised to set up the CEOs with an inspirational speech, following which Dibakar would swoop in to pocket the moolah. The *News Today* team was banking on the event to raise seed capital for the project.

However, the eight-course meal seemed a bit excessive to Nidhi. So did the five types of wine. But since she just could not bear to hear another one of Dibakar's gems— 'spend small to gain small, spend big to gain big'—she nodded along to whatever he said.

'Please make sure you practise the speech with Vikram before the event,' Dibakar said.

'The fact that I've written the entire thing isn't enough?' Nidhi asked, trying to hide her annoyance.

'Delivery is everything, Nidhi,' Dibakar reminded her.

'His delivery is fine. In fact, his post-match interviews are usually pretty good. At least when he's not abusing the journalists,' Nidhi snorted.

Dibakar gave her a patient smile. 'Will you please go over the speech with him?'

Nidhi knew it wasn't a question. She nodded and headed back to her workstation.

So far, Nidhi had done a great job of avoiding Vikram. She hadn't seen him since the last event and didn't intend to see him until the next one. But Dibakar's diktat provided a slight challenge. Maybe she could rehearse the speech with Vikram over the phone.

She called him but he didn't answer. She sighed, assuming it was childish retaliation on his part, but he called back almost immediately.

'Hello, Vikram,' she said formally.

'Sorry I missed your call. I was in the shower.'

Thanks for putting that visual in my head.

'No problem,' she replied, trying not to think about steaming hot water sluicing his bare chest. 'I was wondering if we could practise tomorrow's speech.'

'You don't think I can give a five-minute speech without screwing up?' he asked.

'No, no, that's not what I meant. I'm sure you'll do a great job. I just thought it would—'

'I'm kidding, Nidhi! Of course, we can "practise",' he said, and she could almost visualize the smirk on his face.

'Can we do it now?' she asked.

'Over the phone?'

'Yes.'

'No.'

'Why not?'

'In person.'

'But it will only take—'

'In person,' he repeated firmly. 'Or not at all.'

'Fine,' she relented with a sigh. 'Are you free this evening?'

'Actually, I'm meeting a friend for drinks tonight but I can see you after that. I'll even leave the gate open so you don't have to climb over it.'

Nidhi gasped. 'You've been spying on me!'

'Why don't you just walk in like a normal person instead of climbing over the gate?' he asked.

'None of your business!' she snapped.

'Don't tell me you have a curfew,' he teased.

She kept silent.

'At this age?' he asked, sounding genuinely surprised. 'Wow.'

'Some of us still care about what people think,' she retorted.

'You don't care about what *people* think, you only care about what Balli the Bully thinks,' Vikram said.

Nidhi burst out laughing. 'What did you just call Papa?'

'Dadi and I used to call him that.' Vikram chuckled.

'You've never told me that before,' she said.

'There's a lot I haven't told you, Nidhi,' he replied, and Nidhi could have sworn there was a catch in his voice. 'Will I see you tonight?'

'Can we just do it over the phone, please?'

'Absolutely not,' he said. 'If you can't make it tonight, come over tomorrow and we'll leave for the event together.'

'But the event is in Gurgaon and I was planning to go directly from work. Home is in the opposite direction,' Nidhi complained.

'Tonight or tomorrow. Your choice.'

'Tomorrow,' she agreed reluctantly. 'I'll see you around four.'

Vikram stared at his best friend in utter disbelief.

Shrewd businessman, e-commerce tycoon, raiser of a billion dollars, Rohan Singhal was absolutely, completely, hopelessly in love.

'What should I do?' Rohan groaned, burying his hands in his hair.

Vikram continued to gape at his friend.

'Say something, Walia!' Rohan snapped.

Vikram cleared his throat. 'What's her name?'

'Nitisha Khanna,' Rohan rasped, sliding off his glasses and covering his face with his hands.

'What's she like?' Vikram asked, for the sake of asking *something*.

'She's perfect, man. She's beautiful and funny and smart and fucking awesome,' Rohan said, a pained expression on his face.

'So what's the problem?' Vikram asked.

Rohan chugged his vodka and gave his friend an irritated look. 'The problem is that I'm not a bloody cricketer. Or a goddamn movie star. Didn't you hear a word of what I just said, Walia? She's *perfect*!'

'Just ask her to dinner,' Vikram said, like that was the most obvious solution.

Rohan poured himself another drink and expelled a frustrated breath. 'Is that how it started with Natasha Sahay? Dinner?'

'Don't tell me you've been reading that trash, Singhal! Natasha and I are just friends.'

'So what was the deal with Shaan Kapoor?'

'He was being an asshole. Said some shit, shoved her against a wall.' Vikram ground his teeth, his temper rising just thinking about it.

'That's fucked up, man. The newspapers made it sound like such a love triangle,' Rohan said, his attention momentarily diverted from his own love-struck heart.

'Total bullshit,' Vikram assured him.

Rohan nodded. 'So what's going on?'

This was typical of Rohan. To ask a generic, open-ended question that Vikram could choose to interpret the way he wanted. However, these days, there was only one thing on Vikram's mind.

'Nidhi.'

Now it was Rohan's turn to be shocked. 'The high-school girlfriend?'

Vikram nodded, then felt compelled to correct Rohan. 'She was never my girlfriend.'

'I know.'

Rohan was the only one who knew about Nidhi. He had been Vikram's roommate at the Mumbai Cricket Academy for a year before he moved back to Delhi. Cricket, Rohan had realized after a bouncer broke his nose, wasn't something he wanted to pursue as a career. But the two boys had built a strong friendship in that short duration and ended up staying in touch.

'She's the brand manager on the *News Today* campaign.'

Rohan raised an eyebrow. 'That's a crazy coincidence, dude.'

'Tell me about it,' Vikram muttered, then filled Rohan in on the details of the week gone by.

Rohan shook his head incredulously. 'So we're both screwed.'

'Royally.' Vikram nodded, refilling their glasses.

They sat in silence for a few minutes, attempting—unsuccessfully—to drown their troubles, until Vikram brought up his original concern. 'You've only met this Nitisha girl twice?'

'Yes.'

'*Twice*,' Vikram repeated in disbelief.

'Some of us don't need to know a girl for half our lives before realizing she's the one,' Rohan said pointedly.

Vikram snapped his gaze to Rohan's. 'Fuck you, Singhal.'

Rohan laughed and clinked his glass with Vikram's.

The following day, when Nidhi strode into Vikram's living room dressed in an emerald sheath dress, a slim gold belt around her waist and four-inch-high nude peep-toes, she found him watching a cricket match on his laptop. His back was towards her and he was sitting on the sofa, intently studying a visual of . . . himself.

Narcissist.

Nidhi walked around the sofa and was amazed to see that the expression on his face wasn't an I'm-so-bloody-awesome grin, but a concerned frown.

'Hi,' she said.

He paused the screen before turning to her. His lazy gaze roamed over her curves and his face broke into a slow, admiring smile. 'Wow.'

Nidhi flushed at the compliment, then looked at him in surprise. 'You wear glasses?'

Vikram took off the glasses in question with a self-conscious smile. 'Sometimes.'

'What are you doing?' Nidhi asked, gesturing to the laptop.

'I've been struggling against Dale Steyn,' he said, referring to South Africa's most formidable fast bowler. 'So I was studying some old footage.'

'Oh.'

'What did you think I was doing?' he asked.

'Admiring yourself,' she admitted sheepishly.

'Every time we meet, I think it's impossible for me to sink further in your estimation. And every time you prove me wrong.' He grinned, standing up.

Nidhi watched him slip into his black blazer jacket, admiring how it rested perfectly on his endless shoulders. His hair was brushed up in an elegant fashion, a light stubble coated his jaw, and he looked every bit the glamorous model on the Raymond billboard Nidhi had passed on her way to work that morning.

The complete man, indeed.

'Ready?' Vikram asked.

Nidhi blinked. 'For?'

'The speech,' he said.

'The speech. Right. Yes,' she said stupidly.

He narrowed his eyes. 'Are you okay?'

'Yes. Let's go over the speech.'

A couple of hours later, Vikram went on stage and delivered his speech with the flair and confidence of a professional orator. Nidhi was nodding along in satisfaction until he neared the end. He paused for a long moment and glanced down at his cheat sheet. Nidhi held her breath, sure that he had forgotten his closing.

She was about to signal to the emcee to take over, when Vikram finally spoke: 'Many of you may not know this, but when I was eight years old, I lost my parents in a car accident.'

Nidhi looked at him in shock.

That wasn't a part of the original speech.

'I moved to a new city where I didn't know anyone. I lost interest in school, in cricket, in everything, really. But I was lucky to have a friend who didn't give up on me. A friend who cared about me, supported me, basically badgered the hell out of me till I came around.' He grinned, and polite laughter rang through the audience. 'And I think that's the kind of unrelenting commitment we all need towards this cause. Because there are thousands of kids out there who need the same kind of support and nurturing and . . .' he paused, searching for the right word. He looked straight at Nidhi and added, '. . . love.'

Nidhi stopped breathing.

Vikram returned his attention to the audience. 'Let's take care of these kids; let's educate these kids. Let's educate India.'

He walked off the stage to a deafening applause.

Vikram slid into the chair between Nidhi and Monty, bored of mingling. For the last two hours, Dibakar had paraded him around the room like a show pony, and with uncharacteristic patience, Vikram had smiled, shaken hands and taken selfies with twenty CEOs, their spouses and children.

Nidhi introduced him to the rest of the people at the table. 'This is Anusha, she's a summer intern,' she said, gesturing to a young girl who was staring at him with worshipful eyes. 'And you already know Sam, Khalid and Anoop.'

Vikram opened his mouth, but Monty pre-empted his request and handed him a glass of sparkling wine.

Vikram opened his mouth again, but Monty shook his head. 'No whisky, only wine.'

Vikram turned to the very amused *News Today* team watching the exchange and gave them a sheepish grin. 'I'm a bit spoilt.'

'You're also really behind, man,' Anoop said, raising his glass.

'Yes.' Nidhi giggled. '*Really* behind.'

Vikram turned to her in surprise. 'How much have you had to drink?'

'Three glasses of wine,' she said in a conspiratorial whisper. 'But shhh, I don't want anyone to find out.'

Vikram frowned. 'Have you eaten anything?'

'Four brownies,' she admitted with a smile so endearing that Vikram had to suppress the impulse to pull her into his arms and kiss it off her face.

He nudged a platter of hors d'oeuvres towards her. 'You should eat something else.'

'What's Natasha Sahay like in real life?' Anusha, the intern, asked abruptly, looking star-struck.

'She's amazing,' Vikram said with a warm smile.

'And she has great taste in men.' Anusha blushed, giving Vikram an appreciative smile.

Vikram gritted his teeth, thinking of Shaan Kapoor. 'That's subjective,' he said evasively.

'So modest, Vikram.' Nidhi giggled. 'I think you guys look adorable together!'

Irritated by her compliment, Vikram started to clarify, 'We're not—'

'Not happy about living in *diffrunt* cities!' Monty interrupted, giving Vikram a warning look.

Vikram's expression turned glacial, but he remained silent.

'Was the incident about the twin brothers in England true?' Anusha asked Vikram.

'What incident?' Nidhi asked.

'It was exaggerated, just like every other thing the media reports,' Vikram muttered.

Anusha looked at him with unhidden adoration. 'I heard it on the radio and I thought it was the *sweetest*—'

'How long is your internship?' Vikram asked, attempting to change the subject.

'What incident?' Nidhi repeated.

'These twelve-year-old twins had waited *weeks* for the India–England match at Lord's. They spotted Vikram outside his hotel room and gathered the *courage* to ask him for an autograph,' Anusha said passionately, enunciating every other word and ignoring Vikram's frown. 'Vikram was *dog-tired* after the match—'

'I wasn't *that* tired,' Vikram mumbled.

'. . . with his hands *full* of his cricket gear, but he *promised* the kids that he would drop his stuff at his hotel room and come back. Then he climbed up *five* flights of stairs—'

'I took the elevator.' Vikram sighed.

'. . . and when he came back he found the brothers standing in the *same* spot, their shoulders *slumped* in sorrow, their spirits *defeated*—'

'It really wasn't that dramatic,' Vikram groaned.

'. . . and Vikram asked them, "Don't you want my autograph?" The brothers were *absolutely* ecstatic! They wrote a blog about it titled "Vikram Walia: A Man of His Word" and a radio station picked it up and—'

'Okay, okay, I think we've heard enough,' Vikram interrupted, feeling extremely embarrassed by the unnecessary over-dramatization of a simple event.

It wasn't that Vikram was unaccustomed to female adulation. It wasn't even that the strange combination of reverence and lust in Anusha's eyes was making him shift uncomfortably in his chair—although it was, a little bit. It was the way Nidhi was watching him, with a flicker of admiration in her eyes that took his breath away.

Anusha gave another dreamy sigh. 'And what about the episode with the old couple? Did you really—'

'Let's get you a drink,' Sam said, winking at Vikram as he whisked Anusha away from the table, ignoring her squeals of protest.

Vikram exhaled in relief and absently reached for an appetizer on the platter in front of him. Nidhi slapped his hand away.

'Hey!' he complained. 'What the hell?'

'That's shrimp,' she explained. 'You're allergic.'

A look of pleasant surprise crossed his face. 'You remember?'

'No, I don't!' she denied hastily.

'Clearly, you do,' he said, his voice deep.

'I read it in a magazine,' she clarified.

'Really?' he drawled, sounding amused. 'Which magazine?'

'*Sports* . . . something,' she mumbled.

Vikram's lips twitched with laughter. '*Sports Something.* Sounds important, I better buy a subscription.'

'I don't remember the name of the magazine,' she said, flushing a deep shade of red. 'Maybe it was in the newspaper.'

'Not possible,' he said blandly.

'It's not possible that a journalist asked you what food allergies you have?'

'It's possible they *asked* me. It's not possible I gave that answer.'

'Why not?'

'Because I co-own a seafood restaurant in Mumbai and the PR team has explicitly asked me not to mention the allergy.'

'Oh.'

Amusement danced in Vikram's eyes as he leaned in and murmured, 'Why don't you just admit that you remembered?'

Nidhi rolled her eyes. 'Okay, so I remembered! What do you expect? It's the first time I saw someone go into anaphylactic shock!'

'So why did you lie about it?' Vikram asked, wiggling his eyebrows.

'Vikram!' Dibakar's cheery voice interrupted their conversation and Vikram groaned inwardly. 'I must introduce you to someone very special,' Dibakar said, dragging him away for another session of mingling.

Being kicked off the team was really beginning to suck.

The next time Vikram saw Nidhi, he was no longer just mildly concerned. He was extremely worried.

She was, to put it delicately, pissed drunk.

Vikram charged towards Sam, who was trying to help Nidhi into her car and failing miserably.

'I'll take it from here,' Vikram told him.

'But I need, need, *need* to get her inside the car,' Sam slurred.

Nidhi guffawed even as she started singing, '*Aaja meri gaadi mein baith ja, aaja meri gaadi*—'

Vikram groaned. 'I'll handle it, Sameer. How are you getting home?'

'. . . *mein baith ja. Long drive jayenge*—'

'Car,' Sam said.

'. . . *full speed jayen*ge—'

'You're not driving back.' Vikram frowned.

Sam shook his head. 'Never drink and drive. My chariot awaits.' He gave Vikram a funny little salute and stumbled towards his cab.

'Stop interrupting me,' Nidhi growled. 'It's my favourite song in the whole world! Aaja meri gaadi mein—'

Vikram clamped a hand over her mouth and Nidhi's eyes widened in surprise.

'Shhh,' he said softly, helping her settle into the back seat, before walking around the car to sit next to her.

'Is she okay, Vikram Baba?' Rao asked, flicking a concerned look at Nidhi.

'She's fine, Rao Uncle. Just drunk.' Vikram sighed, closing his door. 'Let's go home.'

As the car sped down the highway, Nidhi whispered, 'Vikramaditya?'

Vikram turned to her, startled by her use of his full name. 'Yes?'

'I'm not drunk.'

'Of course, you're not,' he said, thoroughly amused.

'No, I'm serious. I'm not drunk and I can prove it. Ask me anything,' she demanded.

'Anything?' he asked softly.

'Yes. Like the square root of 350.'

'Okay, what's the square root of 350?'

She furrowed her brow. 'I don't know.'

Vikram laughed.

Nidhi slid a little closer to him. 'Can I ask you something?'

'Anything.' He smiled.

'What's Sachin Tendulkar like in real life?'

'You know what he's like on TV?'

Her green eyes widened with wonder. 'Yeah. Super nice.'

'He's ten times nicer in real life.'

'Kinda like you.' Nidhi giggled. Oblivious to Vikram's look of surprise, she continued, 'I've never met Sachin. He's too important to come to the *NT* office. Even when I worked in the Mumbai office, he never—'

'You worked in Mumbai?'

'Yes, for six months. But he never came to the *NT* Mumbai office. He only—'

'Did you like it?'

'Did I like what?'

'Did you like Mumbai?'

'Not really. Mostly because I didn't get to see Sachin. He only visits important newspapers like the *Times of India* and *Hindustan Times*,' she said, scrunching up her nose.

Vikram smiled. 'You can come to one of my matches. I'll introduce you to him.'

The words were out of his mouth before he realized what he was saying. Did he just invite her to come watch him play?

What next, Walia? Blowing her kisses from your bat?

Nidhi inched closer to him. 'Can I ask you something else?'

'Sure.'

'What hair products do you use?'

Vikram choked. 'Why do you ask?'

'Because your hair always looks so perfect!' she complained, throwing an envious look over his well-coiffed brush-up.

'I, uh, have a regime,' he admitted awkwardly.

'Yes, I saw the photo essay in *Delhi Today* this morning: "How to Get the Walia Look in Under 5 Minutes",' she said, raising her hand and spreading her fingers wide to indicate the number five.

Vikram gave an embarrassed laugh and laced his fingers in hers, bringing their interlocked hands down to rest on his knee. 'I happen to have a good hairstylist.'

'Can I tell you a secret?' Nidhi whispered, resting her head on his shoulder.

'What?' he whispered back.

She giggled. 'You smell really good. Like waves crashing on the beach at night.'

'You smell really good too,' he said with a tender smile.

'But you smell much better than me!' she protested.

Vikram's features softened. 'That's impossible.'

Nidhi slanted him a sceptical look. 'Why?'

'Because nothing in the world smells better than you.'

'Nope. You smell twenty thousand times better than me.'

Vikram laughed. 'You're always saying stuff like that.'

She gave him a quizzical look. 'Stuff like what?'

'"I've told you five million times", "I've been waiting for seventeen hundred hours", "You smell twenty thousand times better than me." Stuff like that.' He grinned.

'Well, you *do* smell better than me. Although . . .' her voice trailed off.

'Although?'

'Although I liked you better when you smelt like a cricket field,' she confessed.

'So did I.'

She shook her head. 'Not the smell of you, but the *you* of you.'

Vikram felt a pang of emotion. 'I'm still me, Nidhi.'

She snorted. 'You pose on magazine covers and date Bollywood actresses. You're hardly the Viks I used to know.'

A thrill of pleasure shot through him at her use of his childhood nickname. 'You called me Viks.'

Nidhi smiled and broke into the all-too-familiar jingle at the top of her lungs. 'Viks ki goli lo, khich-khich door karo!'

Oblivious to Rao's look of unconcealed delight in the rear-view mirror, Vikram draped his arm around Nidhi and pulled her close. 'That's *my* favourite song in the whole world,' he said with an affectionate smile.

Nidhi's eyes lit up. 'You should be the brand ambassador of Vicks ki goli!'

'Great idea.' He chuckled, pressing his lips to her forehead.

She peered at him curiously.

'What?' he asked.

'Your smile is quite . . .'

Vikram raised an eyebrow. 'My smile is quite . . . ?'

'Awry.'

'Yours is quite perfect,' he said solemnly.

She snuggled into his chest and sighed contentedly.

By the time they pulled into the Marwahs' driveway, Nidhi was fast asleep in Vikram's arms. Careful not to wake her up, he said softly, 'Rao Uncle, can you please get the door? I'll carry her.'

He scooped her up in his arms, carrying her out of the car and up one flight of stairs.

He laid her on her bed, took off her earrings and heels, and tucked her into the block-printed dohar blanket. He perched next to her on the bed and brushed his knuckles over her cheek. Her eyes fluttered open and she gave him a sleepy smile.

'Go back to sleep,' he whispered.

Nidhi's eyes widened. 'Risha is right.'

'About what?'

'You *are* hot,' she said in disbelief.

Vikram muffled a laugh. 'I am?'

She nodded and raised her hand to his face, gingerly tracing the outline of his rugged jaw with her fingertips. Her eyes darkened as she placed her thumb over his scar, rubbing it softly.

Vikram inhaled sharply, and she withdrew her hand with a shy smile. He leant down slowly, his lips mere inches from hers, his breath mingling with hers.

'You can't kiss me!'

Vikram's eyes snapped open and he raised his head in confusion. 'Why not?'

'Because,' Nidhi confessed in a clandestine whisper, 'I'm not a good kisser.'

'I seriously doubt that,' he said with an indulgent smile.

'No, it's true,' she assured him. 'Remember the last time we kissed?'

Did he remember!

Vikram nodded. 'We were fourteen.'

Laughter lurked in her jade eyes. 'It was *so* bad that you decided to never speak to me again!'

'That wasn't the reason and you know it,' he said coolly.

'I mean, it was one thing to break my heart, but you didn't have to come barging into my room to tell me—'

'WHAT?'

'. . . that I'm the worst kisser in the world!' she finished.

Astonishment swept over Vikram's features. 'Nidhi, what the *hell* are you talking about?'

'Okay, maybe I'm not *that* bad. I've had some practice since then.' She giggled, sliding her arms around his neck.

His voice went up an octave. 'What did you mean by that?'

'I've kissed *four* boys!' she said proudly. 'And I've had sex with—'

'Nidhi!' he snapped in annoyance. 'What do you mean I broke your heart?'

Nidhi tugged at the front of his shirt, jerking his head down to hers. 'It doesn't matter. Let's kiss and make up.'

Vikram grabbed her wrists and pressed her hands firmly above her head. 'Stop it!'

'Fine.' She rolled her eyes. 'I'll just kiss someone else.'

'The hell you will,' he growled.

A minute ago, Vikram had wanted nothing more than to kiss her, but her unfair accusation had thrown him completely off course. Now he wanted—*needed*—to know what she had meant by that statement. What did she mean *he* had broken *her* heart? What strange and twisted version of that night did she believe?

Vikram debated whether to prod further or to postpone their discussion. A moment later, she made the decision for him when she wriggled free from his grasp and murmured, 'My head is spinning.'

Vikram nodded and stood up. 'You should get some sleep.'

'Goodnight, Viks.'

'Goodnight, Nidhi.'

As he walked out of the room, he thought he heard her hum in her sleep. 'Viks ki goli lo . . .'

January 1991

'Please, Arti,' Balraj begged. 'Don't do this to us.'

She stared at him with the same vacant expression she had worn for over a year. 'I'm not doing anything.'

'The doctors said that the medication takes time. It's a phase—a difficult one—but it will pass, sweetheart,' he pleaded.

Arti gave a mirthless laugh. 'You don't understand. I don't feel anything.'

'Is it because her first word—'

'You don't get it. I don't care that she said "Papa" instead of "Mama". I really don't,' Arti said without emotion.

Balraj's voice was strained. 'It takes some women several years to recover, Arti. And until you feel better, you don't have to be around Nidhi. I'll take care of her, I'll do everything.'

'You already do everything,' Arti said with a hollow laugh.

'Please, sweetheart. Just give it some more time,' Balraj choked, realizing that he was about to lose the battle. Realizing that he was about to lose his wife.

'You are a kind man, Balraj—the kindest I know. You are funny and sensitive and handsome. Someday, you will make some woman very happy,' Arti said, her expression blank.

'Arti, no! Don't say that,' Balraj implored, dropping to his knees before her. He darted a glance at the crib where their daughter slept and lowered his voice. 'I'll do anything.'

'There's nothing you can do. I have dreams.'

'Dreams?'

'Dreams beyond this life—'

'And I will support those dreams!' he promised fiercely.

'I know. But I don't trust myself to pursue them while I am still your wife and still her . . . mother,' she said, choking on the word.

'Take some time for yourself,' Balraj said, trying desperately to make her stay. 'I'll give you your space. I'll give you the money to spend your time anyway you like. I'll give you—'

'I don't want anything from you except my freedom,' Arti said, the stone-cold expression never leaving her eyes. 'I'm sorry for any pain I've caused you.'

'Don't do this to us,' he whispered, his voice strangled with anguish.

'Goodbye, Balraj,' she said, quietly walking out of the room.

Several minutes passed and Balraj stayed hunched on the floor, staring at the carpet Arti had bought on their honeymoon. He watched the rust paisleys swirling against the beige background, like fiery rebels in his idyllic world.

Nidhi gurgled, interrupting his abstract thoughts. Balraj panicked. When did she wake up? What did she see? Although he knew that his daughter was too young to have grasped very much of his argument with his wife, he was still anxious.

Balraj stood up and walked to the crib. He gathered Nidhi in his arms and gave her a little kiss on the cheek. 'Good morning, my Needle-in-a-Haystack!'

Nidhi giggled at the nickname, taken from a bedtime story they had read. 'Why you caw me that?'

'Because I spent years looking for you and then I finally found you.'

'Oh. I thaw because Needle sounds like Nidhi,' she said.

'That too, baby.' Balraj smiled, pressing a kiss to her forehead.

'Where Mama?'

'She's . . . gone,' Balraj said.

Nidhi nodded. 'Okay.'

'Do you miss her?' he asked.

She shook her head. 'Nope.'

'Why not?'

'Because I gaw you,' Nidhi explained with a toothy grin.

Balraj gave her a tender smile. 'And I've got you.'

And, he promised himself silently, I'll never let you go.

March 2014

At the Starbucks located in the Outer Circle of Connaught Place, Risha and Tanvi sat at a corner booth listening to Nidhi's phone conversation with matching expressions of incredulity.

'Yes, Papa. Okay. Of course, I will. I'm sorry, I wouldn't have left if it wasn't important. No, that's not what I meant. Of course, his time is important. Yes, I will. Okay, right away. Did you take your medicines? I'll call you again at night to check. Yes, everything is fine at home. Yes, I have. No, of course, I haven't. I'll see you next week. Bye, Papa.'

Nidhi hung up the phone and took a large swig of her vanilla soy latte. She looked up and saw the looks on her friends' faces. 'What?'

'That conversation was more painful than my morning meeting with Lady K,' Tanvi said dryly.

'He wants me to go out with Kuku Kukreja again!' Nidhi groaned.

Tanvi choked on her macchiato. 'That is the worst name ever.'

Risha took a bite of her double chocolate chip brownie and nodded her agreement. 'The worst.'

'So why does your dad want you to meet him *again*?' Tanvi asked impatiently.

Nidhi bit her lip. 'Because he thinks it's unfair to make up my mind after an incomplete date.'

'Come on,' Risha said. 'When you know, you know.'

A shadow crossed Tanvi's face. 'And when you don't, you don't.'

An uncomfortable moment passed.

Risha spoke softly. 'Hey, Shorty. That's not what I meant.'

Tanvi forced a laugh. 'Don't worry about it.'

Nidhi and Risha exchanged a concerned look. Tanvi and her boyfriend Udayan 'Uday' Sen had been together for nearly three years, but Uday was unwilling to commit to anything serious. In the entire duration of the relationship, Nidhi and Risha had met Uday all of two times, which was still two times *more* than Tanvi's family had met him. The girls didn't know him all that well, but sensed strife in the relationship, and since Tanvi wasn't really one to talk about her feelings, they wisely avoided the topic.

Risha popped the last bit of the brownie into her mouth and responded to Nidhi's unspoken request for advice. 'I think you should be honest with your dad. Just tell him that Kuku is not the right guy for you and meeting him again won't change your mind.'

Nidhi nodded, even though she knew she wouldn't be having that conversation with her father anytime soon. He had sounded extremely upset on the phone and Nidhi didn't want to stress him out further. She would meet Kuku once more and give him a fair chance.

Risha saw the range of emotions play across her friend's face and guessed, quite accurately, Nidhi's next words.

'Maybe that evening was an outlier and he's actually a nice guy,' Nidhi said, forcing a smile.

'Maybe,' Tanvi said, even though she didn't believe in 'nice guys', and doubted that Kuku was one.

'Hey, if all else fails,' Risha said with a grin, 'there's still Sam!'

That evening, when Nidhi reached home, Rao Uncle opened the door for her with an exaggerated flourish.

'Thank you,' she said, puzzled by his unexpected gallantry. She was still wondering what had inspired the change in Rao's behaviour when she spotted Vikram.

He was standing at the main entrance, shoulder propped casually against the door frame, blocking her path. Nidhi turned around and saw Bhimsen and Rao chuckling among themselves. She glowered at them and they sobered immediately, returning to their respective stations.

'Hi,' she said, narrowing her eyes at Vikram's purposeful stance.

'Hi,' he returned with a hint of a smile.

'What's going on?'

'We need to talk.'

'About what?'

'About last night.'

'I'm not interested in talking,' she said calmly.

'You weren't interested in *talking* last night either,' he reminded her, his gaze roving over her lips.

Nidhi was already amply embarrassed by her behaviour the previous night, so his suggestive smile made her flush. 'What do you want to talk about?'

'Us.'

Her pulse quickened. At the finality in his tone, but also at everything that word represented.

Us.

'Go talk to your superstar girlfriend.'

Nidhi wanted to kick herself as soon as the words flew out of her mouth.

'She's not my girlfriend,' Vikram said flatly.

'Excuse me?'

'Natasha is just a friend. Our managers are responsible for those rumours,' he explained.

Nidhi's mouth hung open.

'*Now* can we talk?' Vikram grinned.

'There's nothing to talk about,' Nidhi said firmly.

'Oh, but there is. So either we can talk about it or we can pick up where we left off last night,' he said, revelling in the blush that swept over her cheeks.

'Or we can do neither,' she said testily, walking towards the side entrance of the house.

Vikram pretended to study his cuticles. 'That door is locked and there's no one at home.'

Nidhi turned around to demand an extra key from Bhimsen, but the Trio had prudently skulked away from the impending fight scene.

'Why won't you let me go in?' Nidhi cried desperately.

Vikram flicked her a surprised look. His intention had never been to corner or intimidate her; he genuinely just wanted to have a conversation. Belatedly realizing that arm-twisting would never work with Nidhi, Vikram reassessed his strategy. He glanced at the driveway and an idea struck him. 'Let's play for it.'

'What?'

'A basketball game. If I win, we talk. If you win, we don't.'

'No.'

'Okay,' he said agreeably. 'Then we can stand here all night.'

She glared at him.

'I have no plans. *Absolutely* none,' he said, running a lazy glance over her white silk blouse and black A-line skirt.

She clenched her teeth, resisting the temptation to tackle him to the ground and slug him.

'We can't play on *that*,' she said, trying to reason with him. 'The backboard is all rusty and the net is missing.'

'Scared you'll lose?' He grinned.

'Clearly you've forgotten the ass-whooping you got last week,' she said, referring to their gully cricket match.

'Clearly *you've* forgotten that Mangal made most of the runs,' Vikram pointed out.

Nidhi's eyes shot daggers at him. 'Fine. Let's play.'

She expected to see a smug triumph on his face, but oddly his expression resembled . . . *relief*.

'And,' Vikram said magnanimously, 'I'll even let you go up and change so you can be more comfortable.'

Or so *I* can be more comfortable, he amended silently, scanning her shapely curves.

She returned a few minutes later dressed in a tank top, running shorts and sneakers, her hair pulled back in a ponytail.

'I haven't played in years,' Vikram said, dribbling an old, partially deflated basketball on the driveway and taking warm-up shots.

'Save the excuses until *after* the game, Walia,' she jibed.

He laughed at her ladylike attempt at trash talk. 'First one to 21 wins.'

A few minutes later, Vikram realized that watching Nidhi strut around in short skirts had made him underestimate her athletic prowess. She may no longer be a tomboy, but she had lost neither her athleticism, nor her competitive streak. She was agile and aggressive, and even though Vikram was much taller than her *and* played a sport for a living, she didn't seem intimidated by him in the least. So when they were almost neck and neck at 20–19 in his favour, Vikram was practically embarrassed.

Nidhi faked the ball past him and began her winning lay-up, but Vikram thwarted her attempt by shoving the ball out of her hand with a lightning-quick movement. His elbow made contact with her head and sent her crashing on to the granite, where she landed with a loud thud and a yelp of pain.

Vikram rushed to her side and kneeled down, watching her face with a worried expression. 'Are you okay?'

She blinked.

'Nidhi,' he said, his voice replete with concern. 'Tell me where it hurts.'

'Five,' she rasped.

'Huh?' he said, wondering if the incoherent rambling was a symptom of a concussion.

'That's five,' she said, her voice hoarse.

'What are you talking about?' he asked, inspecting her head for visible signs of injury.

She cleared her throat. 'That was your fifth foul. Which means you're disqualified and I win.'

Vikram gave a sharp crack of laughter. 'You're crazy!'

'Say it,' she insisted.

He rolled his eyes.

'*Say it*,' she repeated.

'Fine, you little weirdo. You win!' he conceded.

Her eyes lit up with satisfaction and Vikram couldn't help but stare into them, fascinated by their jade depths. 'How did you get these eyes?'

Her heart lurched at the huskiness in his voice. 'I think my mother had them.'

His gaze warmed, drifting to her lips.

Nidhi turned her face away from him. 'Let me up,' she said in a breathless voice.

Unwilling to kiss her without her consent, and unable not to, Vikram kissed the tip of her nose instead. A tiny shiver ran through her body and he knew she wanted that kiss just as badly as he did. He pressed his lips to her temple, trailing soft kisses down her jaw. Desire flashed in her eyes and her lips parted slightly. Vikram had merely brushed his lips against the corner of her mouth, when a loud cough made him jerk his head up.

Monty stood at the entrance of Nidhi's driveway and cleared his throat. Nidhi gasped and shoved Vikram aside, releasing herself from the trap of his arms.

Vikram stood up reluctantly and shot Monty an irritated glance. 'What?'

'Natashaji is on the phone,' Monty said, holding up Vikram's cell phone.

Vikram watched the shutters slam down in Nidhi's eyes. He turned to Monty. 'I'll be home in a minute.'

Monty nodded and left without another word.

Nidhi practically sprinted towards the main entrance, but Vikram's voice made her swivel around. 'I'm going to Mumbai tomorrow.' He studied her carefully for a reaction, but her face was expressionless. 'For a week,' he added.

She gave him an uninterested shrug.

'And when I'm back,' he said, more roughly than he had intended, 'we're going to talk.'

Without giving him the satisfaction of a response, Nidhi turned around and walked into the house.

'Great job, Nidhi. This is simply fabulous!' Dibakar gushed.

Nidhi left Dibakar's cabin beaming. It *was* quite fabulous.

Instead of a typical direct mailer, Nidhi and Khalid had worked on a personalized four-page newspaper covering the CEO event. Each CEO would receive a unique front page carrying their photograph with Vikram and a customized headline specific to their company, along with the details of the EducateIndia programme. The centrespread contained an elaborate photomontage of the event and the last page included a donation form and a copy of Vikram's speech.

'I was lucky to have a friend who didn't give up on me.'

Nidhi's pulse raced at the memory of locking eyes with Vikram at the end of his speech. But that was nothing compared to the unbridled hammering of her heart when she thought of their almost kiss after the basketball game.

Even now, her stomach flipped as she remembered his lips fluttering over her jaw and his breath mingling with hers—soft, seamless and very, very hot. And then there was the lazy, unhurried way in which he looked at her, like he had all the time in the world to caress her face using just his eyes.

Nidhi was furious with herself. The previous evening she had run inside the house panting, not from their basketball game, but from the undeniable attraction she felt towards him. He had come waltzing back into her world after twelve years, with that ridiculously charismatic smile and lethally charming personality, and Nidhi had been reduced to a simpering idiot with no control over her feelings. She was like putty in his hands, just as she had been at fourteen. She couldn't wait for the campaign to be over so she could get back to her regular life. A life without Vikram's teasing smile. Or intense gaze. Or electrifying touch.

Nidhi groaned, burying her face in her hands. She was glad about the reprieve his Mumbai trip had provided her. Over the last couple of days, Nidhi had thrown herself into her work without the constant interruption of Vikram's visits, calls or thoughts.

Okay, maybe just the first two.

But now she needed his approval for the four-pager and she had no option but to call him. Nidhi took a deep breath and dialled his number. After several rings, the call went unanswered. Perhaps he was busy.

An hour later, Nidhi tried calling again, and again he didn't pick up. Maybe he was in a meeting.

Two hours went by and Nidhi called him for the third time. When he still didn't answer the phone, Nidhi began to wonder if he was avoiding her calls intentionally.

By late evening, Nidhi's annoyance had heightened to full-blown rage.

What the hell did he think of himself, ignoring her calls like she was some pesky journalist? If he was going to treat her like a journalist, she was going to behave like one. She called Monty.

'Nidhiji! *Kya haal chaal*?' Monty greeted her warmly.

She came straight to the point. 'I've been trying to reach Vikram since morning for an urgent approval.'

'Vikram is, ummm, indisposed.'

'What does that mean?'

'He is not able to come to phone right n—'

'I know what the *word* means,' she snapped. 'I meant, what is he so busy with that he can't take out five minutes to approve a creative?'

'He is busy with . . .' Monty's voice trailed off.

'With?' Nidhi prompted, uneasily aware that it was none of her business.

There was a long pause at the other end before Monty finally said, 'He has met Natashaji after many days, so he is busy with her.'

Nidhi's heart sank.

'Natasha is not my girlfriend.'

Of course, he would lie about that. Because Nidhi was just another girl—a potential fling, a meaningless affair in his string of many. But Nidhi would be damned if she let herself become 'one of Vikram Walia's girls'.

'I see,' Nidhi said quietly. 'A personalized newspaper has to be hand-delivered to each CEO by Monday. I've emailed it to you guys, please have Vikram take a look and let me know if he's fine with it.'

'*Bilkul*, Nidhiji, bilkul,' Monty said agreeably.

'And I may not be available on the phone,' she lied. 'So you can email or text me.'

'Done hai, ji, done!' Monty assured her.

When she hung up the phone, Nidhi dialled Kuku's number.

'Niddy! What a pleasant surprise!'

'I wanted to apologize for cutting our evening short the other day.'

'I understand. How's your friend doing now?' Kuku asked.

'My friend?'

'The one who was unwell.'

'Right, my friend. She's, uh, much better now.'

'Glad to hear that,' he said, and just as Nidhi was about to concede that Kuku might actually be a nice guy, he added, 'Shared hostels are a breeding ground for disease, if you know what I mean.'

Your brain is a breeding ground for stupidity, if you know what I mean.

'Ummm, anyway, I was wondering if we could meet again,' Nidhi said extra cheerfully, trying to mask the reluctance in her voice.

'Yes, of course. I'm in Bangalore for a few days, but we can do dinner on Sunday if you're free?'

'Great. I look forward to it,' Nidhi lied.

After her conversation with Monty the previous night, Nidhi had decided not to humour Vikram's advances, nor encourage any form of non-professional contact.

Too bad if he was her neighbour. Too bad if the thought of kissing him had kept her awake for three nights in a row.

Too bloody bad.

The morning's *Delhi Today* front page only helped strengthen her resolve. The article titled 'Walia's Wild Escapades' was essentially a half-page photo essay dedicated to Vikram's many, *many* girlfriends. One German–Australian supermodel, three Indian supermodels, two TV actresses, one pop star, one former beauty pageant winner, one MTV VJ, even—and Nidhi wondered how he had *ever* convinced her to date him—a famous human rights activist.

And smack in the middle of the collage was a recent photograph of Vikram and Natasha walking outside the Taj Mahal Hotel in Mumbai, sporting trendy sunglasses and holding styrofoam Starbucks cups. Vikram was wearing a white linen shirt with jeans, and Natasha was dressed in a tiny pair of denim shorts and an oversized cricket jersey. A number *thirteen* jersey.

The image was captioned 'Nuts about Vikram'.

So much for 'I don't drink tea or coffee'. And so much for 'Natasha is just a friend'.

Nidhi tossed the newspaper aside and spent the entire day buried in work. When Dibakar asked her for the status of the direct mailer, she told him it was still pending Vikram's approval. She was not his personal secretary and she was done following up. She, however, conveniently forgot to tell Dibakar that she had ignored half a dozen phone calls from Vikram since that morning.

So in the evening, as Nidhi switched the Hindi news channel that blared '*Natu par hue Vikram lattu*' to reruns of *Friends* on Zee Café, she was surprised to receive a call from Dibakar. Especially given how irate he sounded—for Dibakar, that is.

'Nidhi, I'm not blaming you, but Vikram *personally* contacted me! He said he's been calling you since morning,' Dibakar explained.

Nidhi choked. 'That's odd, I must've missed his call.'

'He called you more than ten times,' Dibakar said, sounding strained.

'Ummm, he's exaggerating,' Nidhi evaded. 'You know how these celebrities are.'

'Please call him back immediately,' Dibakar said calmly.

'Sure, Dibakar,' she grumbled, wondering if she could get away with interpreting 'immediately' as 'tomorrow morning'.

'And please inform me once you speak with him,' he added before hanging up.

Nidhi sighed and dialled Vikram's number.

He sounded happy when he answered the phone. 'Finally!'

'What do you want?' Nidhi snapped.

'Why haven't you been taking my calls?' he asked.

'I've been busy,' she said shortly.

'Really? Because Mangal Singh just told me that you've been watching TV for the last two hours,' he said dryly.

Nidhi gasped. 'Are you spying on me?'

'Why haven't you been taking my calls?' Vikram repeated calmly.

'What do you want?' she asked brusquely.

'Why,' he asked again slowly, 'haven't you been taking my calls?'

'I assumed you were busy with your movie star girlfriend!' Nidhi burst out.

'I already told you she's not my girlfriend,' Vikram said patiently.

'I don't care, it's none of my business.'

Vikram sighed. 'Natasha is just a good friend.'

'Really? Is that why you timed your Mumbai trip with hers?' Nidhi threw back.

'Are *you* spying on *me*?' he teased.

'I don't need to. Your personal life is front-page news!' she retorted.

He chuckled. 'Oh, so *that's* why you're upset!'

'I'm not upset!'

'Yes, you don't sound upset at all,' he drawled.

'If you think I give a damn about your harem of supermodels and actresses, you flatter yourself!'

'My *what*?' He laughed.

'I'm hanging up the phone,' she said, and proceeded to do exactly that.

It rang again almost immediately.

'Why can't you leave me alone?' she snapped.

'Why can't you stop being a brat?' he asked cheerily.

'If I'm such a brat, stop calling me. Go call your Filmfare Award–winning girlfriend!' she bit out.

Confusion tinged his voice. 'Nuts and I went to a café together. Why are you making such a big deal about it?'

'You said you don't drink coffee,' she reminded him.

'I don't. But I *do* drink hot chocolate,' he said, amused by her rationale.

She paused, momentarily thrown, before sallying forth haughtily, 'Your personal life is none of my concern. I think you and "Nuts" make a lovely couple.'

'Will you stop saying that?' Vikram snapped. 'I already told you we're not together.'

'I saw the photos!'

'You were meant to, along with the rest of the country. It was a photo op orchestrated by our managers.'

'Really? Because I called Monty yesterday and he said you were "indisposed" and making up for lost time with "Natashaji". I may not be a celebrity, but even I know that's code for *post-coital*!' she spat out.

Vikram laughed at her phraseology.

'Don't you dare laugh,' Nidhi warned. 'She's even wearing your jersey!'

'She's wearing *a* jersey. You can buy them on Shopcart for a thousand bucks. If I didn't get it for free, I would too!'

'Are you telling me she bought that jersey online?'

'No, I gifted it to her after we won the World Cup,' he admitted.

Nidhi went silent.

'Jealous?' Vikram teased.

'Why *would* I be? Natasha Sahay is just another name on the long list of your . . . your *concubines*!'

Vikram burst out laughing. 'Oh, Billi! Where have you been all these years?'

Nidhi froze.

'Are you there?' Vikram asked after a long pause.

Her voice came out as a high-pitched squeak. 'Yes.'

'Natasha and I have the same hair stylist who we visit once a month. I forgot my phone at home yesterday, which is why I was "indisposed",' he explained calmly.

'It's none of my business,' Nidhi reiterated, her tone still sceptical.

'Call Shear Joy in Bandra and ask if Mr O.D. Singh came in for a haircut on Friday.'

'Who is Mr O.D. Singh?'

'Me. It's an alias I use sometimes.'

'Why that name?'

He paused. 'O.D. as in *Odie*.'

Her tone softened. 'You fake-named yourself after Odie?'

Vikram cleared his throat. 'I loved that little guy.'

Nidhi felt herself melt inside. 'Me too.'

'Nidhi,' he began, his voice strained, 'I want us to . . . stop fighting. Is that too much to ask for?'

She paused and considered his words. And when she finally spoke, she was surprised by how much she meant her response. 'No, it isn't. I'd like that too.'

Nidhi spent the next few minutes discussing the creative with Vikram. When she hung up, she felt a strange tightening in her chest. She promptly attributed the feeling to the unexpected reminder of Odie.

At the balcony of his sea-facing apartment in Mumbai, Vikram took a seat next to Monty and spoke in a deceptively calm voice. 'You know I love working with you, right?'

Monty looked up from his tandoori *jhinga* and nodded. 'Right.'

'I do everything you ask me to, no questions asked,' Vikram said, his face expressionless as he watched the waves crash against the rocks.

Even though that was far from the truth, Monty sensed that something much more important was weighing on his client's mind. So, with wisdom acquired over years of working with Vikram, Monty nodded again. 'Right.'

'You ask me to do a dandruff shampoo commercial, I do it. You ask me to attend a politician's kid's birthday party, I do it. You ask me to do a social campaign that pays me nothing, I do it. You ask me to pretend I'm dating Natasha, I do it.'

Monty gulped, a little disconcerted by Vikram's casual tone. 'Right.'

'I know you sometimes go beyond the confines of your job description and do things which you believe are in my best interest,' Vikram continued, and that's when Monty saw the contained fury in his client's tightly clenched jaw. 'But what you said to Nidhi about Natasha was intentionally misleading, and you know it.'

Monty's eyes widened and he instinctively reached for his bottle of pills. 'But, Vikram, I didn't—'

Vikram snapped his gaze to Monty and spoke in a chilling tone. 'If you ever—and Monty, I mean *ever*—interfere with me and Nidhi again, you and I are done.'

Monty's jaw slackened as he absorbed Vikram's words. He stared at his client of seven years and his voice dropped to a low whisper. *'Bhen ki . . .'*

Vikram raised an arrogant eyebrow in inquiry.

Disbelief flashed in Monty's eyes. 'You are in love with her.'

Vikram returned his attention to the view. 'Maybe. Maybe not.'

Monty smiled. 'It wasn't a question.'

'Thanks for doing this, Nuts,' Vikram said, clinking his wine glass with hers.

'Are you kidding me? I'd do anything for a free lunch at Pier 13.' Natasha winked, tossing her long curls over her shoulder before taking a sip of her pinot noir.

'The PR team is clearly thrilled,' he said dryly, tipping his head towards the group of employees beaming their approval at him.

'So are the journalists,' Natasha said, waving to the *Bombay Times* editor seated two tables away from them. 'When's your flight?'

'In a couple of hours.'

'I thought you weren't going back to Delhi until Tuesday,' Natasha said casually.

'Something came up,' Vikram said evasively.

Amusement danced in her eyes. '*Someone*, you mean.'

'I need to see her,' Vikram said, unable to hide his smile.

Natasha laughed. 'You've got it bad.'

'Little bit,' he admitted with a boyish grin.

'I've never seen you like this, sweetie,' she said, squeezing his hand. 'You look adorable.'

'Shut up,' he said, albeit with a lopsided smile. 'Don't make me regret telling you about her.'

'I never thought I'd live to see the day you *voluntarily* go to Delhi,' she teased.

'Hey, I still dislike that city intensely. I could never live there,' he scoffed.

'Never say never,' Natasha said, daintily lifting a spoonful of lobster bisque to her flaming red lips.

Vikram glanced at the spectacular panoramic view of the Arabian Sea through the tall glass walls of his restaurant. 'Mumbai is home.'

'That it is,' Natasha agreed. 'Will you send me a picture of Nidhi later?'

'I intend to drag her out to dinner as soon as I get home.' He grinned.

She raised an amused eyebrow. 'Home?'

He cleared his throat. 'Uh, Delhi.'

'If you say so.' She smirked.

A few hours later, when Vikram landed in Delhi, he was glad Natasha wasn't around to see the goofy grin on his face. He shook his head, slightly abashed by his childlike excitement to see Nidhi. Waves of nostalgia swept over him as he stepped into the car outside the airport. He felt exactly as he had upon returning from cricket camp in Dehradun twelve years ago.

The only difference was that back then he had been a mere teenager, without any experience with the opposite sex. Which is why it surprised Vikram that at twenty-six, after innumerable sexual liaisons with beautiful, accomplished women, he had spent the last week in a state of perpetual arousal after an almost kiss with Nidhi. He hadn't been able to get the image of her pinned under him out of his head. Or the sensation of her heart pounding against his chest. Or the taste of her soft skin on his lips. And he especially hadn't stopped thinking about those startling green eyes.

He was behaving like an infatuated idiot, rushing back to Delhi early just to be with her. But there was a far more compelling reason behind advancing his trip than the overpowering need to kiss her. Vikram was convinced that there was more to the story of their falling-out than the version he had lived with for the last twelve years. And he needed to know exactly what had happened so that they could put it to rest and start afresh.

Nidhi sighed and flopped on to her bed. She had spent the last half hour rummaging through her closet, trying to find an appropriate outfit for her date with Kuku. She glanced at the fuchsia one-shoulder mini dress that hung off her bed and mentally discarded it from her shortlist. The dress was beautiful and showed off her curves, but perhaps it was a bit *too* sexy. And 'too sexy' wasn't the message she wanted to give a guy she had no interest in. She eyed the peach body-con dress sprawled on the floor and rejected it for being too clingy. She had nearly decided upon a sleeveless white sheath dress when her phone rang.

'Hi, Viks!' she said warmly.

Since their conversation about 'Odie Singh' a few days ago, Nidhi's feelings towards Vikram had softened substantially. Circumstances had thrown them into each other's company, and whether Nidhi liked it or not, the fact was that they shared a complex history. True, things had ended on a sour note, but Nidhi couldn't deny the good times they'd seen as kids. And their 'fight' had happened so many years ago that it felt childish to hold it against him. He seemed to have forgotten about it and moved on; so could she. Above all, he had sounded so sincere about wanting to get along with her that Nidhi decided to give it a genuine shot. Who knew, maybe she and Vikram could actually be friends again.

'I'm back!'

'Oh, I thought you weren't back for another couple of days?' she asked, surprised.

'Uh, yeah. I have some work in Delhi.'

'How was Mumbai?'

'Boring.'

Nidhi snorted. 'That's not what your latest tweet said.'

'What tweet?' Vikram asked.

'"Delicious crab cakes and shrimp cocktail with @NatashaSighHigh at @Pier13Mumbai!"'

Vikram sounded amused. 'So you follow me on Twitter?'

Dammit.

'In your dreams,' she lied, reaching for her laptop to open a browser tab so she could unfollow his Twitter account.

Vikram laughed. 'Now don't set about unfollowing me, okay?'

Nidhi froze.

'That *is* what you're doing, isn't it?' Vikram snickered.

Nidhi glanced at her bedroom window and found him leaning casually against the ledge of his own, a roguish grin on his face.

'Stop spying on me!' she hissed, walking over to the window.

'I can't help it. You're very good at ignoring me,' he said, flashing her a white smile.

Nidhi hung up the phone. 'Yes, I am!' she shouted, before slamming her window shut.

To her annoyance, she heard his deep, throaty laugh through the pane.

A couple of minutes later, there was a knock on her door. Nidhi rolled her eyes. 'Come in, Vikram!'

'Hey,' he said, strolling into the room with a wide smile that faded as soon as he spotted the pile of clothes on her bed. 'Are you going out?'

'Yes.'

'Big date?' he scoffed.

'Something like that,' she muttered.

He stared at her in utter shock. 'Seriously?'

She nodded.

Vikram's jaw clenched. 'With Sameer?'

'No way!'

Vikram ran a hand over his face. 'Then with whom?'

'He's a lawyer at Papa's firm,' she said, shifting under his scrutinizing gaze. It was the same look he'd given her after she had inadvertently got him run-out during an inter-school championship when they were ten. The look was an intense combination of restrained anger and bitter disappointment.

'I didn't realize you were the arranged marriage type,' he said casually.

'Neither did I,' she said, forcing a laugh.

'I see you're still pandering to your father's whims and fancies,' he said, sounding irritated.

'There's a difference between pandering to him and protecting him,' Nidhi said.

'What do you mean?'

'Nothing.'

'What, Nidhi?'

Nidhi sighed. 'This morning I spent ten minutes trying to get toothpaste out of my hair.'

Vikram seemed confused by her segue, so she continued, 'Only to realize that it wasn't toothpaste at all.'

'What was it?' he asked.

'A grey hair!' she said, waving an accusatory finger at her scalp.

A reluctant grin tugged at his lips. 'So?'

'So, I'm not getting any younger, Viks. I need to meet guys!'

'And you're going to meet them wearing *that*?' Vikram asked, throwing a horrified look at the fuchsia dress.

'No, most likely I'm wearing this,' she said, showing him the white dress.

'No.'

'What's wrong with it?' she asked, furrowing her brow.

It's too short.

'It's too boring.'

'Hmmm. What about this?' she said, holding up a long lime-green chiffon dress.

'No.'

'Why not?'

Because nothing brings out your eyes like the colour green.

'It's too bright.'

She picked up a red silk dress with a plunging neckline. 'Okay, how about this?'

'No.'

'What's wrong with this one?'

It's too revealing.

'It's too revealing.'

Nidhi groaned. 'You're being a pain, Viks!'

'I'm only trying to help,' he lied.

'Fine. Then why don't *you* pick something?' she said, gesturing to her closet.

'Sure.' Vikram shrugged, sauntering into the walk-in closet.

For the next ten minutes, he rejected a dozen outfits for reasons such as 'too long', 'too pink' and, Nidhi's personal favourite, 'too blah'. So when he finally said 'Aha!', Nidhi turned expectantly to the hanger he was holding up.

She took one look at the outfit he had selected and burst out laughing.

'What?' Vikram said innocently.

'I'm not wearing *that* on a date,' Nidhi sputtered through her laughter.

Vikram seemed affronted. 'Why not?'

She snatched the beige salwar kameez out of his hands. 'Because I wear it to funerals,' she said blandly.

'Don't ask for my advice if you're not going to take it,' Vikram said sullenly, crossing his arms over his chest.

Nidhi narrowed her eyes at him. 'What's the matter with you today?'

'Nothing,' he grumbled, walking towards the door.

'Clearly, it's not nothing,' she said.

'Just a headache,' he said, raking a hand through his hair. 'Enjoy your date.'

Standing at his window a few minutes later, Vikram watched a tall, burly guy help Nidhi into his car.

Vikram noticed, with some irritation, that Nidhi had worn the green dress.

'Balraj Sir didn't steer you towards law?' Kuku asked, slurping on his spaghetti.

Nidhi tried not to focus on the arabiatta sauce adorning his chin. 'On the contrary, he never wanted me to become a lawyer.'

'Why not?'

Because ever since my mother left us to pursue her career, my father is dead against women having demanding jobs.

'Because he wanted me to have a work–life balance,' she said diplomatically, taking a small bite of her baked cod.

Kuku nodded his approval. 'Yes, it's hard to manage such a taxing profession when a woman's primary responsibility is towards her family.'

If this were the morning meeting at *News Today* and one of her male colleagues had made a similar statement, Nidhi would've decimated him. But then again, none of her co-workers were chauvinist assholes.

'I don't mind my wife working after marriage,' Kuku said magnanimously. 'So long as it's not a very demanding job. Sort of like yours.'

Gee, thanks.

Kuku was clearly representative of the vast majority of Indian men, including her own father, who believed that a woman's career was second to a man's, and that women weren't cut out for 'serious' jobs. So Nidhi bit back the scathing retort that was at the tip of her tongue and nodded politely. After all, this was an arranged date, not a job interview.

On the phone last week, her father had sighed. 'Can't I ask even this much of you?'

So Nidhi had been unable to refuse him. And for Balraj's sake, she had actually bothered to put some effort into this evening. She had even spoken at length to her colleague, the marketing insights manager, Sanyukta, who'd had an arranged marriage last year.

'I met several guys before finally saying yes to my husband. The key is to manage expectations,' Sanyukta had said. 'Don't go in looking for perfection. There will always be something you have to compromise on. Either his looks, or his fashion sense, or the fact that he pronounces "bowl" to rhyme with "cowl" instead of "coal",' she had said with grin, referring to her own husband. 'You just have to decide if his flaws are things you can live with, or if they are deal-breakers.'

Kuku had ordered Nidhi's meal for her, which she didn't appreciate, but did it really qualify as a deal-breaker? He didn't know how to eat pasta or pronounce her name, but she could teach him those things. His gaze kept dropping to her breasts, but most guys were like that, weren't they? He had a problem with women drinking alcohol, but so did her father. He clearly didn't give a shit about Nidhi's career, but no one was perfect.

Vikram's face popped in front of her eyes and Nidhi's fork fell from her hand, clattering on to her plate.

Kuku leaned in and gave her a wink. 'At least the law practice will stay in the family.'

I don't remember saying yes, Nidhi wanted to snap, but Balraj's words came back to her, so she took a deep breath and drew a long sip of her virgin mojito instead.

Compromise.

By the end of the evening, Nidhi was seriously beginning to question the 'compromise' strategy.

Kuku insisted on driving, despite having had four glasses of wine. And when Nidhi offered to drive instead, he laughed at the absurdity of her proposal. 'A drunk male driver is better than a sober female driver.'

On top of that, the alcohol had made him a little too *handsy*. When his hand came to rest on her thigh, Nidhi was thankful for the scant protection her long dress provided against his touch.

'Maybe you should use both hands to steer,' she suggested politely, removing his hand.

'Don't tell me what to do!' Kuku barked. When Nidhi blanched, he forced a laugh. 'I'm only joking. Of course, you can tell me what to do. After all, you're my *future wife*.'

Nidhi stiffened. His eyes almost looked *greedy*, like Nidhi was a prize to be claimed, and Kuku the rightful winner.

She grasped the armrest and glanced out the window, slightly relieved to see that they were only a couple of minutes from her home. A moment later, she felt Kuku's finger tracing the curve of her neck. Ignoring her gasp of shock, he hooked his finger in the strap of her dress, sliding it down her shoulder.

'What are you doing?' Nidhi snapped, grabbing his wrist and holding it away from her.

Anger flashed in his eyes. 'Oh, come on! Don't pretend you don't want this. You wouldn't have worn this dress if you didn't,' he said, his rapacious eyes roving her neckline.

How original.

'I think you have the wrong idea, Kuku,' Nidhi said calmly, even as her sense of self-preservation made her reach for the door handle.

'What's the rush?' Kuku asked, bringing the car to a halt outside her house.

The rush is that if I don't get out of your revolting presence this minute, I might throw up.

'I need to get home,' she said firmly, leaping out of the vehicle before he could touch her again.

'Wait!' he commanded.

Nidhi walked backwards, watching Kuku step out of the car and stalk towards her purposefully.

Her back collided with a solid form and she let out a little scream.

'Nidhi?' Vikram said, steadying her shoulders with his hands.

'Viks!' she gasped.

'Hey, hey! You okay?' he asked, his eyes filling with concern.

She nodded emphatically. 'Yes. I . . . yes.'

Apparently, disgust wasn't the only feeling Kuku had invoked in her, Nidhi acknowledged as her arms involuntarily wrapped themselves around Vikram's waist, causing the wave of terror to fade into relief.

Displeasure flashed across Kuku's face at their proximity, but it quickly turned to shock when he recognized Vikram. '*Vikram Walia?*'

Kuku took a step forward and Vikram felt Nidhi's grip tighten around his waist. He pulled her closer, shielding her with his chest.

'I'm Kamal Kukreja. You can call me Kuku,' he blurted, looking a little star-struck in Vikram's presence.

'Hi,' Vikram said.

'Vikram Walia,' Kuku repeated in an awed whisper. 'What are you doing here?'

'I'm Nidhi's next-door neighbour,' Vikram said, and Nidhi was touched when he added, 'and her childhood friend.'

'Oh,' Kuku said, looking dazed.

'It's late,' Vikram said bluntly.

'Yes, it's late,' Kuku agreed sycophantically. 'I'll leave now. I'll call you tomorrow, Niddy.'

Nidhi nodded silently, watching him drive away.

'What's wrong?' Vikram asked, cradling her face between his hands.

'Nothing,' she lied.

'You don't seem like yourself. Tell me what's wrong,' he coaxed gently.

What's wrong is perverts like Kamal Kukreja.

'I . . . it's nothing,' she stuttered.

A dangerous glimmer crept into his eyes, and his face hardened. 'Did he hurt you?'

She shook her head.

'Nidhi,' Vikram said urgently, searching her eyes. 'Promise me you're okay.'

'I'm okay,' she breathed.

Suddenly realizing her arms were still around him, she loosened her grip, preparing to step away. Unwittingly, Vikram's arms tightened around her waist, pulling her closer. Resting his chin on her head, he whispered, 'Stay.'

Nidhi relaxed against his hard chest, revelling in his warmth as well as his heady scent. The steady beating of his heart against her cheek and the soothing feel of his hands on her back brought her breathing back to normal. She felt protected, she felt safe and, after a very long time, she felt *at home*.

Nidhi's eyes snapped open at the intensity of her feelings and she took a step back. 'I better go inside.'

Vikram was reluctant to let her go, but sensing her need for space, he nodded and watched her disappear into the house.

Nidhi sank into the chair at her workstation with a frustrated groan.

Earlier that morning, after seeing a photograph of Vikram and Natasha on Page 3, Dibakar had sent Nidhi on a fool's errand. Her mission was to convince the sports and *Delhi Today* editors to 'tone down' all coverage that showcased Vikram as 'rakish, combative or irresponsible'.

'That's basically everything he does, Dibakar,' Nidhi argued. But the peculiar thing was that the words felt hollow and impotent to her own ears.

'If anyone can convince them, Nidhi, it's you! Run-run,' Dibakar said, giving her two thumbs up for good luck.

She threw back her shoulders and walked into Sukhi's cabin with a resolute smile. Sukhi was lounging on the small plaid couch in his room, looking out the window. Smoking a joint.

'What do you want?' he grunted, without turning away from the view of the Connaught Place skyline.

'Hi, Sukhi,' she said, pasting a pleasant smile on her face.

'I don't have all day,' he said curtly, glancing her way only long enough to scowl at her.

Nidhi came straight to the point. 'Vikram Walia is our brand ambassador, and his personal image directly influences the brand imagery. If we continue to portray him as an irresponsible figure, it will reflect poorly on our brand scores. So, I was thinking, perhaps we could focus more on his contributions to Indian cricket, instead of his ongoing suspension?'

'A puff piece?' Sukhi asked, sitting up.

'Uh, not exactly. But maybe, uh, go a little easy on him?' she suggested.

'What a great idea,' Sukhi said, his haggard face and sunken eyes brightening at the thought.

'Really?'

'No!' he snapped. 'This is a fucking newspaper, not an opinion blog.'

'That's not what I—'

'I don't give a damn about what Walia does *off* the field. I don't care what he wears, where he eats or who he fucks. My job is to cover his cricket and that's what I intend to do,' Sukhi barked.

'Of course. I just meant—'

'Get the hell out of here!' he snarled. 'And if you ever try to tell me how to run my department again, I'll have you fired.'

Nidhi had no doubt he meant it.

She dragged herself to the *Delhi Today* floor, mentally preparing herself for a similar—even if slightly more refined—rejection from the editor, and Risha's boss, Kabir Bose.

'It's just that all these things take attention away from the cause, Kabir,' Nidhi reasoned.

'I understand, Nidhi. But I'm just as concerned about *Delhi Today*'s brand scores as you are about EducateIn's. I don't care what Walia does *on* the field, but there's no way I can ignore the late-night soirées or bar brawls.'

'Of course not. I'm not saying you shouldn't cover his shenanigans, I'm just suggesting that you de-sensationalize the coverage a bit,' Nidhi offered.

'There is a direct correlation between Walia's profligacy and *DT*'s readership numbers,' Kabir said. 'The more reckless he is, the better I look.'

'Ummm, yes. That makes sense, but we're investing a lot of media in EducateIn and it's counterproductive if—'

'Vikram Walia is the crème de la crème of bad boys, and his bad behaviour is good for business.' Kabir chuckled. 'And anyway, today's photograph is just comme ci, comme ça—it's hardly scandalous,' he said, sliding the newspaper towards her.

Ignoring the involuntary pang of disappointment she felt at the image of Vikram and Natasha holding hands at his Mumbai restaurant, Nidhi feigned a nonchalant smile.

'This is simply a photograph of a man in love. Don't you agree?' Kabir asked her.

At their morning chai break under the *NT* building, both Tanvi and Risha had made a similar assessment. Risha had been more reluctant to pass judgement based on a tabloid photograph, but Tanvi was convinced. 'You work for a newspaper, you should know there's no smoke without fire. And *that*,' Tanvi had said pointing to Vikram's face, 'is more emotion on Walia's face than when India won the World Cup. Clearly, the only thing on his mind is the woman he loves.'

As for Nidhi, despite the decade-long hiatus in their friendship, she still knew Vikram far better than she wanted to admit. She knew he had wanted to storm out of the conference room the moment he had laid eyes on her. She knew Anusha's heroic version of the twin boys' incident had embarrassed him. She knew he had lied about having a headache the previous day. She knew the meaning of every single inflection in his tone and every different expression on his face.

Which is how Nidhi knew what Vikram's happy, unguarded smile in the photograph meant. He was in love.

With Natasha Sahay.

So, when Nidhi walked out of Kabir's room, her mood was extremely bleak. Not at the thought of Vikram being in love with Natasha. Not at all. Nidhi was only annoyed because of the unproductive morning she'd had.

On impulse, she sent Vikram a text:

I'm going to kill you.

He replied:

I'm already dying.

She typed back:

What do you mean?

His response was instant:

I'm sick. Come take care of me.

Nidhi rolled her eyes and called him. 'You better not be faking it.'

'I'm not,' he croaked, and Nidhi was startled by how miserable he sounded.

'What's wrong?'

'I have the flu,' he rasped.

'Where's your babysitter?' she asked, referring to Monty.

'He's gone to see the Taj Mahal with his "Cunnayda" wali masi ji,' Vikram said hoarsely.

'Have you seen a doctor?' Nidhi asked.

'No, but I took a Crocin,' he said, struggling to speak through a small coughing fit.

Nidhi sighed. 'Hang in there, let me see what I can do.'

She called Mangal Singh, instructing him to stay with Vikram till she came home. A few minutes later, Mangal called her back to say that he had found Vikram on the bathroom floor, heaving his guts into the toilet.

Nidhi sprang to her feet in alarm. She gathered her stuff and rushed out the door, pausing only briefly to inform Dibakar that she was leaving for the day. Then she called Dr Handa, the family physician, who promised to be there as soon as possible.

By the time Nidhi entered Vikram's room, he was huddled in a blanket on his bed, knees pulled up to his chest. She nodded at Mangal, indicating that he could go back home. She touched Vikram's forehead and yanked her hand back in shock—he was burning up.

'So you're not faking it?' she tried to tease.

'Feels pretty real to me,' he murmured.

'I'm going to call Dr Handa again,' she said, walking towards the door to make the call.

'Wait,' he breathed.

'What's wrong?' She frowned.

'Stay with me,' he said, half coherently.

'You need a doctor,' she said firmly.

His eyes fluttered open. 'I need you.'

Something tugged at Nidhi's heart.

She was used to the charming, flirtatious, self-confident Vikram Walia. She wasn't used to the soft, sweet, vulnerable Viks.

A surge of protectiveness shot through her. It was sudden, involuntary and extremely powerful.

She perched on the bed next to him and took his hand. 'I'm right here,' she assured him.

He laced his fingers through hers and gave her hand a weak squeeze, already drifting off.

'So much for cricketers having great immunity,' she muttered under her breath.

'Come on, Viks,' Nidhi grumbled, trying to help him sit up in bed.

It was a little after midnight and Nidhi had woken him up for the next dose of antibiotics prescribed by Dr Handa. The family doctor had been very reassuring. 'Nothing to worry about, *puttar*—viral is in the air. *Do-teen din dawai khayega*, he will be just fine.'

'Help me out here, Viks,' Nidhi grunted, trying to shift his weight as she placed a pillow behind his head. The man was made of pure muscle.

Vikram pushed himself up on his elbows and slid back on the bed, resting against the headboard. The simple action left him exhausted and he watched through half-open eyes as Nidhi handed him two pills and a glass of water. He opened his mouth weakly and she placed the pills in his mouth, tipping the glass up to help him swallow the tablets.

She felt his forehead with the back of her hand. 'You feel cooler.'

'I feel tired,' he croaked.

She gently smoothed the hair off his forehead. 'Wanna go back to sleep?'

He nodded slowly, slinking down the mattress. 'I feel like I just played a test match.'

Nidhi chuckled and wrapped the blanket around him, watching his eyes flutter to a close.

'I could get used to this,' he murmured sleepily.

She cocked her head in confusion. 'Being sick?'

His response was a low, hoarse whisper. 'Being with you.'

She smiled, loving this open, honest side of him. She started stepping away from the bed to resume her spot on the large armchair, when Vikram's hand clamped around her wrist. 'Don't leave me, Nidhi.'

Nidhi's heart lurched at the raw vulnerability in his voice, and immediately she knew that he wasn't just referring to her leaving his bedside.

'Don't leave me again,' he whispered.

Again? Nidhi frowned. She hadn't left *him*, he had left *her*. She opened her mouth to correct him, but his grasp on her wrist tightened. She sat on the edge of his bed and softly pressed her fingertips to his chiselled jaw. 'Never,' she promised.

He expelled a long, relieved breath and closed his eyes.

Nidhi sat next to him for a long time and only when she was certain that he was asleep, she whispered, 'I could also get used to this.'

Nidhi was woken up the next morning by the sound of Vikram's irritable grunting. He was flinging off the blanket, complaining about the heat. Nidhi felt his cool forehead, guessing his fever had broken, but took his temperature just to be sure. She waited for him to finish eating a Bourbon biscuit before handing him his pills. She then asked Mangal Singh to keep vigil while she went home to shower and inform Dibakar that she would be working from home.

An hour later, Nidhi returned with her laptop and stationed herself on the sofa in Vikram's living room, sending out emails and taking calls.

By late afternoon, when a freshly showered Vikram dragged himself down the stairs, he was surprised to find Nidhi sitting cross-legged on his couch, eating Maggi. 'You didn't go to work?'

'Just making sure you don't die. Only because you're the brand ambassador,' she said, sticking her tongue out at him.

His lips quirked into a smile. 'You could've just left Mangal with me.'

Resisting the temptation to ruffle his gorgeously styled hair, Nidhi sighed dramatically. 'Trust me, I tried.'

Vikram chuckled and slid on to the sofa next to her.

'How are you feeling?' she asked.

'Pissed off. I've had two bowls of palak ka soup since morning and you're eating Maggi?' he accused, snatching her fork and digging into the bowl of noodles.

He lifted his feet up to the coffee table, and Nidhi followed suit. They looked at each other.

A second later, in perfect synchrony, they lowered their feet.

Nidhi raised an eyebrow. 'Dadi?'

Vikram assumed a high-pitched feminine voice. '*Vikramaditya Singh Walia, if you want those feet to remain attached to your legs, remove them from the table this minute!*'

Nidhi laughed. 'That sounds just like her.'

They sat in silence for a few minutes till Vikram noticed Nidhi's pensive expression.

'What are you thinking about?' he said, shoving another forkful of noodles into his mouth.

'You know,' she began softly, 'a few days before Dadi passed away, I was teaching her how to use the Internet.'

Vikram looked up with a startled smile. 'Really?'

'She intended to follow you on Twitter so she could know what *you* were saying, as opposed to what the media was saying about you.'

Pain flashed across his features. 'I wasn't a good grandson.'

'That's not true, Viks,' she said softly.

'Dadi took me in when no one else wanted me,' he said, his voice thick with emotion. 'And I didn't even make it to her funeral.'

Nidhi heard the self-loathing in his voice and spoke gently. 'You were busy winning the World Cup, Viks. I'm sure Dadi would have understood.' When the guilt still didn't leave his eyes, she added, 'If you had *lost*, on the other hand . . .'

Vikram laughed.

Nidhi squeezed his hand. 'She was very proud of you. We all were.'

Are.

'Dadi always said that you took your charm and resilience from your Punjabi father, and your pride and hot temper from your Rajput mother.'

Vikram turned to her in surprise. 'She spoke to you about Ma?'

Nidhi nodded. 'Sometimes.'

'Dadi never mentioned her in front of me,' Vikram said. 'Nothing nice, anyway.'

'People change with time, Viks,' Nidhi said softly.

They sure do, he thought, draping an arm around her shoulders. They sat in companionable silence until Nidhi suddenly giggled. Vikram turned to her inquiringly.

'Did you know Dadi loved reading Mills and Boons?' Nidhi asked. When he shook his head, she continued, 'She used to wrap the books in old newspaper and when I asked her why, she said it was because of the "sex scenes" on the cover. The year I turned thirteen, I couldn't resist any more, so I stole one of her books and peeled back the newspaper. The cover had an illustration of a bare-chested man and a well-endowed woman. And do you know what they were doing?'

Enamoured by her infectious enthusiasm, Vikram gave her a curious smile. 'What?'

'The man was kissing the woman's neck. So, for the longest time, I thought *necking* is how babies are born,' she admitted with an embarrassed laugh.

He gave her a dubious look. 'Wait, *do* you know how babies are born?'

'Ha ha,' she said blandly. After a pause, she added, 'Dadi was the strong female influence in my life.'

'No wonder you turned out like this,' he teased, placing the empty bowl on the table.

Nidhi rested her head on his shoulder and Vikram rubbed his jaw against her temple, breathing in the fruity fragrance of her shampoo.

'I saw you, you know,' Nidhi said. 'Four years ago.'

'Where?'

'Here. You were sitting in the garden with Dadi, eating breakfast.'

'And where were you?'

'I had walked over to say hi to her, but . . .'

'But you saw me, so you went back home.'

She nodded.

'I used to visit Dadi all the time. It's surprising that we never bumped into each other,' Vikram said. Then he saw her sheepish smile and realization dawned upon him. 'You avoided me on purpose?'

'Yes.'

He gave an understanding nod. 'Probably for the best.'

'Why did Dadi call me "Billi"?' Nidhi asked suddenly.

'You don't know?' he asked, surprised.

She shook her head.

'Because of your eyes.'

'Oh,' Nidhi said, disappointed by the simple explanation.

'They're beautiful,' he said quietly.

And all of a sudden, Nidhi was no longer disappointed.

She cleared her throat. 'How long will you be in Delhi?'

'I can't wait to leave,' he groaned. 'I hate this city.'

'Why?'

'I just do.'

'You don't hate Delhi.'

Vikram smirked at the conviction in her voice. 'I don't?'

She shook her head. 'I think you have a lot of painful memories associated with the city. Your parents, Dadi . . .' Her voice trailed off, and Vikram wondered if she had been about to add her own name to the list. 'The day it stops representing pain, you won't hate Delhi any more.'

Vikram nodded, agreeing with her logic. 'I guess you're right. I may not always hate it, but I could never live here again.'

'Come on! Don't you just love all this open space?' she said, waving her hands at the large living room.

Vikram chuckled. 'Yes, that's one of the few perks. Also, my friend Singhal lives here.' He then told her all about Rohan, from the first time they had met in Mumbai as teenagers to their most recent drinking session the previous week. 'He's madly in love with this girl and has been stressing about asking her out. Apparently, he took one look at her and knew he wanted to spend the rest of his life with her.'

Nidhi scoffed. 'That doesn't happen in real life.'

An indescribable expression crossed his face. 'Sometimes it does.'

She looked away. 'In any case,' she said, trying to keep the mood light, *'you're* not the marrying type.'

Nidhi remembered the cosy photo of Natasha and Vikram from the previous day's paper, and though it tore at her to think about it, she wondered if the right girl might make him the marrying type. And whether Natasha was that girl . . .

That damn photo!

'Really?' Vikram asked, keeping his tone blank. 'What type am I?'

'The type to entertain Brazilian escorts,' she blurted before she could stop herself.

His eyebrows snapped together. 'God, Nidhi! Stop reading all that garbage. You, of all people, should know that most of what gets reported by the media isn't true!'

'So they weren't Brazilian escorts?' she challenged.

'They were,' he said.

'And they weren't photographed leaving your apartment?'

'They were, but I didn't ord—invite them!'

Vikram was silent for a few moments, and she could see him struggling with a decision. He rubbed the muscles at the back of his neck and exhaled deeply. 'Some of the married guys in the team invited them, and they obviously didn't want their wives to find out, so I didn't bother to correct the media reports.'

Nidhi stared at him, aghast. 'You took the fall for them?'

He gave her a tight smile. 'It's called "taking one for the team".'

'It's called "turning a blind eye"!' she returned.

He took a deep breath. 'Look, I don't condone infidelity, but I would never betray my teammates. Those guys are the only family I've got.'

You've got me.

The words almost tumbled out of her, but she swallowed them back.

'And while we're on the subject,' Vikram continued, 'all those stories of my so-called affairs and one-night stands are grossly exaggerated!'

'So you didn't sleep with that MTV VJ with the five dozen tattoos and piercings?' she asked sceptically.

He gave her a roguish grin. 'I said "exaggerated", not "false".'

Nidhi threw a pillow at him and he laughed.

'I think you're feeling much better now,' she said, standing up primly. 'I'm going home.'

'I'm feeling sick again, I want to cuddle,' he said with a pout, raising his arms in a childlike gesture.

Nidhi smothered a giggle. 'I'll send Mangal, you can cuddle with him.'

Over the next two days, while Vikram's health got progressively better, his mood got increasingly worse.

Since leaving his home that afternoon, Nidhi had been avoiding him. He hadn't seen her around, she wasn't taking his calls and her responses to his text messages were limited to monosyllables.

According to Bhimsen, her father had returned from Mumbai, and Vikram suspected that was the reason for her cold attitude. Balraj Marwah had never liked Vikram and it was possible that Nidhi was trying to prevent a confrontation between them. But Vikram had never been one to watch the game from the sidelines, so he padded up and decided to face his adversary head on.

'I'm going to Nidhi's!' he yelled to Monty, walking towards the door.

'Yes, yes,' Monty said, his voice dripping with sarcasm, 'go and enjoy the match on a fifty-inch flat screen LED, while I am stuck with this twenty-five-inch piece of junk. The picture tube is so bad, Dhoni's jersey is appearing red!'

Vikram shrugged. 'So buy a new TV.'

Monty gaped at him.

'What?' Vikram said impatiently.

'How long are we going to stay here?'

Vikram gave him an impish grin. 'Long enough to invest in a new TV.'

Monty shook his head in resignation.

'Try Shopcart,' Vikram called to him laughingly as he walked out of the house. 'They have some great deals!'

At the Marwahs' gate, Bhimsen rushed forward to inform Vikram how 'very-very glad' he was to see his health restored. Vikram just gave him a quick wave and a smile, too eager to see Nidhi to stop and make conversation.

'Where's Nidhi?' Vikram asked Mangal Singh inside the house.

But Mangal Singh was so pleased to see him that he ignored Vikram's query and asked a pressing question of his own. 'Watching the match, na, Vikram Baba? Today Dhoni's century is 100 per cent sure!'

'Yes, yes, 100 per cent,' Vikram said distractedly. 'Where's Nidhi?'

'Look at that! Fours and sixers, one after the other!' Mangal beamed.

'Where's Nidhi?' Vikram repeated.

'She is watching the match in the living room and . . .'

Vikram didn't hear the end of the sentence because he was already halfway to the living room. He lingered in the doorway, studying her engrossed features as she watched a replay of the last shot while gorging on a bowl of popcorn. Dressed in a pair of yoga pants and a loose T-shirt, her hair pulled back in a messy ponytail, Vikram thought she was the most beautiful girl he had ever laid eyes on. He wanted nothing more than to kiss her.

He cleared his throat loudly.

Nidhi turned towards him and Vikram could've sworn that happiness flickered in her eyes for the briefest second before it was replaced by wariness. 'What are you doing here?'

'I thought we could watch the match together,' he said, casually walking over to the sofa and plonking himself next to her.

She leapt off the sofa. 'Are you crazy? Papa is at home!'

'So?' He quirked an eyebrow.

Good question.

'So, I don't know. It's late and he might not like it that I have company,' she finished lamely, her eyes darting to the door.

Vikram patted the spot next to him. 'Come on, Nidhi. It's been years since we watched a match together. It'll be fun, I promise.'

Nidhi sat down reluctantly, strategically placing the bowl of popcorn between them.

Vikram casually shifted the bowl on to his lap and scooted next to her, his leg grazing hers.

'Stop being such a *darrpoke*,' he said, tossing a kernel at her.

'I'm not scared of anything!' she protested huffily.

'If you say so.' He shrugged, shoving a fistful of popcorn into his mouth.

Nidhi returned her attention to the mid-match analysis.

'I think India is still twenty–thirty runs short,' said one of the panellists. 'It's a flat batting track and Sri Lanka has great power hitters at the top, so the target set by the Indians seems achievable. This is where Vikram Walia would've come in handy. He brings both pace and stability to the Indian middle order.'

'Oooh!' Nidhi grinned, elbowing Vikram in the ribs good-naturedly.

He rolled his eyes.

'Yes, that's true,' another panellist added. 'He is also great at giving his team those skyscraper overs at the end. Too bad he can't keep his temper in check.'

The presenter chuckled. 'As the winner of our Himani Navratna Cool Talc slogan contest suggested: "Keep calm. Unless you are Vikram Walia!"'

He waited for the panel's hearty laughter to subside before adding, 'On that note, up next is a collection of Walia's temper tantrums over the last year brought to you by Eveready Batteries—Give Me Red.'

Vikram groaned as the screen cut to a minute-long montage of his on-field altercations. Cursing furiously at the Sri Lankan captain. Exchanging heated words with an Australian fast bowler. Verbally abusing cricketers from three other nations. Giving the finger to members of the crowd and the press.

'Wow,' Nidhi breathed, completely transfixed as the video montage played out to a heavy metal score. Vikram tried to grab the remote to change the channel, but she snatched it out of his reach.

In all these years, Vikram had never felt ashamed of his actions—on *or* off the field. The press had written all kinds of things about him—right and wrong, true and false—and he had borne it all with an indifferent shrug. But somehow, today, as he watched the look on Nidhi's face, he had the unprecedented urge to defend himself. 'You're confusing my persona with my personality.'

'I'm surprised that a person whose vocabulary contains words like *that*,' Nidhi said, gesturing to the TV screen where Vikram was now giving a mouthful to the Pakistani wicketkeeper, 'knows the difference between "persona" and "personality"!'

'We had the same English teacher,' Vikram tried to joke. 'So my vocabulary is as good, or as bad, as yours.'

'Clearly, your Hindi is much better,' Nidhi commented as the montage came to a close with a dramatic back-to-back replay of Vikram shoulder-butting the umpire and muttering the choicest curses on his way out.

Vikram caught the smile in Nidhi's eyes and relief shot through his pores. 'So you don't think I'm an ill-tempered jerk?' he asked, still needing reassurance.

'Of course, I do.' She chuckled and, when his face fell, added, 'But you shouldn't feel bad about it.'

'I don't. Or I didn't, until now,' he confessed.

She shrugged. 'You've always been aggressive on the field.'

'Don't judge me by my aggression on the field,' he said in a husky whisper. 'I can be *very* gentle off it.'

'Nice innuendo,' Nidhi said dryly.

He opened his mouth to make another teasing comment, but was interrupted by Balraj Marwah's booming voice. 'Good evening, Vikram.'

Vikram turned his head towards the door and saw Balraj enter the room. He rose to his feet languidly and held out his hand. 'Uncle! It's so good to see you.'

Shock crossed Balraj's face at the warm greeting, and he shook Vikram's hand automatically. 'I heard you were in town, but I wasn't aware that you would be visiting us today,' Balraj said, insinuating that Vikram was an uninvited guest.

'Actually, I'm staying next door,' Vikram said cheerily, noticing the flicker of surprise on Balraj's face before his features composed into a blank expression.

'How wonderful,' Balraj said, his curt tone belying his words.

'Nidhi and I are watching the match. Would you like to join us?' Vikram smiled, sinking into the couch with natural ease, as though it was *his* couch. *His* home.

Balraj stiffened. 'Unfortunately, I cannot. I have a prior commitment.'

'That's too bad.' Vikram grinned.

Balraj's eyes darted to his daughter before locking with Vikram's. 'Will you be staying for the entire match?'

'I would love to,' Vikram said, deliberately mistaking the question for an invitation.

Balraj turned the blast of his frigid glare on Vikram and, as clearly as if he had spoken, commanded the younger man to get out of his house. It was a look that had sent Vikram scurrying out of the Marwahs' home several times as a kid, avoiding eye contact and mumbling apologies along the way.

But Vikram was no longer a nervous teenager.

Very slowly, very deliberately, he propped his feet up on the coffee table and draped an arm on the couch behind Nidhi.

Balraj's eyes flashed and he spoke in a silky voice. 'I trust you will conduct yourself as a gentleman in my daughter's company?'

'Cricket is a gentleman's game. And I,' Vikram said, laying a hand on his heart, 'am a *thorough* cricketer.'

The sarcasm wasn't lost on Balraj and he raised an angry eyebrow in warning.

Frantically trying to think of a way to defuse the situation, Nidhi jumped in with, 'What time will you be back, Papa?'

'Late,' Balraj said vaguely, and without moving his eyes from Vikram's, he emphasized, 'I'm meeting the *police commissioner* at the Gymkhana.'

Vikram gave him an amused smile. 'Tell him I said hi.' Satisfied when astonishment momentarily cracked Balraj's icy facade, Vikram continued, 'We collaborated on a traffic campaign two years ago, and he just couldn't get enough selfies with me!'

Shocked and annoyed that his attempt to goad Vikram hadn't affected him in the least, Balraj turned around and left the room, fists clenched at his sides.

Nidhi exhaled audibly and Vikram turned to her. 'Why are you so high-strung around Balli the Bully?'

'No, I'm not,' Nidhi denied automatically.

'Yes, you are. You're very different around him and very different around me or any of your other friends,' Vikram said.

'Childhood habit, I guess.' Nidhi smiled weakly.

Vikram nodded. 'You were always careful around him as a kid, but it seems to have gotten worse, when it should've gotten better.'

'What do you mean?'

'People are supposed to open up to their parents when they grow up. Ironically, you seem even more reserved, almost *timid* around him. You're less like a billi, more like a *chooha* in front of him.'

'I'm not scared of him. I just . . . don't want to upset him,' Nidhi said.

Vikram watched her carefully, sensing that she was holding something back. He was about to gingerly probe further, when Nidhi said with an admiring smile, 'The confrontation was clearly a breeze for you, though.'

Basking in the warmth of her approval, Vikram forgot his original concern and slung an arm around her shoulders.

They watched the second half of the match over pizza and hot chocolate fudge sundaes from Nirula's. As the post-match analysis drew to a close, Vikram helped Nidhi clear the table. Mangal had already retired to his quarters and Bhimsen was snoring away happily at his station.

'Walk me home?' Vikram said, unwilling to leave her side.

Nidhi giggled. 'Why? Scared you'll get lost?'

'Yes, without you,' he said, his tone sombre.

She shifted under his gaze. 'Stop saying stuff like that.'

'Why?' he said, taking her hand and raising it to his lips.

Because I'm just another girl for you. But you're not just another guy for me.

'Let's go,' she said, snatching her hand away.

Confused by her sudden aloofness, Vikram followed her out.

'Oh, look, we're here! It only took three seconds,' she said dryly.

'Tuck me in?' he said, his eyes twinkling with humour.

'Fine,' she muttered and followed him up the stairs, too tired to argue.

As soon as she walked into his bedroom, Vikram grabbed her wrist, spun her around and pinned her against the door.

Nidhi gasped. 'What are you doing?'

'We need to talk,' Vikram said firmly, placing his hands on either side of her.

Nidhi paused. Then she sighed. 'We do.'

'We do?' he repeated, surprised by her concession.

She fiddled with her hair. 'Yes.'

'Okay, you go first.'

'I'm getting engaged.'

He dropped his hands. 'What?'

'To Kuku,' she said, looking at the floor.

Vikram's entire body went rigid with shock. 'What the hell are you talking about?' he snapped, trying to contain his rage. And his fear.

He couldn't lose her—not now, not again. Not *ever*.

Nidhi raised her eyes to his, surprised by his tone. 'Kamal Kukreja, the guy I—'

'I know who the fuck he is!' Vikram snarled. 'Why the fuck are you getting engaged to that piece of shit?'

'Stop cursing,' Nidhi said calmly.

He took a deep breath. 'Why are you getting engaged to him?'

'Because Papa thinks he's a good match and—'

Vikram's hands clamped down on her shoulders with such force that Nidhi thought her head would snap off. 'For once in your life, Nidhi, stop thinking about what your father wants and focus on what *you* want!'

Unshed tears stung hers eyes and she shook her head. 'He only wants what's best for me.'

'Bullshit!' Vikram exploded. 'Why the hell do you let him dictate your life like this?'

'Because I can't lose him,' Nidhi said in a strangled whisper.

Vikram felt an uneasy prickling at the back of his neck. 'What do you mean?'

Nidhi paused, as though assessing her words. 'Papa had two heart attacks after you left, Viks. The first one happened a week before my twelfth-standard board exams and the second one happened when I was in Mumbai.'

Vikram stared at her in shock. 'That's why you moved back to Delhi?'

She nodded. 'I can't lose him, Viks.'

Vikram took a deep breath. 'I get it, Nidhi. Trust me, I do. I grew up without parents and it's not something I'd wish on anyone. But the solution isn't to spend the rest of your life with someone you don't even like, let alone love.'

'If it makes Papa happy, it's worth it,' Nidhi said, feigning conviction she didn't feel.

'The two things aren't related, Nidhi,' Vikram said, uncharacteristically calm. 'Marrying someone your father approves of isn't a guarantee of his good health.'

'I'm not willing to take a chance.'

'You're being ridiculous!' Vikram bit out, tightening his grasp on her shoulders.

Nidhi was as shocked by the force of his words as she was by his harsh grip. She swallowed and pushed her chin up. 'Let me go, Vikram.'

'No.'

'Yes.'

'You can't marry him.'

'Why not?'

'Because.'

Nidhi gave a mirthless laugh. '"Because"? *That's* a convincing argument.'

'You want a convincing argument? I'll *give* you a convincing argument!' Vikram growled, right before his mouth swooped down on hers in a possessive kiss. He cupped her face in his hands, claiming her lips with a passion that stunned her. The kiss was hungry and intense, but it was also coaxing. Like he was *actually* trying to convince her that he was the only man in the world she should ever kiss.

And he was very, *very* convincing.

When Vikram lifted his mouth, Nidhi's fingers instinctively flew to her lips to stifle a moan.

What a waste of the last twelve years, she thought. Because *damn*, this man could kiss.

Her entire body trembled with anticipation and she yearned to taste him again. She longed to fuel the fire that had started as a small ember over a decade ago and blazed into a full-fledged inferno the moment his lips had touched hers.

Vikram pulled her into his arms and she burrowed into his neck, breathing the rough, masculine scent of him, feeling the thundering of his heart against hers.

After a few moments, when sense prevailed, the first emotion to wash over Nidhi was guilt. She lifted her head and drew away, walking past him to take a seat on the edge of his bed. 'This is wrong,' she whispered, staring at her hands.

'This is right, Nidhi,' he said huskily.

'I can't do this to him,' she choked.

'You barely know him,' Vikram said, trying not to lose his cool.

'Not Kuku! I mean *Papa*. I can't do this to Papa,' she said miserably.

Vikram's restraint broke and his voice shook with fury. 'Your father is a tyrannical busybody who thinks it's his birthright to interfere in the lives of others!'

'That's unfair!' Nidhi flung back.

'Really?' Vikram said with cold disdain. 'Then twelve years ago, why did he *proactively* seek me out to tell me what you had said about me.'

Nidhi's face flushed with embarrassment. 'Why are you bringing this up now?'

'Because we never talked about it. We need to talk about it,' he said firmly, sitting next to her.

'I thought we were over it!' she cried, feeling humiliated.

'I never got over it, Nidhi,' Vikram said quietly. 'I was heartbroken.'

Nidhi raised her shocked gaze to his. '*You* were heartbroken? You were the one who broke *my* heart!'

'What are you talking about?' he said harshly. 'Your father told me that the only reason you were friends with me was because you felt sorry for "poor little orphan Vikram". And you only kissed me out of pity.'

'No,' Nidhi said in a choked whisper. 'No!'

The realization that followed hit Vikram like a ton of bricks. He saw the torment in Nidhi's eyes and he knew. He knew that every word Balraj Marwah had spoken to him that night when he was fourteen and hopelessly in love with this sweet, loyal girl had been a lie.

'You didn't say that,' he stated flatly.

Tears streamed down her cheeks. 'I didn't, Viks. I would never—'

'I know,' he said gently, pulling her into his arms.

'I swear, I never—'

'I know, Nidhi,' he said in a ragged whisper. 'I know.'

She sobbed against his chest, drenching the front of his shirt with her tears, and Vikram let her cry. He rubbed her back and whispered softly. 'I'm here, Nidhi. I'm right here.'

She cried like her heart was about to break, and Vikram held her, powerless to comfort or console her. He cringed as Mangal's words came back to him.

'*Every morning the dustbin was full of used tissue papers.*'

A wave of anger swept through Vikram—at her callous, heartless father. And then he remembered Nidhi's guilty expression that night.

'*Is it true, Nidhi?*' Vikram had asked. '*Is that really how you feel about me?*'

Vikram raised her chin with his index finger and gazed into her eyes. 'So what exactly did you admit to that night? What did you tell your father?'

'I told him that I loved you.'

Amid his astonishment, a wave of pleasure shot through Vikram. But he didn't have an opportunity to process either emotion, because another sob shuddered through Nidhi and when she looked at him through her veil of tears, desolate and defeated, Vikram had to physically fight back the tears forming in his own eyes.

He gathered her gently in his arms, and for a brief moment, Nidhi felt like she was fourteen again, sitting on his porch and crying in his arms, taking comfort in his embrace. Except that he was no longer a gullible, powerless little boy. He was a man—a strong, self-assured, but also unbelievably gentle, man.

'I c-can't believe Papa would d-do that to me,' she hiccupped. 'You were my best friend.'

'I still am,' he said with such finality that a fresh set of tears welled up in her eyes.

He shook his head and cupped her face in his hands. 'Don't cry, Nidhi. I can't take it any more,' he begged, his voice hoarse with emotion.

Nidhi made a valiant effort to hold back her tears. She clung to him to keep from crying, to keep from falling apart. She rubbed her cheek against his shirt and slid her hands over the muscular width of his sculpted shoulders, trying to absorb some of his pain.

She lifted her gaze to his and the stormy intensity in her eyes was his undoing. When she raised her mouth to his, Vikram inhaled sharply. When she brushed her lips over his, he groaned. When her tongue darted boldly between his lips, he lowered her on to the bed, giving her complete control of his mouth. And his heart.

I love you, he thought.

He swirled his tongue around hers, exploring the warmth of her mouth, learning the taste of her. It was the moment he had built up in his head for years. How many times had he woken up unable to breathe, panting, gasping from a dream in which he was doing exactly this? And more.

Nidhi belonged with him.

I love you.

The words rose inside his chest, strangling him with their need to be said.

Nidhi's eyes locked with his, as though she had heard the unspoken proclamation. And that's when Vikram saw it. The forest fire in her eyes. Except this time it wasn't anger that had set her eyes ablaze. It was desire—unconcealable and untameable. She moulded her body to his, fitting herself perfectly to his hard contours.

'Vikram,' she breathed softly.

And in that moment, Vikram felt complete. Just a kiss with Nidhi had shattered him like nothing he'd ever experienced. They were both completely clothed and yet Vikram had never felt so wholly satisfied in his life.

'Stay with me,' he whispered. She hesitated and he pressed his mouth to her collarbone. 'Stay . . . please.' She was about to voice another concern, but he pre-empted it by placing a finger on her lips. 'You can jump over the gate in the morning,' he said, flashing one of his famous crooked smiles.

And just like that, Nidhi was convinced. 'Okay.'

Vikram let out a breath of relief and touched his forehead to hers. 'Thank you.'

Vikram woke up in bed, alone.

He smiled at the first thought that crossed his mind.

I told him that I loved you.

His eyes snapped open.

Nidhi had loved him. And whether she was ready to admit it or not, she *still* loved him.

Vikram had felt it last night, in the way she responded to his kisses. And he had felt it several times over the last month, in every suppressed smile and every teasing remark. Heck, even in every snarky quip and sarcastic insult that came out of her sexy mouth.

Unfortunately, Nidhi's opinion of Vikram's character was vastly influenced by what she had read in the papers. But she was smart enough to realize that there was seldom more than an iota of truth in tabloid gossip.

How often had a brand appearance with a female celebrity turned into a 'dinner date'? Or a conversation at a gym been reported as 'couples' spa'? Or a party he had shown his face at for barely an hour turned into a 'booty call'? Ironically, Vikram's interaction with the majority of women he was photographed with had been limited to a polite greeting.

True, he couldn't deny that he had slept with a few women, but the number was nowhere close to what was estimated by the media. And if he'd had even the slightest inkling that he would find Nidhi again, he would've led his life very differently till this point.

His entire body hardened with pleasure as he replayed the events of the night gone by.

Nidhi always looked so proper and put-together that the memory of her hair sprawled on his pillow in a careless disarray made his heart leap with pride. He loved just how improper she had looked last night—wild, primitive, carefree. Just like the girl he had grown up loving.

'I told him that I loved you.'

Twelve years ago, this beautiful, brave girl had admitted to loving him. And he had thrown that love in her face by telling her that she was a stupid tomboy whose kisses meant nothing to him. And that he hated her.

Although Vikram had tried to control his anger for Nidhi's sake earlier, he now felt a fresh surge of fury at Balraj Marwah. The man's ruthless sadism and selfishness made Vikram's blood boil. Last night, Nidhi had turned her pleading eyes to him and whispered, 'Maybe it's all a big misunderstanding. Maybe Papa didn't mean it?'

The most important relationship of Vikram's life had almost irreparably been destroyed by that man, so Vikram was far from feeling charitable towards Balraj Marwah. But the pain in Nidhi's eyes had made him swallow his scathing summation of her father's connivance. 'Maybe,' he had gritted, even though he didn't believe it.

Perhaps, Vikram thought with a twinge of humour, denouncing her evil father wasn't the best way of endearing himself to the girl he loved.

The only girl he had ever loved.

Nidhi dropped her head on Risha's coffee table. 'I can't do it.'

Risha stretched out her legs on the couch and took a sip of her Kingfisher Ultra. 'Then don't.'

Nidhi gave her a look.

'Stop being a baby, Nidhi,' Tanvi snapped impatiently. 'Just say no.'

'I tried!' Nidhi whined.

'Try harder,' Tanvi retorted bluntly.

Risha gave Tanvi a warning look. Over the last hour, the girls had gone through two kathi rolls and two beers each, while Nidhi updated them on what they had started referring to as 'The Kuku Catastrophe'.

'You're talking about the *rest* of your life, Nidhi. Marriage is no joke.' Risha frowned.

'I know,' Nidhi whispered miserably. 'But you didn't see the bitter disappointment in Papa's eyes when I told him I didn't want to marry Kuku.'

'So he'll be disappointed for a while, then he'll get over it.' Tanvi shrugged.

What if he doesn't? Nidhi thought to herself, as Tanvi continued, 'And anyway, arranged marriage is for chumps. Learn from Risha, she has been avoiding matrimonials from her parents for years.'

'Thank you, thank you!' Risha grinned, blowing kisses to her imaginary fans.

Tanvi opened her mouth to say something, then stopped.

'What?' Nidhi probed.

Tanvi paused. 'You have to learn to say no to your father, Nidhi.'

Nidhi nodded, absently picking at the residual pudina chutney in her plate with her index finger. 'I don't want to go out with Kuku again. He creeps me out,' she admitted.

Risha raised an eyebrow. 'What do you mean?'

'He's a bit . . . *handsy*.' Nidhi cringed. 'And it makes me uncomfortable. I'm supposed to meet him tomorrow night, but I really want to get out of it.'

Tanvi narrowed her eyes. 'Brushing-his-hand-against-yours-casually handsy or attempting-to-grope-you-without-your-permission handsy?'

'The latter,' Nidhi admitted with annoyance.

Risha saw the temper flare in Tanvi's eyes and quickly turned to Nidhi. 'Did you tell your dad about that?'

'No.'

'Why not?'

Because it's not worth giving him another heart attack over.

'I didn't want to freak him out.' Nidhi shrugged. 'And maybe it was a weird one-off thing because he'd been drinking.'

'Don't be ridiculous! Being a creepy asshole is never a one-off,' Tanvi snarled.

'I agree. You need to tell your dad about it,' Risha said firmly. 'I seriously doubt he wants you to spend the rest of your life with a drunken lech.'

Nidhi pursed her lips. 'It means a lot to Papa. He thinks Kuku is a "sensible" choice, and if I marry him, the law firm will stay in the family.'

'I'm sure your dad cares more about your happiness than about finding an heir to his corporate throne,' Risha said. 'Right, Shorty?'

'Right,' Tanvi muttered unconvincingly.

Nidhi sighed in frustration. Why did Kuku have to be so obnoxious?

'I have an idea,' Risha began, and Nidhi felt a wave of affection at her friend's enthusiasm. 'How about you invite your dad on the date? Ask him to join you guys for dinner, so he can witness first-hand what a jerk Kuku is!'

Nidhi's eyes lit up. 'You want me to sabotage the date?'

'Yes,' Tanvi said emphatically.

'No,' Risha said, rolling her eyes. 'I just want you to encourage Kuku to drink enough to show his true colours.'

'I think I can manage that. Papa absolutely *despises* public scenes, so when Kuku starts misbehaving at the restaurant, it will automatically be a deal-breaker,' Nidhi said hopefully.

'Exactly!' Risha chuckled, rubbing her hands with glee. 'Now, here's what you should do . . .'

Nidhi's 'date' was not going as planned. Her father's assistant had called to inform her that 'Mr Marwah and Mr Kukreja will be stuck in a meeting till late' and that he had cancelled the reservation at House of Ming and asked Mangal Singh to cook dinner at home instead.

So much for a public scene, Nidhi grumbled to herself.

She was about to reach for her phone to call Risha when a tennis ball whizzed into her room, thwacking her on the forearm. She winced and rubbed her arm, purposefully walking to her window to chastise the culprit. But the 'culprit' wasn't a group of young kids playing on the street.

It was one annoyingly handsome cricketer, standing at his bedroom window with a bat in one hand, tennis ball in the other and a grin on his face.

'No wonder you're off the team!' Nidhi yelled. 'Your aim sucks.'

'On the contrary.' Vikram smirked, throwing the ball in the air, smacking it with his bat and sending it careening into her room. It missed Nidhi's ear by a hair's breadth and this time she knew that was exactly what he had intended.

The arrogance of this man!

'What do you want?' Nidhi snapped.

'I want to know,' he said, reaching for another ball, 'why you're avoiding me. Again.'

'Don't you dare!' she warned, watching him toss the ball in the air.

He caught it in his hand and lowered his bat. 'So tell me.'

'I'm not avoiding you,' she lied, avoiding his eyes.

The ball came swooshing in through the window, ricocheting off Nidhi's shoulder into her room.

'Ow!' she yelped, rubbing her shoulder. 'What the hell is wrong with you?'

'Answer my question,' Vikram said, throwing another ball in the air and letting it see-saw on his knuckles before tossing it back up and catching it deftly in one hand.

'I'm not avoiding you!' she hissed. 'And stop throwing your balls at me.' Vikram burst out laughing and Nidhi flushed. 'That's not what I meant.'

'Pick up the phone,' he said, reaching for his cell phone without moving his gaze from hers. He redialled the number he had tried half a dozen times since the morning.

Nidhi picked up. 'You are so annoying!'

'And you are driving me crazy with this blow-hot-and-cold attitude,' Vikram said, sounding frustrated.

'I don't know what you're talking about,' she said, turning around so he wouldn't see the blatant lie on her face.

Another ball flew in and smacked her, this time on her behind.

She whipped around, her green eyes blazing with anger.

'Okay, okay. Sorry!' Vikram laughed, enjoying the fire in her eyes. *This* was his Nidhi. Well, not *his* Nidhi, but the Nidhi he had grown up with. Fiery, tempestuous, passionate.

'I swear to God, Viks, if you do that one more time, I'll close the window and never open it again,' she threatened.

'That was the last ball,' he assured her. 'Will you please tell me what's bothering you? Why aren't you talking to me?'

'I've been busy,' she evaded.

'Really? Because I can see twenty dresses sprawled on your bed. Another date tonight?' he joked.

'Actually, yes,' she said quietly.

He dropped the bat. 'What?'

'Kuku is coming over for dinner,' she said, trying not to sound guilty.

'You're not seriously going through with this?' Vikram snapped. Then he lowered his voice an octave. 'Not after what happened between us.'

Nidhi swallowed, pushing her back against the wall next to the window, out of his view.

'Nidhi?' he said, his voice pained. 'Look at me.'

She took a deep breath and turned around to face him, fighting to keep her expression composed. 'We were both emotional that day. It didn't mean anything.'

'Bullshit!' he bit out. 'You know it did.'

'No, it didn't,' she said, her voice breaking.

'Don't do this to us, Nidhi. The first time was bad enough, I won't be able to take it again,' he said softly.

'I'm sorry,' she whispered, hanging up the phone. She half expected another tennis ball to fly in through the window, but it didn't.

Instead she received a text from him:

Enjoy your dinner. But after that, we need to talk.

She replied:

There's nothing to talk about.

He ignored that and wrote back:

I'll be waiting, Nidhi. You know I will.

'Are you sure you don't want another drink?' Nidhi asked Kuku sceptically, even as her father shot her a sharp look.

'Yes, I'm certain, Niddy,' Kuku responded with an amiable smile. 'I'm driving.'

Nidhi's eyebrows shot up. *Really? That didn't stop you last time.*

Kuku was a completely different person in front of Balraj. He was polite, restrained and not once did Nidhi catch him gawking at her breasts. He nodded along obsequiously to almost everything her father said, and Nidhi was beginning to realize why Balraj was so keen on Kuku. Because he would be a puppet in her father's hands.

Balraj threw back his head and laughed at something Kuku said, slapping him on the back affably.

Nidhi felt the proverbial noose tighten around her neck.

'Niddy?'

'Yes?'

'Are you okay? You look kind of pale,' Kuku observed.

'Just a little tired,' she yawned, hoping he would take the hint and leave.

'Would you like to go for a drive?' Kuku asked. 'Some fresh air will do you good.'

What fresh air? We live in the most polluted city in the world.

When she didn't immediately respond, Kuku turned to Balraj and added, 'With your permission, of course, sir.'

'Sure,' Balraj said with a friendly smile. 'You're practically family.'

'No!' she burst out and her father narrowed his eyes at her. 'I mean, maybe we can go for a walk instead,' she amended helplessly.

'Sounds good,' Kuku said with a suggestive smile.

Nidhi noticed his leer and re-evaluated the wisdom of going for a walk with him alone. The street was fairly well lit and she knew most of the neighbours. So at least it would be safer than jumping out of a moving car, if it came to that.

How was she considering marrying a man she was *afraid* of? Nidhi wondered in disgust. Was she so spineless? Was she so scared of disappointing her father that she was willing to sacrifice her happiness, maybe even her safety?

Her feelings for Vikram aside, she did *not* want to marry Kuku. And she intended to tell her father that immediately. Or at least as soon as this ridiculous moonlit stroll was over.

Nidhi followed Kuku out of the house wordlessly, keeping a careful distance between them.

But Kuku's intention, as it turned out, was not to walk.

He grabbed Nidhi by the shoulders and pinned her against his car, parked a few feet from the Marwahs' gate.

Panic clawed at Nidhi and she swallowed back her gasp of shock. 'What the hell are you doing?'

'Oh, come on, Niddy,' Kuku chortled, a greedy glint in his eyes. 'There's no use acting coy now. You want this as much as I do. You've been trying to get me drunk all night.' Nidhi swallowed guiltily and he added, 'Don't think I haven't noticed.'

'It's not like that, Kuku,' she said, trying to keep her tone composed and casual even as she internally shuddered at the thought of getting physical with him.

'We're practically engaged,' Kuku said, leering at her breasts.

'No, we're not. And we never will be,' Nidhi snorted, shoving hard at his chest.

Kuku stumbled back in shock and his face flashed with anger at her rejection. He clasped her wrists in a death grip and gave her a menacing smile, 'Not only will we get engaged, we'll get *married*. And then there will be no room for shyness or resistance in our relationship.'

Nidhi broke into a cold sweat, recognizing the clear intention in his tone. 'No,' she choked as he pulled her head back roughly with one hand, using his other hand to trap her against the car, making her skin crawl. 'Stop!' Nidhi rasped, as his fingers bit punishingly into her flesh. She looked around frantically, for Bhimsen or a neighbour or even a stray passer-by. Ignoring her plea, Kuku slid his hand down her neck, over her collarbone, until it came to rest on her breast.

'Get off me, you asshole!' she snapped and was furious with herself when her warning came out as a terrified squeak instead of an ominous command. Terror rose in her throat as his sweaty palm covered her breast through the fabric of her wrap dress. 'Stop or I'll—' Kuku's mouth came smashing down on hers, drowning her threat as his hard body pressed tightly against hers. Tears of pain and humiliation sprang to Nidhi's eyes and she struggled to break away from the vicious assault of Kuku's fleshy mouth. She fought to draw some oxygen into her lungs, to find her voice, to scream for help, but she was no match for his brute strength.

'You fucking piece of shit!' Vikram's voice boomed a split second before he grabbed Kuku by the neck and slammed him against the bonnet of the car. Cold, raw fury flashed in Vikram's eyes as he thrust his arm against Kuku's throat, pinning him down and cutting off his oxygen supply.

Kuku's eyes widened with fear. 'No,' he croaked, shaking his head.

Vikram lowered his face to Kuku's, his eyes blazing with violence. 'Do you even know the meaning of that word, you son of a bitch?' he spat out savagely right before his fist came crashing down on Kuku's jaw with a loud crack. 'If you *ever* touch her again,' he warned in a dangerous voice, 'I will rip you apart limb by limb!'

Kuku sputtered, trying to choke out a response.

'Do you understand?' Vikram bit out, raising his fist again.

Kuku nodded emphatically.

'Let him go,' Nidhi whispered, still gasping from Kuku's onslaught.

Vikram was so consumed by his rage that it took him a moment to register Nidhi's presence. The colour had drained from her cheeks and she stood with her arms wrapped around herself, shivering. She looked so damn fragile that another bout of anger swept over Vikram.

He lifted Kuku by the collar and thrust him aside, causing him to stumble on to the road. 'Get the fuck out of here!' Vikram roared and Kuku leapt into his car, hurriedly starting the ignition.

The car sped away and Vikram reached for Nidhi, but she shook her head. He nodded and stood next to her, waiting for her hands to stop shaking and her breathing to stabilize.

'I heard tyres screech. What happened?' Balraj asked, striding out of the house. 'What did you do to her?' he demanded of Vikram, noticing Nidhi's petrified expression.

'What did *I* do to her?' Vikram snarled. 'What did *you* do to her? You've taken her strength and spirit and crushed it! What kind of father are you?'

'How dare you!' Balraj thundered.

'You did it twelve years ago and you've done it again!' Vikram scathed.

Balraj turned to his daughter. 'What is he talking about, Nidhi?'

Nidhi stared at the ground, unable to find her voice.

Vikram glared at Balraj. 'That fucking son of a bitch . . .'

'Stop!' Nidhi warned. 'Please, Viks. I don't want to stress Papa out.'

'And even after all this she's still thinking about *you*!' Vikram snapped in disgust.

'What happened?' Balraj demanded, panic creeping into his eyes. 'Did Kuku do something to you?'

Nidhi nodded and Vikram's heart broke at the cold, lost expression in her eyes. Balraj caught Vikram flexing and unflexing his right hand and saw the redness around his knuckles. 'Did you hit him?'

'Not as hard as I wanted to,' Vikram said bitterly.

Balraj held his hand out to Nidhi. 'Let's go home.'

Nidhi ignored his hand, but walked into the house. Balraj gave Vikram a curt nod and followed Nidhi inside.

Balraj Marwah sat on the couch next to his daughter and handed her a glass of whisky.

'Drink this,' he said quietly.

Surprise flickered in Nidhi's eyes. 'But I don't . . .' Her voice trailed off.

'I know you drink alcohol, Nidhi,' Balraj said dryly.

Nidhi took a large swig from the glass and turned to face him. 'How did you find out?'

'Just because your loyal Trio is sworn to secrecy doesn't mean I don't have eyes,' he said blandly.

She gave him a puzzled look.

'Until a few years ago, I used to pay your credit card bill,' he reminded her with a wry smile. 'And since then, I've seen you jump over the gate several times.'

Nidhi flushed. 'Why didn't you ever say anything before?'

'Why didn't *you*?' he countered.

'I didn't want to upset you. You always say drinking—'

'Not that!' he said bitterly. 'Why didn't you say anything about Kuku?'

She stared into her glass. 'I tried.'

'I'm sorry,' Balraj whispered, his face a ravaged mask of regret. 'I'm so sorry.'

Tears welled up in Nidhi's eyes and she tried to blink them back with a final swallow of her drink.

'What did Walia mean that even after all this you're still thinking about me?' Balraj asked. When Nidhi remained silent, he continued, 'Is it because of my health? Did you agree to marry Kuku because you thought I'd have another heart attack if you refused?' Balraj pressed, his voice a pained mix of shock and self-contempt.

Nidhi ignored his question and said, instead, 'I don't want to marry him.'

Balraj gave her a hurt look. 'You think I would let you marry him after this?'

Tanvi's words came back to Nidhi. *'You have to learn to say no to your father.'*

And then there was the harsh truth Vikram had thrown in her face two nights ago. *'For once in your life, stop thinking about what your father wants and focus on what you want!'*

'That's the point,' Nidhi responded. 'It's not your decision to make. It's mine.'

Balraj sank back into the sofa. 'I see.'

'I've spent my entire life trying to make you happy, doing things you would approve of. I've spent every moment trying not to upset you, disappoint you or let you down. I'm tired, Papa. Tired of always second-guessing myself, tip-toeing around you, feeling guilty even when I haven't done anything wrong, trying to make you proud—'

'I *am* proud!' Balraj said, and the ferocity in his voice took Nidhi by surprise. 'But I'm also constantly scared. I just want to . . . protect you.'

'Is that what you were doing twelve years ago?' Nidhi shot back. 'Protecting me from Vikram?'

Balraj's jaw clenched and he looked away.

'Instead of protecting me, you hurt me in the most unimaginable way possible. He was my best friend, Papa. My *only* friend. Not only did you take him away from me, you left me alone to pick up the pieces of my broken heart.'

Balraj heard the quiver in her voice and spoke in a flat tone. 'You're still in love with him.'

Nidhi nodded. 'I never stopped loving him. And I think I never will.'

'He's a spoilt rich playboy and his interest in you is nothing but a passing fancy!' Balraj snapped, his face turning red with anger.

'Calm down,' Nidhi warned and was oddly touched when Balraj took a deep breath before continuing in a more reasonable tone. 'He'll use you like a plaything, toss you aside when he's bored, and move on to the next girl.'

His words slashed through her heart, but not because Nidhi thought they were true. She had worked for a newspaper long enough to know that stories of Vikram's numerous flings and sexual encounters were mostly embellished. But it wasn't just the rational part of her brain that rose to his defence. It was also her heart. It was the years of knowing him that assured her that Vikram wasn't the use-them-and-lose-them type. So it wasn't his string of past relationships that bothered Nidhi. What bothered her was the look on Vikram's face in that photograph with Natasha.

'This is simply a photograph of a man in love.'

'That's more emotion on his face than when India won the World Cup.'

'Clearly, the only thing on his mind is the woman he loves.'

Those words had haunted Nidhi for days, and she could not discount them. Because Vikram could deny that relationship all he wanted, but Nidhi knew him well enough to recognize his expression in that photograph.

Vikram loved Natasha.

'Nidhi,' Balraj began urgently. 'He had a bad temper as a kid, but his rage has only gotten worse as an adult. He's a bully!'

Nidhi bit back a smile. 'He's not a bully.' *And neither are you.*

'You're a sweet, sensible girl who needs to be with someone who will care for you.'

'He *does* care for me, Papa. And,' she added calmly, 'he doesn't lose his temper without reason.'

'He's not right for you, Nidhi,' Balraj persisted.

Because he doesn't love me. 'I know,' she responded.

His eyebrows shot up. 'You know?'

She gave a little laugh. 'Yes, I know.'

Her father nodded, evidently relieved.

'But that still doesn't give you the right to interfere,' she warned lightly.

Balraj pulled her in for a brief hug. 'Okay.'

'Thank you,' Nidhi said.

'Thank *you*,' he replied.

'Come in!' Nidhi said in response to the soft knock on her door the following morning.

Vikram nudged the door open with his shoulder, walking into the room with two cups of Starbucks coffee in his hands. Or, if Nidhi had to guess, one cup of coffee and one cup of hot chocolate.

'Hey,' he said softly, glancing at the empty spot next to her on the bed.

Nidhi nodded, giving him tacit permission to sit. He kicked off his sporty flip-flops and settled in beside her, folding his knees up to his chest before handing her a cup.

Nidhi took a long sip of the warm coffee and sighed contentedly. 'How did you know what kind of coffee I like?'

Vikram gave her an embarrassed smile. 'Your friend Risha talks quite a bit.'

'And did Risha also tell you what time I woke up this morning?' Nidhi asked, tipping her head towards her open window.

He threw her a guilty look and sipped his hot chocolate. 'Did you sleep well?'

Nidhi heard the slight catch in his voice and responded to his unasked question. 'I'm doing okay, Viks. I was a little shaken up last night, but I had a long talk with Papa and I felt much better.'

The tension left his body and he gave her a relieved smile. 'I'm glad.'

'How's your hand?' she asked, taking another gulp of her latte.

He glanced down at his swollen knuckles and shrugged. 'I've seen worse.'

'Thanks for yesterday, Viks. If you hadn't—'

'If I hadn't punched him, you would have. And *that* would've hurt much worse,' he said with an exaggerated shudder.

Nidhi smiled and rested her head on his shoulder, drinking her coffee in silence, inhaling the familiar scent of him. The scent that would drift out of her life as abruptly as it had wafted in, she realized with a flash of pain.

Vikram felt her stiffen against him. 'What are you thinking about?'

'When are you going back to Mumbai?' Nidhi asked.

'I have to attend the disciplinary hearing next week, but I can fly back to Delhi immediately after.'

'Why?'

'Firstly, if all goes well, I'll be playing the South Africa series, and the first match is at Feroz Shah Kotla.'

'And secondly?' she probed.

Secondly, I'm insanely in love with you and want to spend the rest of my life with you.

He grinned to himself, imagining her shocked reaction if he voiced that sudden, ardent proclamation. 'You know secondly.'

She knew. And as much as it pained her to steer the conversation in that direction, she also knew it had to be done. 'Tell me.'

'Because I want to spend time with you,' Vikram said softly, rubbing his jaw against her temple.

Nidhi jerked her head away from his shoulder. 'No.'

He narrowed his eyes, somewhat confused. 'No?'

'Whatever this is,' she gestured between them, 'it's not real.'

'What do you mean?' he asked, looking genuinely baffled.

'I mean, it needs to stop. The flirting, the peeping through my window, the bringing me coffee . . .' she explained.

He rolled his eyes. 'You're being ridiculous.'

She held up a palm. 'No, *you're* being ridiculous. We're friends, but what do you think is going to happen between us?'

'Someone woke up on the wrong side of the bed today,' Vikram teased, yanking on a strand of her hair.

'I'm serious,' she bit out and it was the determined glint in her eyes that made Vikram sit up and pay attention to her words. 'I've had enough of this.'

'Enough of *what*, Nidhi?' he said in a silky voice.

'I don't want you to spend time in Delhi because of me,' she evaded.

'Why not?' he snapped.

Because you don't love me. 'Because I just don't,' she said vaguely.

Vikram's eyes burned into hers. 'I want to be with you.'

Nidhi's heart slammed against her ribs.

'I want you in my life, Nidhi,' he said simply.

'I don't want you in mine.'

He looked like she had slapped him.

Nidhi turned away, trying to shield herself against the hurt in his eyes.

'Why?' Vikram asked, his tone carefully blank. When she said nothing, he added, 'Is it because of your dad?'

'No, this has nothing to do with him. It's my decision.'

'What made you arrive at this decision?' he asked sarcastically. 'And don't tell me it's because you don't have feelings for me.'

Nidhi lifted her chin but couldn't look at him when she responded. 'I don't.'

'Really?' he challenged in an icy tone. 'If you'll give me two minutes, I'll prove you wrong.'

Afraid that he would succeed if he tried, she placed a hand on his chest to keep some distance between them. Vikram's large, calloused hand covered her dainty one and Nidhi stared at the vision, mesmerized against her will. Her heart soared at what their hands represented— trust and togetherness; loyalty and love.

Vikram watched the emotions flit across her face and he lowered his mouth to hers. He traced the seam of her lips with his tongue, urging them to open. His hands reached around her midriff, seductively tracing her contours, inching up towards her breasts. Nidhi's resolve began to weaken as she found herself relishing Vikram's hands on her body. She was seized by a sudden desire to yield to him—to lean into his muscled chest, to wrap her legs around him, to have his mouth feast on her skin . . . Alarmed by the intensity of her own cravings, she fought against the magnetic lure of his mouth and the relentless thudding of his heart against hers.

'Kiss me back,' he whispered, his mouth curving up in a sexy smile. And when she still hesitated, he added huskily, 'Please, Nidhi.'

It was the soft plea in his voice that made her capitulate. She parted her lips, welcoming the sweet invasion of his tongue, whimpering helplessly against his mouth. She clenched his shirt between her fists, clinging to him as he possessed her mouth with a stormy passion that drove her wild. She arched her head back, and as he lowered his mouth to her neck, Nidhi saw the humour lurking in his eyes. 'Oh no!' he quipped dramatically. 'We're necking! Shouldn't we use protection?'

For some reason it was the joke—the reminder of their shared history, of their first kiss and the way it had ended—that made Nidhi pull away from him. 'Stop,' she said, and felt a stab of disappointment when he obeyed immediately. 'We can't do this,' she said reluctantly.

'Okay,' he mumbled distractedly, already lowering his mouth to hers.

Nidhi pushed him away and leapt off the bed.

Vikram stood up and raised an eyebrow.

'I meant what I said, Vikram. I don't want you around.'

'Now that we've established it's not because of your lack of feelings for me,' he said with a smirk, 'may I know the real reason?'

Because you don't love me! 'Because there's no future for us,' she said.

A look of genuine surprise crossed his face. 'Why not?'

'Because I'm not a supermodel, or a Bollywood actr—'

'I don't want a goddamn supermodel, Nidhi!' he snapped. 'I want *you*.'

Her heart gave a little leap at his words, desperate to believe him. 'I can't compete with your girlfriends, Vikram,' she reasoned. 'I'm not some hot and glam—'

'I don't want you to compete with anyone! And I don't want you to be anything other than yourself,' Vikram said in a strangled voice, taking her hands in his. 'You are enough for me, Nidhi. In every way.'

'It won't last,' she said and, trying to lighten the mood, added, 'and anyway, just imagine what gorgeous babies you and Natasha would—'

'Don't!' he said harshly. 'Don't turn this into a joke, Nidhi.'

She looked at their entangled hands, letting the silence linger, before she threw back her shoulders and spoke in a smooth voice. 'You and I both know that I'm your latest source of entertainment, and you'll get bored of me as soon as the next Miss India comes traipsing into your life.'

He released her as if she'd burned him. 'Is that what you think of me?'

'I've read the tabloids.' Nidhi shrugged.

'That's not what I asked. I asked if that's what *you* think of me,' he said stiffly.

No! Nidhi wanted to scream. *Because you are loyal to a fault and you would do anything to protect the people you care about. And I can see how much you care about me. But that isn't enough, because you don't love me. And when it comes to you, settling for anything less than love will destroy me.*

'Yes.'

Vikram nodded, his face wiped clean of all expression. He walked away from her slowly, pausing for a split second when his hand found the doorknob.

'Wait!' Nidhi called out to him.

Hope flickered in his eyes as he turned around, waiting for her to take back her words, to change her mind, to admit how she really felt about him.

'Can we still be friends?' she pleaded helplessly.

He gave a hollow laugh. 'No.'

And with that, he walked out of her room. And out of her life.

Nidhi collapsed on the floor. She pressed her chin to her chest and sobbed. She cried till her eyes were dry and her heart was empty. She cried till she felt exactly as she had felt the last time Vikram Walia had left her.

Completely and utterly alone.

'Are you listening to me, Vikram?' Monty asked urgently.

Vikram nodded, even though he hadn't heard a single word.

Four days had passed since their return from Delhi, and Vikram's state of eerie calm was beginning to worry Monty. Vikram hadn't lost his infamous temper even once since landing in Mumbai, but then again, he had barely spoken at all. He hadn't stepped out of the house, except to go to the gym, and he had been eating all his meals mechanically, like he couldn't taste the food.

And Monty would have let all these things go if it wasn't for one rather alarming anomaly—Vikram's unprecedented insomnia. For as long as Monty had known Vikram, his client possessed the enviable ability to fall asleep as soon as his head touched a pillow. Vikram could sleep at any time, any place, and wake up from the deepest slumber without an alarm clock or a complaint. And yet, lately, Vikram had been drinking himself into a stupor, well into the wee hours of the morning.

'Vikram, I'm serious. This is important!' Monty said frantically.

Vikram looked away from the television and gave his manager his attention. 'What?'

'This,' Monty said, waving the newspaper under his nose.

Vikram shrugged. 'Ignore it.'

Monty's chubby red cheeks turned a dark shade of crimson. '*Ignore* it? This man works for one of the biggest law firms in country, and two days before your disciplinary hearing, he is pressing assault charges against you! How can I *ignore* it?'

'Because it's true,' Vikram said, snatching the newspaper from Monty and tossing it on the coffee table. 'And I don't give a damn.'

'Lekin can you at least tell me what happened that day?' Monty pressed.

He thought he saw pain flash in Vikram's eyes, but it was gone before he was certain. Vikram was still wearing the same stony expression he had worn over the last four days.

Monty tried to recall the events of their last day in Delhi.

'Good, you are back early!' Monty had beamed at Vikram when he returned from Nidhi's house. 'Come to drawing room, I have *ultimate* surprise!'

'We're going back to Mumbai.'

Monty's face fell. 'When?'

'Today,' Vikram said, his voice devoid of emotion.

'But I just had new TV installed,' Monty tried to reason.

'Book the first available flight,' Vikram had said, his expression unreadable.

Monty narrowed his eyes. 'Did something happen with Nidhiji?'

Vikram levelled a hard stare at his manager. 'I never want to hear her name again.'

'Lekin Vikram, *hua kya*?' Monty asked, wiping sweat from his brow.

The calm in Vikram's voice had been chilling. 'This conversation is over, Monty. Permanently.'

So even now, Monty didn't dare to bring up Nidhi. But his client's stubborn silence was making it very difficult for him to do his job.

'Can you please tell me what happened?' Monty repeated.

'Leave it, Monty,' Vikram said, reaching for the remote control to change the channel.

Monty took a deep breath and reached into his pocket for his anti-anxiety medication. Very calmly, he placed the bottle on the table without opening the lid. That got Vikram's attention.

Monty gave him an atypically serene smile. 'Can I ask you one question?'

Vikram lifted an eyebrow. 'Can I stop you?'

Monty ignored that. 'Do you ever want to play professional cricket again?'

Vikram continued to stare wordlessly at the television and if it weren't for his knuckles turning white around the remote, Monty would have assumed Vikram hadn't heard him.

So that's a yes, Monty thought.

'You are loose cannon who cannot control his temper on or off field. You are nothing but spoilt young kid who has let fame and success go to his head. And your ego is much bigger than your game,' Monty said calmly.

He saw the murderous glint in Vikram's eyes and raised his hands defensively. 'That is what BCCI will say. I know Shaan Kapoor deserved that punch and pro*beb*ly that Kuku fellow did too. Lekin as far as BCCI is concerned, both assaults were unprovoked, making them very serious. BCCI *will* extend ban, Vikram. It is no longer "maybe pro*beb*ly" situation. It *will* happen, unless you can explain both incidents to the public.'

Vikram covered his face with his hands, dragging them through his hair. He knew Monty was right—this time the shit had got real. He knew he was trapped.

But his choice was no choice at all. Perhaps it was his Rajput genes, or his mother's voice in his head, reminding him that the one thing in life that took precedence over all else was loyalty. So Vikram decided that he would gladly throw his career out the window before he threw his friends under the bus. He would not talk to the media about Natasha's abusive relationship with Kapoor. And he would die before he talked to them about Nidhi.

Even though she thought he was a womanizing scoundrel.

Which, he admitted fairly, was the truth. Or *used to be* the truth. Because since the day Nidhi had come back into his life, Vikram hadn't touched another woman. Hell, he hadn't even *thought* about another woman. But since the day she had told him to get out of her life, Vikram hadn't thought about Nidhi either.

He hadn't visualized her with toothpaste stuck in her hair while brushing his teeth every morning. He hadn't thought about her drunken singing while pouring his fifth whisky last night. He hadn't thrown out his fruit-scented shampoo because it smelt like Nidhi. He hadn't ripped up the full page EducateIndia ad because it had reminded him of Nidhi's ferocious reaction to the idea of Photoshopping his scar. The kids playing basketball in the gym hadn't brought back the memory of his game with Nidhi and the almost kiss that had followed it. And he certainly hadn't spent every single one of the last four nights being haunted by her fathomless green eyes.

Who was he kidding? He hadn't *stopped* thinking about Nidhi since the day he left Delhi. And the permanent ache that had settled in his chest was a constant reminder of her rejection.

In a way, Vikram was glad he hadn't told her that he loved her. But at the same time, he regretted it more than anything in his life. Maybe if he had confessed how he felt about her, she wouldn't have blown his heart to smithereens.

Bullshit.

She didn't trust him. She trusted the media's version of him. She believed a bunch of gossip columnists over him. Her opinion was that Vikram was capable of hurting her. She genuinely believed that he could *hurt* her! Vikram would sooner rip his own heart out than let a hair on Nidhi's head come to harm. And that was why he couldn't tell the media about what had happened with Kukreja.

Vikram turned to Monty and drew a long, tortured breath. 'I can't.'

Monty gave him a sympathetic smile, oddly laced with a hint of pride. 'I cannot say I am surprised.'

'I'm sorry, Monty,' Vikram said remorsefully.

Monty rose and placed a hand on Vikram's shoulder. 'Don't worry. We will think of something else.'

'Wait, what?' Risha repeated, her brown eyes widening.

Nidhi sighed. 'Rish, come on.'

'No, seriously. Can you please repeat what you just said?'

Nidhi rolled her eyes. 'Vikram and I have—'

Risha raised her palms. 'Hang on. Vikram *Walia*? The cricketer? The sixth-richest celebrity in India? *GQ*'s Man of the Year? *Vogue*'s Sexiest Abs? *People* mag—'

Nidhi cut her off with a groan. 'I can't believe you know all that.'

'It's my *job* to know all that,' Risha scoffed. 'Page 3, remember?'

'Yes, I remember,' Nidhi muttered, taking two cups of tea from the chai wala below their office building and handing one to Risha.

'Where's Shorty at dramatic moments like these?' Risha asked.

'Having a dramatic moment of her own. Apparently Lady K is on the verge of decapitating Shorty for failing to get A.R. Rahman for the sangeet,' Nidhi said dryly.

'But he never performs at weddings,' Risha reminded her.

'Exactly,' Nidhi said. 'Which is why Shorty is now on a flight to Chennai with Lady K to "invite" Rahman to the wedding as a friend of the family.'

Risha rolled her eyes. 'Rich-people problems.'

Nidhi nodded in resignation. 'Poor Shorty.'

'Anyway, please continue,' Risha prompted. 'You were saying that you and Vikram are childhood sweethearts.'

'I was saying no such thing!' Nidhi denied fervently. 'Vikram and I are childhood *friends*.'

Risha raised her eyebrows. 'Oh, really? So the fact that his jersey number is thirteen has *nothing* to do with your birthday being on the thirteenth of June?'

'Of course, not . . .' Nidhi's voice trailed off.

She had never considered that before. Vikram had used thirteen as his jersey number since they were teenagers.

'It's just a coincidence,' Nidhi said, even though the strange sensation at the back of her neck told her otherwise. 'Vikram is a nonconformist, and he probably picked the unlucky number just to scandalize the whole country.' Risha gave her a doubtful look and Nidhi repeated firmly, 'We're just friends.'

'So the googly eyes you were making at his shirtless photo this morning were completely platonic, then?' Risha asked, deadpan.

Nidhi tried to hide her blush behind a long sip of her chai. 'By the way, that image was completely inappropriate for the story.'

'I know.' Risha shrugged. 'But Kabir believes that Walia's six-pack will get us more eyeballs than yet another snapshot of the Shaan Kapoor video. What's with Walia and punching people, anyway?'

'Kuku deserved it,' Nidhi said quietly, avoiding Risha's eyes.

Risha looked at her in alarm. 'Why?'

Nidhi bit her lip. 'He tried to . . . grope me.' Then she added with disgust, 'Outside my own house, no less.'

Risha gasped. 'God, Nidhi! Why didn't you tell me?'

'I'm okay, Rish. Really,' Nidhi said, surprised that she meant it.

Risha gave her a hug. 'Is that the reason your eyes are all puffy?'

'Honestly? No,' Nidhi said with a sad smile.

'So you didn't spend the entire weekend crying over Kuku?' Risha asked.

'I did spend the entire weekend crying,' Nidhi admitted. 'But not over Kuku.'

'Shit,' Risha whispered. 'You're in love with Vikram?'

Nidhi nodded, trying to swallow the lump that had permanently lodged itself in her throat since the day Vikram had left.

'And he doesn't love you back?' Risha asked.

Nidhi shook her head. 'He loves Natasha.'

'I don't know about that.' Risha frowned.

'Shorty thinks so,' Nidhi reminded her.

'Shorty's judgement is clouded, thanks to that commitment-phobe she has wasted three years with,' Risha rebutted.

'I can't risk it, Rish,' Nidhi said, unable to keep the pain out of her voice. 'I've loved him for nearly half my life and I can't gamble my heart on the off-chance that he's not in love with Natasha. Because, frankly, that's not even the real issue. The issue is that he's not in love with *me*.'

'He's an idiot,' Risha said so fiercely that Nidhi smiled in spite of herself.

'I texted him this morning to apologize for the Kuku debacle, but all I got in response was a message from his manager asking me to address all future communication to him instead of Vikram,' Nidhi said miserably.

Her thoughts went to the photograph of Vikram that Miss Malini had posted on Twitter the previous day. He was stepping out of his gym in Mumbai, his features perfectly composed behind his four-day-old stubble, looking impeccable even in his workout gear. But there was one thing about his appearance that had seemed terribly out of place—his hair. His usually perfect hair had looked a tad messy.

Even the day Nidhi had found him curled up in a ball from the flu, his hair had looked like it had been professionally messed up a few minutes before. And when she had left him sleeping in his bed the morning after they had kissed, his sexy bedhead had been a sight to behold.

His dishevelled appearance bothered Nidhi because it implied that Vikram had been raking his hands through his hair—something he had done several times during the last few overs of the World Cup. Nidhi recognized the stressed-out gesture all too well.

Of course, he probably had a lot of things on his mind at the moment—his suspension, the disciplinary hearing and now Kuku's ridiculous case against him. But for some reason, the thought of Vikram's rumpled hair made Nidhi feel terribly guilty.

And then Nidhi remembered something that made her guilt subside. The expression on Vikram's face in that photograph with Natasha.

'Clearly, the only thing on his mind is the woman he loves.'

Which is why, no matter how tempted she was, Nidhi couldn't risk a temporary affair with Vikram. Because there would be nothing temporary about it—not for her.

Risha took Nidhi's empty styrofoam cup and tossed it into the garbage can. 'Wanna get out of here?'

'I really do,' Nidhi said.

Nidhi stormed into her father's study without knocking. 'Did you do this?' she demanded, slamming the newspaper on his desk.

Balraj looked at her in surprise, more shocked by her tone than by her interruption.

'Did you do this, Papa?' she repeated, her green eyes blazing.

'Sit down,' Balraj said calmly.

'No, I will not sit down,' Nidhi said, raising her chin defiantly.

'Sit!' her father snapped.

'Answer my question first. *Then* I'll sit,' she persisted.

Balraj stifled a smile at her temerity. 'You look so much like your mother right now.'

Nidhi blinked. 'What?'

Balraj's expression softened and he spoke gently. 'Nidhi, sweetheart, will you please sit down?'

She sat mechanically, a little stunned by the reference to her mother.

'Now tell me, in a *calm* tone of voice, what you're talking about,' Balraj said.

'You mentioned my mother,' Nidhi blurted, momentarily forgetting the reason she had barged into his study.

Balraj sighed and stood up, walking towards his bar. He poured himself a whisky and turned to Nidhi inquiringly. She shook her head, impatient to get back to the topic that had been taboo in their home for over two decades.

Balraj tossed back his drink in one large gulp and poured another, bracing himself for the discussion. 'What do you want to know?'

'Anything. Everything,' she said, feeling like a child who had been asked what she wanted for Christmas.

'You have her eyes,' he said softly. 'And her smile.' Nidhi nodded eagerly and he tipped his head towards the newspaper she had flung on his desk. 'And clearly her temper.'

'Why did she leave?'

Balraj sighed. 'We've been over this, Nidhi. She left because her career was too important to her and she did not want the responsibility of a family to hold her back from achieving her goals.'

'When did she leave?'

'When you were two and a half.'

'Did you try looking for her?'

Balraj's jaw clenched. 'Initially I was obsessed with tracking her down—I wasted years trying to locate her, not to mention lakhs of rupees. Then I spent the next decade being terrified that she would come back to claim you. I spent every day until you turned eighteen looking over my shoulder, for your mother.'

For the first time, Nidhi looked at Balraj and saw not the indomitable force that controlled her life, but the insecure, vulnerable father who, for years, had lived with the irrational fear of losing his only child.

Nidhi swallowed the emotion clogging her throat. 'Do you know where she is?'

'I honestly don't. I signed divorce papers a few years ago and sent them to a law firm in Paris. I believe she was touring with a theatre company somewhere there, but I have not kept track,' Balraj said bitterly.

Nidhi nodded, realizing the conversation was probably as hard for him as it was for her. But there was one other thing she wanted to know, and because she couldn't count on her father ever speaking about this again, she had to ask now. 'After she left, did she ever . . .' Nidhi's voice trailed off.

Balraj's knuckles tightened around his glass as he correctly predicted Nidhi's next question. 'Did she ever ask about me?'

Balraj considered lying.

'Tell me the truth, Papa,' she said, watching the struggle on his face. 'I can handle it.'

Balraj looked at her and spoke honestly. 'No. Never.'

Nidhi raised her chin and said softly, 'Her loss, right?'

Pride shone in her father's eyes as he walked around his desk and faced her. 'Damn right. You may look like your mother, but you are your father's daughter,' he said, leaning down to kiss her forehead.

Nidhi flushed at the unexpected display of affection.

Balraj cleared his throat and returned to his chair. 'Now, tell me, what has made you so upset?'

'Kuku has pressed charges against Vikram and he's already in the middle of a controversy that might affect his discip—'

'Kuku dropped the charges an hour ago,' Balraj told her.

Nidhi was surprised. 'How do you know?'

'The only reason he pressed charges in the first place was because I fired him. Petty revenge on his part, but also a colossal mistake.'

'Why?'

'Because no one messes with you and gets away with it,' Balraj said gruffly.

Nidhi smiled. 'Thanks, Papa.'

'He thought he would get some free publicity off Walia, but it didn't take a lot to change his mind,' Balraj said wryly.

'Did you bribe him?' Nidhi asked sceptically.

'No. But I did threaten to divert all of Marwah & Mehta's legal resources towards ensuring his total destruction,' Balraj said with disgust.

Nidhi expelled a breath of relief and stood up. 'Thank you.'

'Nidhi?' Balraj added, as she walked towards the door. 'I want to make one thing very clear. My actions had nothing to do with Walia. I didn't do it to protect him, I did it to protect you. I still don't approve of him.'

Nidhi nodded and walked out the door.

'Chalo, at least one disaster averted!' Monty said, tossing back two pills with his lassi.

Vikram grunted without looking up from his cheese omelette.

'No more of this Kukreja-Shukreja nonsense. Now we only need to deal with Shaan Kapoor,' Monty said, attacking his aloo parantha with both hands.

Vikram took another bite of his omelette and washed it down with a large gulp of orange juice.

'Please tell me you are planning to shave before tomorrow's hearing?' Monty grimaced.

Vikram nodded, his gaze still focussed on his plate.

'So sad that Natashaji is in Dilli tomorrow,' Monty said conversationally.

Vikram gave him a warning look that clearly stated 'Don't go there' before saying, 'She's promoting her new film, Monty.'

'No, no,' Monty clarified, 'I was not talking about her making an appearance before BCCI. I was only saying for moral support-shupport.'

'That's what I have you for,' Vikram said with a lacklustre smile before returning his attention to his breakfast.

Monty gave his client a long look before bravely venturing into a sensitive subject. 'We have got offer for your house.'

'Huh?' Vikram looked up.

'Your Lajpat Nagar kothi,' Monty clarified.

Something flashed in Vikram's eyes before he nodded. 'Sell it.'

Monty gave him a surprised look. 'Lekin I have not even told you price.'

Vikram shrugged. 'I trust you, Monty.'

'It is only first offer, Vikram. And it is two crores less than asking price. I think we should wait for—'

'Sell it,' Vikram said tersely. 'I want to put that chapter of my life behind me.'

'But what about when you go back to Dilli?'

'I have no reason to go back to Delhi.'

'Of course, you do.'

Vikram raised an eyebrow.

Monty gave him an innocent look. 'South Afreeka series.'

'So what?' Vikram said. 'We'll be staying at a hotel like the rest of the team.'

'Yes, I just meant . . .' Monty stood up without finishing his thought and wiped his butter-soaked fingers on a napkin. 'I will make some calls. Then we can close this Dilli chapter forever.'

Vikram raked a hand through his hair and nodded. 'Right. Forever.'

News Today Office Messenger Chat
Participants: Risha_K, Nidhi13

Risha_K: You'll never guess what the Bollywood editor just told me!

Nidhi13: Salman Khan is in jail?

Risha_K: Guess again.

Nidhi13: Sanjay Dutt is out of jail?

Risha_K: You suck at this.

Nidhi13: At least give me a hint!

Risha_K: It's about a Bollywood actress who is currently promoting a film in Delhi.

Nidhi13: Oooh. Madhuri Dixit?

Risha_K: Yes, because this is the early nineties.

Nidhi13: Hey, I love Madhuri!

Risha_K: So do I. But it's not her. Think of someone under the age of thirty.

Nidhi13: Alia Bhatt?

Risha_K: I didn't say under *twenty*.

Nidhi13: Just tell me already.

Risha_K: Natasha Sahay just gave an exclusive to Kabir. Apparently she was in a 'turbulent' relationship with her ex and it's totally obvious she's talking about

Shaan Kapoor! Didn't I tell you he was sleazeball?

Nidhi13: That's why Vikram punched him???

Risha_K: While she didn't say that in so many words, she strongly hinted at it. And she only gave the interview on the condition that Kabir release it on the website immediately and do a longer follow-up in the newspaper tomorrow.

Nidhi13: Vikram's disciplinary hearing is tomorrow, so she's obviously trying to protect him!

Risha_K: One moment she's here to promote her movie and the next moment she's *volunteering* an interview. Kabir is ecstatic!

Nidhi13: That's weird.

Risha_K: Of course not. He has every reason to be thrilled. It's the first time *Delhi Today* has bagged such a big scoop!

Nidhi13: No, I mean it's weird that Kabir is calling me right now. BRB.

'Can you please come to my cabin immediately?' Kabir said on the phone, sounding frantic.

Nidhi took the one flight of stairs down to the *Delhi Today* floor, wondering why Kabir's first instinct after procuring the biggest scoop of his life would be to call *her*.

Nidhi knocked on his door. 'You wanted to see . . .' Her voice trailed off as soon as she caught sight of the guest seated on the small love seat in Kabir's cabin.

'Come in, Nidhi!' Kabir said with a bright smile. 'Meet Natasha Sahay.'

Nidhi turned to the tall beauty in the pristine white pantsuit. Natasha's trademark waves had been straightened and pulled back into a high ponytail, and she wore nude makeup that accentuated her smooth skin and sculpted cheekbones. Her thick-winged eyeliner and smoky-grey eyeshadow brought out the distinct gold flecks in her otherwise brown eyes.

The Indian media was not exaggerating when they called her the most beautiful woman in the country. Because Natasha Sahay was absolutely breathtaking.

Nidhi resisted the temptation to glance down at her boring black slacks and grey satin blouse. 'Hi. I'm Nidhi.'

Natasha stepped forward, and, for a split second, Nidhi had the uneasy impression that she was about to *hug* her. Instead, Natasha took a step back and shook Nidhi's hand with a warm smile. 'It's so nice to finally meet you.'

'"Finally"?' Nidhi asked.

'I've heard so much about you,' Natasha explained, and when Nidhi's eyebrows shot up, she added, 'from Kabir.'

'I'm a big fan of your work,' Nidhi offered politely.

'That makes one of us!' Natasha winked.

Nidhi gave a surprised laugh.

'Natasha is very interested in the EducateIndia programme and wants to know how she can be a part of it,' Kabir said, gesturing to the love seat.

Both women sat down and Natasha said, 'I have room in my brand portfolio for a social cause, and I was wondering if you could share some details about the programme. I've heard so much about it from Vikram.'

Nidhi stiffened at the mention of his name, but nodded. 'Sure, I'd love to. We started the progr—'

'Kabir,' Natasha turned to him. 'Don't let us keep you from pressing matters, sweetie.'

Kabir understood the politely worded dismissal and sprang to his feet immediately, making a graceful exit from the room.

'I don't really want to talk about EducateIndia,' Natasha said as soon as the door clicked shut.

Nidhi gaped at her. 'Oh.'

'I mean, I'd love to. But not today.' Natasha smiled.

So this is what a celebrity mood swing looks like.

'Okay.' Nidhi shrugged. 'No problem.' She started to stand, but Natasha clasped her hand to stop her. Nidhi looked at her in confusion.

'I wanted to see you in person,' Natasha said.

Nidhi observed the twinkle in Natasha's deep brown eyes and the glow on her flawless skin and spoke tentatively. 'Oh-kay.'

'I've heard so much about you from Vikram,' Natasha explained.

Oh. So that's what it's about. Marking her territory.

Nidhi gave her a polite smile. 'Don't believe everything he says. I'm not *all* bad.'

Natasha laughed. 'There's that sense of humour he keeps talking about. I can totally see why he's crazy about you.'

Nidhi choked. '*What?*'

'During his last Mumbai trip, you're all he could talk about. He told me about your—'

'He was talking about *me?*' Nidhi blurted.

Natasha gave her an amused smile. 'He went on and on about the colour of your eyes. He couldn't decide if they are jade or emerald. And now I can see why,' Natasha said warmly. 'They're a little bit of both.'

Nidhi stared at her, slack-jawed.

'I heard all about Odie and the Trio and also five hundred reasons why Vikram is *never* playing basketball with you again,' Natasha said, rolling her eyes.

Then she did the strangest thing. She reached out and squeezed Nidhi's hand. And the gesture was all too similar to the one in the photograph.

'This is simply a photograph of a man in love.'

'He was talking about me,' Nidhi whispered.

'Clearly, the only thing on his mind is the woman he loves.'

'He was talking about *me*,' she repeated, as the realization sank in.

Natasha nodded. 'It was the first time in years that he seemed . . . at home. I'm so glad you both have finally found each other again.'

Nidhi stared at her blankly.

'And I'm sorry for catching you off guard like this,' Natasha said with a helpless smile. 'Next time let's plan properly and do lunch or dinner?'

Nidhi cleared her throat, finding her voice and her manners. 'Yes, I'd like that very much. And it was a pleasure to meet you, Natasha. I can see why Vikram is so fond of you.'

'I'm lucky to have a friend like him,' Natasha said, a shadow crossing her face. 'He's been there for me through a very tough period in my life.'

'And I can see that you're repaying the favour,' Nidhi said, referring to the interview.

But Natasha shook her head. 'Honestly, it's the least I can do. Cricket is his life.'

'Thank you,' Nidhi said.

'Of course. I would never let Vikram throw his life away,' Natasha said, a strange catch in her voice.

Nidhi reached out and gave Natasha an awkward hug, and Natasha hugged her back warmly before reaching for her bright orange Hermès clutch. 'I better go. I have to catch a flight to Ahmedabad.'

The moment Natasha left, Nidhi sank into the love seat, her entire body alive with the heartbreaking realization that Vikram loved her.

He loved her!

Nidhi remembered his face, white with strain, when he'd held her after her date with Kuku.

'Promise me you're okay.'

And the way he'd leapt to the defence of his adulterous teammates.

'I don't condone infidelity, but I would never betray my teammates. Those guys are the only family I've got.'

Nidhi had wanted to tell him how wrong he was. She was his family, always had been and always would be. She almost laughed when she recalled his annoyance at the aggressive video montage.

'You're confusing my persona with my personality.'

Vikram was kind and loyal and protective. And the whole world could confuse his persona with his personality, but Nidhi would never doubt his strength of character again. Because she would never forget the biting fury in his eyes when he had threatened Kuku.

'If you ever touch her again, I will rip you apart limb by limb!'

Her expression softened at the memory of Vikram lying in bed, delirious with fever, his expression vulnerable.

'Don't leave me again.'

Her body almost shook with emotion when she thought of the gentle way he'd held her in his arms as she sobbed her heart out.

'Don't cry, Nidhi. I can't take it any more.'

And the raw ache in his eyes when she had asked him to let her go.

'I don't want a goddamn supermodel. I want you!'

She wanted him too. So much.

'You are enough for me. In every way.'

And he was enough for her.

Monty dug into his third helping of biryani and studied his client, who was seated on the other side of the room with his teammates.

On the one hand, Vikram had proclaimed that he was done with Nidhi—permanently—and forbidden any mention of her. But on the other hand, he hadn't so much as cracked a smile since the day of the disciplinary hearing. The BCCI had given him a clean chit with a fair warning after Vikram promised to 'behave himself'. Barring the practised smile Vikram had given the paparazzi outside the BCCI headquarters, he had worn the same impassive expression for the last ten days.

The entire team was in Delhi for the match against South Africa, and the first session in the nets was scheduled for the following morning. And while Vikram seemed relaxed with his teammates after his brief hiatus, he was not participating in the good-natured ribbing or friendly trash talk. The guys were on his case about his recent transgressions and Vikram had borne the jokes—their own and the ones they found on social media—with a sporting but half-hearted smile.

Monty glanced up and saw the captain of the Indian cricket team walking towards him, and he immediately put his spoon down, bracing himself for the inevitable interrogation.

'What's wrong with him?'

Monty, who usually subscribed to the why-use-ten words-when-you-can-use-fifty philosophy in life, came straight to the point for the no-nonsense captain. 'Girl trouble.'

'What?'

'He's in love.'

'He's . . . in love?'

'Yes.'

'*Walia* is in love?'

Monty held up his palms in a don't-look-at-me gesture. 'And it is one-sided.'

'Impossible,' Captain whispered in disbelief. 'Natasha?'

'No. Childhood sweetheart.'

'Ouch.' Captain turned around and strode purposefully towards Vikram, who, currently surrounded by six other players on a round table, was eating his dinner.

'*Yeh achha wala hai,*' the wicketkeeper chuckled, reading off his phone. '"Why will the entire South African line-up be wearing helmets? Because who knows when Walia will punch someone! #WaliaKoGussaKyunAataHai"'

The rest of the guys laughed at that and Vikram gave a slight smile.

'Chalo, that's enough, boys,' Captain said and the hearty laughter subsided into suppressed guffaws. 'Come with me,' he told Vikram, who put his fork down and followed his captain to a quiet corner.

'I need to know you have your head in the game,' Captain said bluntly.

Vikram nodded emphatically. 'Of course, I do.'

'You'll steer clear of *ladai-jhagda*?'

'Yes.'

'You'll cut down on *gaali-galoch*?'

'Yes.'

'And you'll handle your girl problems?'

Vikram raised an eyebrow.

The steadfast captain returned his glare.

Vikram's jaw tightened. 'I don't have girl problems.'

'Then stop behaving like a goddamn chick on her period.'

'I'm not—'

'Whatever it is, Walia—fix it.'

Vikram nodded, but didn't say anything.

'I can't have my star batsman moping around like this,' Captain added, to take the edge off his reprimand.

'May I get back to my dinner now?' Vikram gritted.

Captain nodded and watched him walk away, making a mental note to tell the rest of the guys to lay off Walia for a bit. The poor guy really did look whipped.

Nidhi walked in through the gate of the Feroz Shah Kotla Stadium in Delhi, trying to hide her nervousness behind her oversized sunglasses. For the hundredth time since that morning, the sheer absurdity of her plan made her want to run away and lock herself inside her house.

Risha was right. Nidhi should've just stalked Vikram at his hotel. But the security there was too tight.

She had already tried.

Since Vikram was avoiding her calls, she had tried to reason with Monty, but Monty was quite firm in his refusal to help her. 'So sorry, Nidhiji,' he had said sincerely. 'I really want to help you, but I cannot. Vikram has banned me from talking about you and Captain Sir has issued strict instructions not to disturb-shisturb Vikram's focus. I hope you understand.'

She didn't understand. She didn't understand at all. But Monty had sounded so helpless that instead of shouting at him, Nidhi had thanked him politely and hung up the phone.

And so she had to go with her last resort—confronting Vikram at the stadium after net practice.

'Just flash your press card and walk in confidently,' Sam had advised her last night. 'Don't make eye contact with the guard.'

'I'm going to stick out like a sore thumb. Too bad there are such few female sports journos.' Nidhi had sighed.

'Yes, the players would definitely respond much better to them,' he said with a pointed look at her legs.

She rolled her eyes. 'I just hope I can get inside the stadium.'

'I've already told Piyush to look out for you,' he said, referring to the *NT* cricket correspondent on the field.

She gave him a quick peck on the cheek. 'Thanks, Sam.'

'Break a leg.' He smiled.

Now Nidhi was wishing that she had *actually* broken a leg. It would be less painful than a potentially public confrontation with Vikram. Nidhi smoothened an imaginary crease on her turquoise green dress, trying to brush away the sense of dread that had taken over her.

What if Vikram didn't want anything to do with her?

What if he thought she was 'disturbing-shisturbing' his focus?

What if he didn't love her?

Nidhi's confidence dwindled with every step around the circumference of the boundary and she seriously reassessed the wisdom of showing up at the stadium. If their positions had been reversed, Nidhi would not appreciate Vikram confronting her at her office. After all, this was his 'place of work' and Nidhi didn't want to make a scene in front of his 'colleagues'.

If at all there *was* a scene. Maybe he would just pretend not to recognize her like that first meeting at the *NT* office.

Panic rose in her throat.

Perhaps, she would just camp outside his hotel and pounce on him like all the other crazy people. What's the worst that could happen? Nidhi was entertaining visions of jail time and restraining orders when she spotted Vikram.

Her stomach gave a little flip as she saw him shuffle a football before passing it to one of his teammates.

Nidhi presumed that the serious part of the practice session was over because the guys were tossing around a football, seemingly to unwind after a gruelling morning in the nets. Vikram laughed at something one of his teammates said and the familiar, throaty sound sent a jolt down Nidhi's spine. She was about to turn around and make a run for it when he caught sight of her. Even though she couldn't see his eyes behind his sunglasses, Nidhi was certain that he'd seen her because he froze in his tracks.

Nidhi took off her own sunglasses and waved to him, relieved when he did the same. He tipped his head towards the stands, away from the nets, and Nidhi walked in that direction, her legs watery and unstable.

'Hi,' she said.

'Hi,' he responded, his expression inscrutable.

'How are you?' she asked, yearning to touch his handsome face.

'I'm fine,' he said coolly, shoving his hands into his pockets.

She glanced around the nets uneasily. 'I'm sorry for bothering you here, but you haven't been taking my calls.'

He shrugged. 'I've been busy.'

Nidhi stared at something behind his shoulder and her jaw slackened. 'Is that *Virat Kohli*?'

Vikram stiffened. 'Did you come here to ogle the players?'

Even though his face was a mask of granite, Nidhi heard the jealousy in his voice and felt a stab of hope. Resisting the overwhelming urge to throw herself into his arms, she gave him a sweet smile. 'Not originally.'

'Then why are you here?' he demanded.

'I came to apologize,' she began bravely, hoping she was appealing to the laid-back *raat-gayi-baat-gayi* Punjabi half of him and not the staunch, unforgiving Rajput half.

His expression softened a little. 'For what?'

'For what happened with Kuku. I'm glad it didn't affect your discip—'

'It's fine,' he said abruptly. 'It wasn't your fault.'

She nodded, looking down at the ground. 'I know.'

Vikram watched her carefully, as though expecting her to say something else. When she continued to study the grass on the field, his face hardened. 'If you don't mind, I have to get back,' he said tersely, turning around.

'Wait!' she cried, placing a hand on his arm.

He jerked his arm away and snapped his gaze to hers. 'Nidhi, if you have something to say, say it. Otherwise, I'd like to get on with my day. *And* my life.'

'I do have something to say,' she said, stubbornly raising her chin. 'I'm really sorry about the things I said the last time I saw you, Viks.'

Barring the clenching of his jaw when she addressed him by that name, his expression remained unreadable.

'I didn't mean it,' she added softly.

Vikram scoffed. 'The part where you said you didn't have feelings for me or the part where you said I was a spineless man-whore?'

Nidhi cringed at the memory. 'All of it.'

He gave her an indifferent shrug. 'It doesn't matter.'

'It matters to me,' she said firmly.

'Why?'

She met his eyes. 'Because I'm in love with you.' Vikram stared at her and she gave a helpless laugh. 'I'm so in love with you, Viks. I've loved you since I was eight years old. I never stopped loving you. And now I've screwed up every—'

Vikram's mouth descended on hers and he pulled her against his chest in one swift motion. He kissed her like his life depended on it. He kissed her as though kissing her was the only way to keep her from disappearing again. And Nidhi kissed him back urgently and brazenly, pouring her soul into that one kiss. When they finally parted, Vikram cradled her face between his palms. 'I thought I'd lost you, Nidhi,' he said gruffly. 'I thought I'd lost you forever.'

Her eyes gleamed with unshed tears. 'Me too.'

'I love you,' he whispered achingly, touching his forehead to hers. 'I love you so damn much.'

'Let's not screw this up again, okay?' she murmured against his mouth.

Vikram raised his head and gave her a pointed look. 'Does your father know?'

Nidhi knew instinctively that the answer to that question was important to Vikram, because it would help him gauge how sure Nidhi was about him. But Nidhi had never been surer of anything in her entire life. 'He has the gist, but I postponed the closing argument until later. I thought we could do it together.'

'Great. I'd like nothing more than to see his expression,' Vikram growled.

'Be nice,' Nidhi warned. 'You'll be dating his daughter.'

He gave her a tender grin. 'I intend on doing a lot more than just dating her.'

'Best to keep that to yourself,' she muttered.

A loud clicking sound made Vikram pull away from her. 'Shit. I forgot about the press!' he said, absently rubbing his jaw.

'The *what*?' she gasped.

'There are a bunch of reporters right behind us,' he said.

Nidhi groaned. 'Is there any chance they didn't . . .'

She looked so distraught that Vikram almost wanted to lie. 'There's a *chance*,' he evaded.

'My face is going to be in tomorrow's newspaper, isn't it?' she ventured.

'It's probably already on Twitter,' he admitted, searching her face for signs of regret.

'So much for taking it slow,' she said dryly.

Vikram gazed into her eyes. 'I've waited twelve years for this, Nidhi. I'm done taking it slow.' He saw the shy longing in her green eyes and started to reach for her, but Nidhi took a step back, cocking her head towards the press enclosure. He sighed and let go of her with great reluctance. 'I should get back before the guys notice I'm gone.'

Nidhi cleared her throat and pointed behind him. 'Ummm, I think they already did.'

Vikram turned around to find the entire Indian cricket team standing in a row watching him and Nidhi. The moment they caught his eye, they started hooting and whistling wildly.

Nidhi blushed and Vikram shot his teammates a disgusted look. 'Very mature, guys,' he called to them, following it up with a rude gesture, but the cheering only got louder.

Vikram shook his head, muttering under his breath. 'Goddamn world champions behaving like a bunch of *chu*—'

Nidhi gave him a look and he grinned sheepishly.

'I think you'd better go.' She sighed.

Vikram nodded and turned around. Then he turned back. 'Nidhi?'

'Yes?'

'Don't go too far, okay?'

She heard the poignant implication in his request and shook her head. 'Never.'

His face broke into a boyish smile as he sprinted back to his teammates, only to face louder cheers, friendly chokeholds and back slaps.

It almost felt like they had won a match.

But to Vikram, it felt a whole lot better.

Two months later . . .

'Bhimsen?'

Bhimsen continued to snore.

'Bhimsen? Unlock the gate!'

'Dekha Hai Pehli Baar, Saajan Ki Aankhon Mein Pyaar . . .' continued to blare in the background.

'Bhimsen!'

Clearly, this was not working. The only option was to jump over the gate and call the trusted comrade to the rescue.

'Hello?' Nidhi whispered into the phone.

'Hey,' Vikram whispered back. 'I'm going to jump over the gate now. Can you unlock the side door?'

'I'll be right there.'

Vikram climbed over the Marwahs' metallic gate with practised ease and jogged up the driveway to the side entrance.

'Hey,' Nidhi whispered when she opened the door.

Vikram shoved his hands in her hair and started to pull her forward for a kiss, but Nidhi placed her hands on his chest and gave him a little push. 'Papa is still awake, so we need to be super quiet.'

Vikram groaned. 'I thought you said he was warming up to me?'

Nidhi shushed him and he followed her into the house, tip-toeing his way across the long lobby. He was mentally congratulating himself on yet another successful attempt at sneaking into his girlfriend's house undiscovered, when . . .

'Hello, Vikram.'

Vikram froze at the sound of Balraj Marwah's voice. The man was seated on the couch in the living room, strangely enough, with his back towards Vikram.

Does Balli the Bully have eyes at the back of his head?

'Hi, Uncle,' Vikram called to him sheepishly, and Nidhi leapt behind the large mahogany door, clamping a hand over her mouth to keep from exploding into giggles.

Balraj stood up and turned around, striding out to the lobby. He held out his hand formally. 'Good to see you.'

'Same here,' Vikram said, struggling to keep a straight face.

'How long are you in town?' Balraj asked, his tone lacking its usual curtness.

'I'm flying to England tomorrow, so I just, uh, came to say bye to Nidhi,' Vikram improvised.

Balraj raised an eyebrow. 'I see. Like you've been saying bye for the last three nights?'

Shit.

Vikram started to fabricate an explanation, but Balraj pre-empted the lie with a shake of his head. 'Let's talk when you return from England. We need to reach a mutually agreeable arrangement.'

Vikram stiffened.

'An arrangement,' Balraj added hastily, noticing the ominous glitter in Vikram's eyes, 'that will hopefully put an end to all this sneaking around.'

Vikram blinked. 'Huh?'

'I'm going to bed now,' Balraj said meaningfully, walking up the stairwell. 'Goodnight.'

And though Vikram wasn't certain, he thought he saw Balraj's shoulders shaking.

Vikram turned to Nidhi in utter bewilderment. 'Was your dad *laughing*?'

'Told you he's warming up to you,' Nidhi teased, taking his hand and pulling him up the stairs. She flopped on the bed inside her room, and was surprised when Vikram didn't immediately jump in next to her and claim her mouth in a long, torrid kiss.

'Something on your mind?' she asked, watching his dazed expression.

'Did your dad mean what I think he meant?' Vikram asked.

'Given that you've dropped the M-word two thousand times in the last two months, I thought it was best to prepare him,' Nidhi said awkwardly. Ignoring the uneasy sense of foreboding, she added, 'Don't worry, we'll take it one step at a time.'

Vikram sat next to her on the bed. 'Am I to understand that you think I'm getting cold feet?'

'Are you?' Nidhi asked.

He took her hand in his and gazed into her eyes. 'If it were up to me, I would marry you this minute. You know that.'

Nidhi smiled at that. When he still seemed distracted, she shifted uneasily. 'Is there a problem?'

He nodded. 'Yes. A very big one.'

'What?' she asked, watching a grin tug at the corner of his mouth.

'I could never live in Delhi,' he said, pressing his lips to her fingertips.

'I could never live in Mumbai,' she breathed.

He sobered. 'I'm serious.'

'So am I. I can't leave Papa alone, he doesn't deserve that.'

Vikram opened his mouth to tell her exactly what Balraj Marwah deserved, when Nidhi slipped her arms around his waist and snuggled into his chest. Even though he could feel his resolve crumbling, he glanced down at her and raised a challenging eyebrow.

Suddenly, Nidhi pinned him to the bed and straddled him between her legs. Vikram looked up at her in surprise. She leaned down and whispered against his mouth. 'It would mean a lot to me.'

Vikram's face broke into a lazy smile. 'When you put it that way . . .'

ACKNOWLEDGEMENTS

Several individuals deserve special mention for helping me through this project.

To my family—thank you for being my most ardent cheerleaders.

Thanks also to my amazing friends—Nidhi Arora and Rohan Sehgal—for dropping everything to text or video-chat with me at odd hours.

I am grateful to Sakshi Bahadur Oberoi and Arjun Fauzdar for lending their faces to the cover of this book. And to the immensely talented Angad B. Sodhi—only you could bring out the best in them!

I owe tremendous thanks to Nidhi Tuli for sharing her experiences as a sports journalist and bringing a touch of realism to my work of fiction.

Finally, thank you to the team at Penguin Random House India—Devangana Dash, Cibani Premkumar, Varun Tanwar and Tarini Uppal—for your professionalism and patience. And especially to my editor, Ambar Sahil Chatterjee—for dealing with the time difference, agreeing to disagree and always pushing me to do better!